AS THE POPPIES BLOOMED

"Boyadjian vividly conjures the specific sensory details of the Armenians' lost world.... Powerful and sensitive, this tragic novel helps illuminate a historical episode still too little known or acknowledged."

—*Kirkus Reviews*

"Exceptionally well written, *As the Poppies Bloomed* is a compelling read from first page to last and clearly documents author Maral Boyadjian as an especially gifted storyteller who will leave her readers looking eagerly toward her next novel. Very highly recommended."

—*Midwest Book Review*

"Maral Boyadjian's debut novel, *As the Poppies Bloomed,* is a fictionalized account of her family's experience during the Armenian Genocide of 1915.... That is perhaps why this lovingly written and sometimes lyrical account of the events in the small village of Salor seems so real—at times the characters almost jump off the page.... A story of love, loss and in the end salvation—the best type of story we have to remind ourselves of some of the worst, and best, aspects of the human condition."

—Christopher Atamian, *Huffington Post*

"Cultural and historical details add depth to this love story.... A moving work."

—*Foreword Reviews*

"*As the Poppies Bloomed* is a beautiful novel. Maral Boyadjian paints a gorgeous picture, with intricate detail.... With her host of characters, we are able to get to know and love a whole village, from the youngest baby to the matriarchs, the patriarchs, the goat herders, and the freedom fighters.... She also provides some valuable insight into the Armenian Genocide, which is a tragic part of history that is seldom taught or understood in the average American psyche. This is a tale of love and loss that will also satisfy any history buff."

—*Portland Book Review*

A NOVEL OF LOVE IN A TIME OF FEAR

As the

POPPIES
BLOOMED

MARAL BOYADJIAN

SALOR PRESS

For information, address:

Salor Press
E-mail: info@salorpress.com

For foreign and translation rights, contact Nigel J. Yorwerth
E-mail: nigel@PublishingCoaches.com

Library of Congress Control Number: 2014917133

ISBN: 978-0-9911241-0-7

10 9 8 7 6 5 4 3 2

Cover design: Nita Ybarra

To the grandchildren of Krikor Haroutinian—
Mshak, Nahreen, Krikor, Kareen, Marie, Kevo, and Tamar.

I know that wherever you are, Dad, you are so, so proud.

CHAPTER 1

Salor, Sassoun 1913

On the same day that the village headman's older daughter was to wed, his younger daughter hid in an abandoned well.

Anno clung to the well's solid top blocks. It was a well that had not been used by the villagers during her lifetime, and the bottom, she knew, was hard and dry. Her fingers pressed the edges of the blocks and she willed herself to keep her head out of sight. Her forearms were scraped, bleeding into the sleeves of her blouse, but Anno felt no pain at all. All that mattered was that she was not seen.

And as Anno hung in the well, she felt the rise of stinging, bubbling anger. Anger that all she had planned should end like this, all because of that meddling Old Mariam.

Anno's arms and shoulders were burning now with exertion. She slowly, creepingly, felt around the inside of the well with her right foot, searching for something to push against to take the load from her arms. She knew she must stay there until Old Mariam passed, and Old Mariam's pace was very, very slow.

Tears filled her eyes when she wondered if she would even have the strength to pull herself out when it was finally safe.

Flashes of the morning activity came to her in split seconds. She had waited until all the relatives and neighbors had focused all their attention on her sister, Lucine, the bride. She knew that she would have no more than thirty minutes from that moment until her absence was noticed, and so she had soundlessly and purposefully left through a back door. She had walked close along the outer walls of the stable and away from the cluster of village homes, then up a short dry slope to her and Daron's meeting place, this abandoned well.

Daron, too, would slip away as soon as he had received his signal. Takoush, Anno's closest friend, would move outside Anno's father's front door to the road, casually look to her left and then to her right, seemingly searching for a stray guest, and then turn back inside.

But Anno and Daron had had such little time to plan. They had forgotten Old Mariam's treks to her favorite field for collecting her grasses and herbs.

Anno's foot rested against something solid. She pushed against it tentatively with the ball of her foot and exhaled sharply. She dared not look down, but her foot was most definitely pushing against some solid protrusion. Then she lifted her body by inches until her eyes topped the well. Looking right and left, she could no longer see Mariam's hunched figure among the grasses. Without hesitating, she pushed herself out of the well, immediately, while she still had the strength to do so, because her arms were numbing dangerously. She slumped on the dry grass and cold perspiration streamed down her face and back.

And it was just this way, with her mouth hanging open, hair streaking the sides of her face, slumped against the well's wall, that Daron found her.

Anno's index finger shot up and lay against her lips to warn Daron not to cry out. He instinctively bent over double and ran to her side, dark brown eyes staring wildly into her face. He imagined the worst, because Anno was not one to frighten easily.

"Old Mariam walked by. I had to hide." She nodded behind her to the well. "There was nowhere else. I almost fell in." She stopped a moment to breathe again. Her mouth was dry and the words came slowly. "She did not see."

Daron swallowed once.

I almost fell in, she had said. *She did not see.* And in response he could not cry out in case someone heard, and he could not hold her, in case someone saw.

Instead, Daron gently pushed the long, matted hair off her face and lifted her hands. They both saw the blood for the first time, and Daron took his handkerchief from his pocket and dabbed at the red droplets, occasionally pressing down to stop the flow. For a long moment, he neither spoke nor looked up. Anno turned away from the anger in his face and watched his large olive-skinned hands working over hers.

"This must stop," he said finally, looking straight into her eyes.

She nodded sadly back at him, knowing he did not mean the blood.

"Either your father agrees or he does not. Nothing can be as bad as what happened here today. What if you had fallen in?" He gripped her shoulders. "Anno, what if you had fallen in?"

With his words, they both imagined her arms tired, her hands and fingertips surrendering their grip as she slipped and scraped rapidly and endlessly down past the cold, forgotten walls of the well to its rock-hard bottom. And they imagined, at that moment, having lost each other, having no more reason to spare their families shame by meeting in secret places, speaking but not touching. Rising to her knees, Anno and Daron embraced for the first time, and their faces touched.

"I will speak to my father today. Today. Do not worry," Daron whispered. And to further prove how confident she should be in him, he kissed her slowly. First her temple, then her eyelids, and finally, her mouth.

"Now go," Daron said, pulling Anno slowly to her feet. "This is not how they should find out about us, hiding behind an old well."

They were able to smile now, despite their own poorly made plans.

Still feeling his kisses, Anno could not speak.

"I will go first. Count to ten, then follow," Daron told her, and noticing now that she was standing limply, not her true straight self, he held her arms anxiously.

"Can you walk? Are your legs hurt?" He searched her, up and down.

"No. No. Of course I can walk." Anno pulled herself up. "We must return now." She held his shoulders and slowly turned him around.

With one last look around the dry slope, Daron left. Anno waited until she could see him no more, counted to ten and followed. Her knees were weak for a number of reasons, but her heart was happy.

CHAPTER 2

Lucine, headman Vartan's older daughter, was well accustomed to being the center of attention. But today, on the day of her wedding, things were disconcertingly different.

As the daughter of an important family, she had learned at an early age that her behavior and manners must be above reproach at all times. She knew that even when she played or worked among family members or girls her age, she was observed. She did not mind. In fact, she enjoyed it. She expected it. Her thick, wavy hair was always neatly braided down her back, and the wisps around her temples wound into enviable shades of golden brown. Her eyes were an unexpected green, and her skin, pale. With these unusual fair features, she would likely have been watched anyway.

Today, however, the attentions cast upon Lucine were not silent observations and whisperings, or even heads nodding in approval. Today, the women of her own family and of her future husband's family were critical. They were fingering her hair, her wedding dress, turning her to the left and around and volubly expressing all opinions.

"Her headpiece has slipped once already. It will fall in her face and we will all be shamed," someone warned.

"That is because too many coins have been sewn on the front. And whose work was that?" her father's sister queried loudly.

Lucine's face burned with embarrassment. She had insisted on the many embellishments around her face despite her mother's warnings. She looked at her mother now.

Yeraz, Lucine's mother, was not tall. Nor was she particularly stout. But no one would ever say she was a small woman. In fact, with dark brown braids coiled high on her head, her back and shoulders straight, her wool skirt long and full, the people rather considered the wife of the headman to be stately. Wise and stately.

The people of mountainous Sassoun, and their little village of Salor, had worked and fought together, celebrated, suffered, and mourned together on this land for centuries. Every person there had been part of numerous weddings, baptisms, and funerals. Yeraz Vartanian was no exception. Although Lucine was the first of her four children to wed, every aspect of the traditional betrothal and wedding was very clear and familiar to her. And so, she had thought to see her eldest daughter's wedding celebration through quite smoothly, but instead, she found herself, on this first day, already losing patience and narrowly controlling her tongue. She purposely spoke little, not trusting herself and her temper. She knew she must appear not to mind the women and their thoughtless criticisms so that no one would have reason to gossip later. And most importantly, Lucine would become even more flustered if her mother showed any agitation, because Yeraz was rarely, if ever, agitated.

"Marie," Yeraz spoke to her husband's sister. "You are the most skilled with the needle. Take Lucine's headpiece and remove some of those coins. You will know which ones." Yeraz passed the dishlike red velvet headpiece and it floated from hand to hand as if it were a crown.

Marie's bosom swelled with pride at Yeraz's compliment. She reached for the piece with both hands.

"It would be a sin if this headpiece hid our girl's lovely eyes. I will fix it. All of you do something else," she stated generously, and was further pleased to turn and find the arms of several eager young girls outstretched, offering her a wide choice of scissors, needles, and thread. She showingly chose her tools, rejecting the first two needles for no true reason, and sat down smugly to work.

Yeraz now turned her attention to her new in-laws, *khnamis*. There were about a dozen various female relatives, including, of course, Lucine's future mother- and grandmother-in-law. They were eating sweets from trays laid out before them by neighbors who had prepared and delivered them to the bride's father's home just as Yeraz herself had done for countless other weddings.

Yeraz's eyes flickered over the emptied rows of sticky trays and doubted there would be enough left to last them to the next day.

Father Sarkis, who had arrived earlier to bless Lucine's wedding garments, poured a bit of oghee, a local spirit made from mulberries, into his cup and sipped it with satisfaction. He clutched his cup to him and seemed pleased to be here among the women for the moment. He knew that friends and male members of the family had taken the groom, the *pesa,* to the bathhouse to be bathed and shaved, and that he did not need to partake in the jokes that would take place there. So for the time being, he was most content to be where he was. He would join the bride's father and other relatives in the small, walled courtyard soon, but not just yet.

Takoush's voice, pensive and sweet, rose above the others'. She clasped her hands against her heart and allowed her body to sway slightly as she began a song that had been sung for centuries. First she sang the role of a young bride leaving her mother to go live in a faraway village and then that of the mother comforting the daughter with words of love and encouragement. The guests sang along and many wept for daughters who had indeed left.

Yeraz paid no attention to the ballad at all. Lucine, blessedly, was moving exactly fourteen houses up the road to make her new home with Avo and his large family. And although it must be accepted that

she would be their bride now, their *hars,* Yeraz knew of many oppor-
tunities that would arise, and yes, be created, to share precious moments with her eldest daughter. When she herself had left her parents'
village many years ago, she had sworn to herself that her daughters, if
she were blessed with any, would never go so far.

Yeraz, for the moment, was more concerned with her younger
daughter's whereabouts. Anno's place should have been with her family every passing moment of this day. But a while ago she had tugged
on her mother's arm and told her that she must "run" to the outhouse.
Yeraz had looked at her daughter in alarm. "Are you ill, Anno?"

Anno, desperate to avoid questioning, had merely shaken her
head and left. That had been quite some time ago.

Yeraz thought it unwise to wait for Anno any longer, and with a
sweep of her arm she indicated to the guests that it was time to place
the veil on the bride's head.

Fingers were licked and cups were drained. Vests, velvet aprons,
sleeves, and skirts were straightened as all the guests turned toward
the bride.

"Quickly now!" someone called out.

"Gather closer. Where is the bride's father? Call the brothers. Call
the men!"

The three village musicians who had been silent during Takoush's
song now started a lively dance tune and the men filed in singly from
the garden. Some had arms already outstretched, fingers extended,
entering to the tune of the music.

"Smile, my daughter," Yeraz whispered in Lucine's ear. "You
are lovely. Stand straight, be brave, and bring honor to your father's
home." Yeraz kissed both Lucine's cheeks and turned to find Anno at
her side.

Anno's eyes filled with tears as she squeezed Lucine's hands, kissed
her and backed away.

Outstretched arms held a long, simple white veil. Lucine stood in the middle of the room and waited. The musicians quickened the tune and all the guests formed a large circle and danced around the bride. The veil was circled atop the bride's head three times before being placed on her head. Next came the red velvet cap, perfectly altered. The coins framed Lucine's face but with no danger of the cap sliding askew. She smiled gratefully at her aunt. Marie smiled back and gave a large nod and wink.

With a sudden surge of confidence Lucine whirled and, with arms outstretched and hands gracefully turning at the wrist, daintily began to dance toward her brothers. With heels marking the floor, both came forward to meet her and the threesome danced a tight circle while the crowd clapped and cheered.

It was at this moment that Old Mariam came through the door with her two sons and their wives. Anno had just begun to breathe normally again and feel a bit of joy in the day when she saw the woman. All turned black again and she shrunk back into the wall.

Mariam had changed from her old black skirt and blouse to a slightly newer, less faded version of the same. Her head was bare, and her long gray hair, still thick and shining with cleanliness, formed a neat bun at the back of her head. She was greeted warmly not just for her age, but because she was truly loved for herself. She was a frequent visitor to Vartan's home and had been the midwife at the birth of all his children. But since a short hour ago, Anno had forgotten all of this. She had forgotten all the kindnesses the woman had shown her; she only saw her as one more person able to thwart her and Daron's plans.

"The groom is just up the road." Mariam chuckled. "Their voices can be heard around the world."

Everyone looked to Yeraz to take the next traditional step.

Yeraz looked at her husband. Vartan, standing close to Lucine, now waited until the room was silent and then commanded, "Lock the door."

Their eldest son, Raffi, went forward and turned the key loudly.

A cheer went up and one of the women turned to Lucine and started to sing. Everyone joined in loudly. Outside, the drum and horn could be heard as the groom's family arrived and pounded on the door.

CHAPTER 3

*A*vo's dagger slapped his thigh as he walked. It was unfamiliar to him, this being the only day in his life he could legally arm himself, and he reached down to still it once more as they approached Vartan's door.

Beside him, Avo had felt his father twist and search behind them anxiously for the dozenth time.

Avo had enjoyed joking and laughing all morning. Each toast had centered on his and his family's favorable and enviable qualities. He felt as if he were basking in the sun. He labored hard with the animals and the crops and felt he had been waiting for this acknowledgment for a long time.

He had been fully scrubbed at the bathhouse, and this year's oghee had been passed around again and again while layers of his wedding attire were presented to him to wear.

He wore a wide blue *shalvar* with black and red embroidery on the sides and a matching tunic with a high, round collar. At his waist was a wide, twisted cloth over which came a single leather belt that housed his dagger. His leather boots were covered with embroidered cloth to his ankles, and were so soft he had already glanced down at his feet twice in amazement, until he had caught his father frowning at him. His head was bare and his dark, coarse hair curled unusually generously today from the steam of the bath.

Avo had watched closely as Mihran, the ironsmith, had sharpened his dagger the previous week. When he had finished, Avo had asked him to sharpen it one more time.

The Turkish soldiers thunder through our villages at their whim and we cannot arm ourselves against them and their ruination, Avo thought with disgust. *Yet, against the Kurds whose clans live in the mountains and valleys of Sassoun, the government allows us to arm ourselves for only these brief hours, against the kidnapping of our brides.*

He felt the weight of his new responsibility lay on his shoulders.

It had not been his idea to wed Lucine. Shortly after he had entered his eighteenth year, his parents had stood before him and announced that they would be sending someone to Vartan Vartanian's home to ask for her hand in marriage to Avo. They had quietly observed him for any reaction. Avo, stunned and not prepared to answer, remembered focusing on his father's thick, upturned moustache. *It must be trimmed again, soon,* he had thought foolishly.

Still they had waited. It was ultimately not Avo's decision whom he married, they all knew that, but if they were to have a reluctant bridegroom, it was better to know of it now.

Avo had eventually nodded. He knew they had chosen well for him.

"The time has come!" a man behind Avo called out.

"We have come to pluck the lovely flower from your garden," another spoke.

"Our groom here is impatient," the men laughed.

From inside the house, Raffi's voice responded loudly, "And why should we let you enter?"

There was more banging. The village houses, made of mud bricks and stone, had few windows, and even those were small and high. It worked to their advantage during attacks, but for now, Avo's family did not have the convenience of peering through the windows.

"We have a gift for the mother of the bride, of course!"

"We are giving you the first daughter of the house, the light and joy of her parents' hearth," they called from inside.

The musicians played a short dance tune. Whistling and clapping could be heard from the courtyard.

Inside, Lucine's palms were wet. Outside, Avo was wondering if this part of the wedding tradition had ever ended badly.

Coins were offered, then jewelry made of coins and still the door did not open. The music continued.

Lucine searched the guests' faces. No one looked concerned at all. Was it only herself? How long would this go on?

And suddenly the music stopped and there was silence. The godfather's voice in the courtyard was now heard clearly inside the house.

"We would like to honor the mother of the bride for raising such a daughter. On behalf of the Avedissian clan, we thank the honorable Vartanian family for raising this girl to be a good Christian and a good Armenian. We have not forgotten that our khnami Yeraz came to our village from as far away as Karabagh to wed our honorable headman, Vartan. And from the very first day of that union, we have known her to be a model wife and mother and a blessing to our village. And so we offer her a humble reminder of her childhood."

Lucine had not taken her eyes off her parents during this announcement. Would they at last open the door?

Yeraz's face softened and Vartan nodded toward his sons. Both walked solemnly forward and opened the door.

Amid music and clapping, two of Avo's cousins walked in holding a rug. It was nearly three feet wide by five feet long, with such a joyous blend of deep reds, oranges, and yellows that everyone gasped in appreciation. Smiling faces turned toward Yeraz as her eyes expertly took in the details of the rug. She would have known that this rug had come from her parents' village even if it had been mixed in with a dozen others.

She could almost smell the turmeric and berries as she gazed at the colliding shades of yellow. How many stained hands had sorted the walnut shells to obtain that inky black, she wondered, remembering her own mother's hands, cracked and dyed and busied. Deep hennas created the orange, indigo created the blue, and, of course, the crushed cochineal supplied the red on which she had locked her eyes. The field of the rug contained two large medallions outlined in black. Emerging from the sides of the medallions were leaves and tendrils of flowers in a soothing blue.

Yeraz wanted to reach out and stroke the soft pile, but knew better than to show excessive pleasure in the gift. Bolting the door in want of a gift was only the first jest of many to begin the celebrations. It need never be a gift of extraordinary value such as this one, because so many of the villagers were without the means to procure such things. It would be shameful for Yeraz to linger now, but she was nonetheless very moved by Avo's family's thoughtfulness.

Avo's father was kissing both of Vartan's cheeks now, and Yeraz called to Raffi to roll and store the rug. It was time to make their way to the church.

OLD MARIAM SLOWLY followed along with the wedding party. She had a place of honor, toward the front.

There used to be so many more of us, she thought as she walked. *Thousands and thousands more.*

The roads were always dusty and dry in late summer, but soon, the rains would flow into the cracks and the dust would clear away once more. Snows would cover the mountains and hills of Sassoun and beyond, ensuring a spring landscape of several shades of green and rivers and streams bursting with water.

Would she witness another spring, she wondered? Would any of the blessed people she walked with now, young and old? This morning she had thought not.

Her daughters-in-law had been surprised to see her prepare to leave the house with her old square handkerchief, which she used only for gathering herbs and grasses.

"There is still much to be gathered," she had announced matter-of-factly and left. She enjoyed her position of matriarch. She had earned it.

Her kerchief nearly full, she had been bending low to pluck the last few hollyhocks when she had looked up in time to see Vartan's youngest daughter scramble over the walls of the old, dry well. Again she felt her heartbeat quicken, just remembering.

Thinking Anno was being chased by a raiding band, Mariam had wildly searched the hill. Who was trying to harm the child? She listened for the sound of horses. Should she scream for help? They were too far away for the villagers to hear. She had remained crouched and hidden, but had almost, twice, decided to stumble toward the well and pull the child out before she slipped. And then she had seen him. The merchant's boy.

It had been clear at once to Mariam what they were attempting. Had she not been so frightened by it all, she might have chuckled at the sight of them. But there really was nothing Vartan and Yeraz would have thought amusing had they known of Anno's whereabouts that morning. Mariam shuddered at the thought. Daughters must be, above all else, chaste. And Vartan would see to it, with his last breath, that his daughters were.

She stopped abruptly in the middle of the road and turned. Where was the child now? She saw only Raffi, several groups behind, not laughing and singing with anyone. His body straight and his arms loosely at his sides, he scanned the hills around them with his black eyes, searching out movement.

Mariam understood at once where his attention was, as did all the villagers. The Turkish government had separate laws for the Christian citizens than for the Muslim. They had learned to be ready to defend themselves.

Mariam watched as another young man, Aram, closed in behind Raffi. But Raffi did not to turn to acknowledge his friend. Mariam thought it odd how Aram's mouth curved forcibly and the friends stood paces apart. Then Raffi suddenly uttered something and pulled Aram to him in the crook of one powerful arm. Aram's head fell against his friend's.

Mariam's curiosity was piqued, and she forgot Anno for the moment. Raffi was studying his friend in sympathy, searching his face. Then, when he noticed more than a guest or two walk past them and turn, he realized the attention they had attracted. His head lifted suddenly and his eyes locked with those of Old Mariam.

Mariam, unflinching, looked frankly back at him.

Raffi pulled at Aram, and the men began walking again. Mariam dropped her gaze and slowly turned her body toward the church once more. Behind her, she did not see Aram kick at a tiny pebble, nor did she hear him hiss, "If she is unhappy, I will take his eyes out."

Nor did she hear Raffi's even reply: "Let her be safe. Let her be sheltered. Let her be respected. It is enough. You and I have work to do."

Old Mariam wondered what they had been murmuring. Unease was always with her regarding Raffi's doings. To her, he was still a babe in Yeraz's arms. She remembered well the day he had been born.

CHAPTER 4

Sassoun 1894

Yeraz could hardly breathe. Arms were pushing, almost lifting her from behind. She tried to take great gulps of air but instead felt the dust coat her mouth and make its way deeper down her throat.

She was flanked by women and children scrambling up the mountainside. But Yeraz could not scramble. She was eight months pregnant, heavy and slow, and the Turks and Kurds had come.

Vartan had had news that thousands of Greeks had already been massacred throughout the Ottoman Empire.

"Will they come here, Vartan, to Salor?" she had asked, clutching his arm.

"I do not know," he had answered dully. "It is as if we are citizens of nowhere at all."

From a distance, Yeraz heard short, sporadic sobs and only that. She looked around her, amazed at how silent the children were in their climb.

The rocks beneath her feet slid against the ungiving soil and she nearly dropped onto her hands. A distant neighbor caught her by the waist and waited mutely until she could steady herself.

She dragged one foot after another, then rested. Ahead, several babies were shifted from one back to the next as the mothers tired. It did not matter which back, whose child.

Their destination was clear. Away. High and away. Yeraz struggled again to walk.

"With each step I am moving further away from Vartan," she panted to herself. He had rushed out the door to fight the Turks and their throngs of mercenary Kurds with his bare hands and a heart filled with rage at the lifetime of living with the same rights as a stabled beast.

Up ahead, a woman cried out sharply. The child on her back was slipping, her delicate arms giving way.

"Do not worry, Yeraz," Vartan had whispered nights ago. "The fedayees will be with us."

Her hopes had risen. "How many, Vartan?" In all of Turkey, concentrated mostly in its eastern, rural portion, there were no more than 200 young fedayees, freedom fighters, whose entire lives were dedicated to the defense of the Armenian villagers.

"A few." In fact, only four had arrived in their little village of Salor. Watching her shoulders slump, he had continued. "They will help us organize. We will form some self-defense."

Yeraz and the women had been climbing for hours. It was nearly noon now. They had thinned themselves out to almost single file as the mountainside steepened further. The summer grass was dry and blade-like in places and their backs were bent against the heat. Yeraz's head covering had dropped long ago. Their men would hold back the attack for hours. If they were to be followed, it would not be for some time.

Old Mariam was near. Yeraz could hear her words of encouragement.

"This is the way. Keep your eyes on the shades of grass," she directed.

They had stopped scrambling frantically a while ago. Now, they had all slowed and began to seek water. They could not continue without it. The women scanned the slopes around them for areas where the grass grew green. Their mountains were full of streams. They should find one soon.

Yeraz had grown used to the stabs of pain in her lower belly. She simply ground her teeth in silence until they stopped. She did not care about the pain. Just let there not be blood, she prayed.

Mouths hung open in thirst and the women spat on the parched ground, trying to clear their throats of dust. Some dropped to the ground retching.

Yeraz thought only of Vartan. She remembered his face as she had seen it just this morning at early dawn. He had thrown open the door of their sleeping room and taken two quick strides to her mattress. She had not even known that he had been out already because her sleep had been so heavy and deep these last weeks. He had knelt and wrapped his arms fully around her waist and pulled her to a sitting position. Astonished, she tried to speak, but his eyes told her everything. He was pulling her boots on and lacing them, all the while shouting directions to all the women of the household. They must leave, now, up the mountain and not return until he came after them.

"Go now! Do not look back. Take nothing. There is no time," he instructed. And for a fleeting moment, he did something he would have only done in utter darkness and privacy, he laid his head on Yeraz's breast and kissed her stomach. And suddenly on his feet again, he was gone.

The person in front of her stopped. Yeraz stopped as well and leaned against a ledge. For a long while now, they had walked beneath the shade of vultures' wings. The large black birds had glided above them and patiently blinked at the newly arrived clusters of desperation. Yeraz focused on one now.

"You will not get me," she said silently. "Nor will you get Vartan's child." She protected her stomach with both arms. Hopelessness was something her people had always lived with. But they had not died because of it. Turks. Vultures. It seemed all the same.

A cry went out. Yeraz looked ahead. Kurds, perhaps? No. She sensed excitement. Vartan's mother, who had never for a moment left her side, did so now. She pushed ahead and disappeared. Yeraz did not move. She had been told not to. Mariam appeared at her side now and smoothed the hair off her forehead. Marie, Vartan's younger sister, sat at Yeraz's feet. Dust, finely and deeply layered, coated the girl's shoes and skirt, and her cheeks burned frighteningly. How Vartan adored that child. Yeraz reached out to stroke her head, but her hand dropped in mid-air. The child was too far.

The line began moving. Wild goats had been seen ahead. Water was near.

"Walk, Hars, walk." Her mother-in-law reappeared and pulled her along excitedly, a bit hard. Yeraz followed, her legs slightly parted now as the blood that had started to flow ran thick and warm past her knees to her ankles.

She allowed herself to be pulled several feet more before she protested. She lifted her skirts to hear Vartan's mother exclaim.

"It is all right. It is all right," the older woman kept repeating after her initial shock. Yeraz felt herself led away from the single file of women she had stood with. "There is a bit of shade over there. Lie down in the shade. Here."

The pain in her groin had not eased when she finally lay down. It increased in waves. Through eyes blurred with pain, she watched Mariam work over her.

Water, cool, blessed water, was brought to her lips and wiped across her forehead and neck. Her head tossed with the pain. Her fists clutched brittle blades of grass.

Visions of a story came to her, of a young woman, like herself, giving birth in a church. A church that the Turks had packed with villagers and then set fire to. They had carried the young woman in with arms and legs splayed and sealed the door after her. Yeraz screamed.

"Hush your screams," Vartan's mother told her fervently, close to her ear. "You must not scream."

Yeraz writhed in silence until dusk fell. She pushed one last time and a baby emerged into her mother-in-law's blood-filled palms.

"It is a boy," she heard Mariam say.

"A boy." She took this in slowly. The baby was not dead, then. She heard its weak cry.

A boy, she thought more clearly. Their firstborn, and he would be named after his paternal grandfather. Yeraz actually began to feel some joy lying there on the ground, with rocks censuring her every move and a vulture blinking at her from the branches. She smiled and the bird's image blurred as tears gathered in her eyes.

"And we will have more." It was as if she spoke to Vartan. "We will have many more children to replace those who will surely die today. And the next will also be a boy, and he will be named Vrej, *revenge*."

ihran cursed his wife loudly, happily damning her and her entire clan, those within earshot and without. In his rantings he always gave preference to his mother-in-law. He loathed her and it flew off his tongue easily.

"Let the donkeys have their way with you! You and your mother! Let them drop feces into your mouths. Aha! And your sisters. They are not better than you."

Mihran would usually have stopped here, but not today. It was a rare opportunity he had today.

"Do you think I do not know how they whisper when my back is turned? And their husbands too! Line them side by side and not a full pair of genitals will you find. Aakkhh." He shook his head in disgust and lifted both heavily muscled arms. "If it were not for these, you would have all starved by now! Remember that."

When he had wed the eldest daughter of the house, his father-in-law had looked at Mihran's thin shoulders and shaken his head. But Mihran had trudged with him to the forge daily and had learned to be a better ironsmith than the old man had ever been.

"Only God knows what I have endured at your hands. Let Him strike you blind. All of you! You deserve it. In a houseful of prostitutes and pimps is where I have lived. Nothing more than that!"

Mihran always like to throw a thing or two to ensure everyone's full attention to the end. He looked around the sparse room. The stool? No. There were only two, and it hurt his backside to sit long on the floor cushions. The lamp? It would be too difficult to replace. There were some books, but he could never purposely damage a book. His wife's knitting? He realized this indecision was ruining his chances of cowing the females further, so he made long, decisive strides toward the water jug. It was across the room and very near to where his mother-in-law sat scowling at him. He picked it up and smashed it inches away from her feet. Water splashed everywhere as it shattered on the floor.

Good, Mihran thought to himself. Her skirts were left soaked in places now as well.

"Tooh!" he made a last disgusted spitting noise in her direction and left the tiny house.

He walked down the road a bit and halted. He had forgotten his fez, and he preferred to keep his balding head protected from the weather. But it did not matter. He would need a better reason than a head covering to go back to that bunch just now.

He rubbed his temples. Why had he not had a drop of luck in his lifetime, he wondered for the hundredth time?

This part of the village was empty now and quiet. Far away, he heard singing and loud shouts from the wedding celebration. His children, Aram and Takoush, were there, and most of his neighbors. It was why he had been able to empty his heart a little without being heard. But he did not feel better for having done it. Still, it was necessary.

He and his wife would soon have to make their own way to the church square, as well, to join the party. Vartan was a good man, and had been a friend to him, but he could not go just now. He must find some peace first. Mihran moved off the road and slipped through a narrow opening between the walls of two houses.

He paused, thinking he heard his wife call after him, but moved on again. It was only the barking of a dog.

These narrow passages could be found here and there throughout the entire village. They were narrow enough for a person to fit through, but never horses or field animals. Running along the width of the houses, they served the villagers as escape routes or for relaying messages. He used one now as a shortcut.

Once among the trees that ringed the village, he put his hands behind his back and listened for the familiar hum. And scent.

The trunks of the pines around him were thick and solid. The needles crunched and bent under his feet and he felt awkward, as always, disturbing the silence and serenity here. He weaved slowly through the trees. The wide branches cooled the air as well as his temper. He liked to trail his fingertips along the rough bark as he walked past. It was his silent greeting and his grateful acknowledgment of their acceptance.

He would not have to go far now. He sniffed the air. Which would he detect first? The scent or the hum? It was a game he remembered playing long ago, with his mother, before she died. The skin on his scalp and forearms tingled happily. He heard them.

Still on the edges of the wooded area where light filtered abundantly through the branches of the pine, fir, and oaks, Mihran stood before a cluster of hives. This year, there were six thriving colonies, all firmly built into the hollows and crevices of the proud trees. Many of the villagers kept hives near their homes. Honey was a staple for them and their favorite sweetener. But these wild forest hives were Mihran's own special discovery.

It was time to harvest, but not today. He had wandered here for solace only. He moved closer and stood only a foot away from one of the hives. He had built his immunity to stings months ago, in the early spring. He had quickly rubbed cool mud on them, over his arms and neck. Once, he remembered well, he had had to drop his shalvar down to his ankles and slap away the young bee clinging to his inner thigh. No amount of cool mud had eased that sting for hours.

The worker bees moved in and around the cells of the hive, hundreds at a time. The large queen, Mihran knew, was somewhere about. Where else would she be, impervious and proud? Mihran eyed the drones concernedly. It was a dangerous time for them, for the drones were the only males of the colony and their sole reason for existence was to mate with the queen. The mating, Mihran knew, took place somewhere in midair, and immediately afterwards, the drone would fall paralyzed to his death.

"Huh," Mihran thought, as he remembered his own box-shaped wife and her thin, pursed lips. The only matings he had ever known had been like death.

For the drones, time was running out. Soon, they would be thrown out of the hive to die.

Mihran took a step back suddenly and forced his thoughts away from the luckless drones. He was not like them at all, he realized, as he remembered his brave, healthy son. Aram and Takoush were his reason for surviving in that household whose women would never let him forget that he was a *dan pesa,* a penniless groom. He had been an orphan for so long, sheltering under this roof and then that. He had had no hope of acquiring a house of his own, so he had come to live in the house of his bride, something that was almost never done in any Armenian village. It had been almost twenty years now, and they had pecked and needled him about it, nearly every day. And every day, he had swallowed their poisonous words and carried on with his work, because of his children. And now, it was time to harvest more honey for trade.

CHAPTER 6

Daron kicked up straw as he nervously paced up and down their small stable. He appreciated the cool darkness inside. He could not stop perspiring, and the hens stopped to peck at him suspiciously now and then. It had been two hours since he had seen Anno at the well and his shirt was soaked down his back and under his arms. He kept picturing Anno's fingers finally releasing their hold on the blocks, grasping at nothing but the gravelly belly of the well and then falling, endlessly falling.

He would speak to his father today and put an end to their risk taking.

He was practicing different ways of introducing this subject.

"Hayrig," he thought he would use the formal way of addressing his father. "Baba" sounded childish just now. "Have I not done well in helping you with your trade and in the fields? Do you not think I could continue to do well on my own soon? I could ease your burden then."

No. Daron shook his head. His father would dislike this round-about way. They did not need to speak of livelihood. Buying, selling, trading was what his father had always done, and his grandfather before him. This was not the problem. The problem was that Anno was the village headman's daughter and Daron's family was not well known to them. And that, Daron decided, straightening his shoulders and kicking decidedly once at the ground, was just something his father would have to cope with. Swinging around toward the house, he went in search of him.

Daron's father, Mgro, sat on a cushion by the cylindrical stone oven built into the ground. The top of the furnace was level with the floor of the house. In this *toneer* all household baking took place, and it served as a sort of central heating system as well. However, just now the toneer was not lit, but covered with a round piece of wood topped with a clean cloth and turned into a low table. There, Mgro sat with his father and younger brother and their ever-present cups of oghee. Their presence did not deter Daron.

Their entire family shared a roof and he had learned from birth that grandparents, aunts, and uncles were as parents to him. And all the children, consequently, were equally the responsibility of all adults.

Daron lowered himself to one knee a few feet from the table and waited in silence for his presence to be acknowledged. The men were discussing the value of traveling to Moush or Van once more to bring more goods before winter came. Their people were so self-sufficient that Mgro's business depended on special occasions like weddings or christenings, and the season for those was nearly over. They stopped speaking when Daron approached the table. He knew it would be left to his father to deal with this interruption.

Mgro looked at Daron. Daron resisted the urge to bow his head as he had been taught to do when speaking to an elder. He instead met Mgro's gaze and was relieved to see good humor there.

"Hayrig, I have something to discuss with you that is very important to me," he began.

Daron sensed his grandfather leaning in to better hear and wished his sweat-soaked shirt did not cling so closely.

"I am listening," Mgro answered evenly.

"I have ended my seventeenth year, as you know. I have been

considering for some time now that I would like to be married. I wanted to be certain before I spoke of it. Now, I am certain. I would like to marry." Before anyone could interrupt, Daron took a step forward and continued. "I would like to marry Headman Vartan's younger daughter."

Daron paused. He did not expect to glean a hint of his father's thoughts by looking into his face. He never had been able to. Mgro's profession had called for one important lesson to be learned early in life and that was not to allow facial expressions to betray his true emotions. Emotions, his father had told him, were a private thing that could not be avoided. Everyone had them. They could be suppressed. Actions, however, made the man, or ruined him.

Mgro motioned with his arm for Daron to sit down. At first, Daron thought to sit on the straw matting covering the floor, but wanting to be on the same level with the other men, he went to fetch a cushion.

"Vartan's younger daughter? The small, dark one?" Mgro questioned.

Was she dark? Daron was nonplussed. He remembered comments made from his father in passing. Mgro liked fair-skinned women and Anno was small, yes… He caught himself. This was not important. He knew they both spoke of Anno and so they must continue.

"Well, yes, that is Anno. Her hair is dark," he conceded, "if that is what you mean." He was about to say that her eyes were not dark at all, and in the sunlight they were a warm, golden brown, but he should not seem so familiar. This was dangerous. He drew himself up and started again, this time remembering his training. He wiped all expression from his face and spoke as if he were describing the characteristics of a tool.

"Yes, yes," Mgro interrupted. Daron realized Mgro knew very well of whom he spoke. Was his father perhaps simply searching for time to think?

"Daron, there could be a problem here. Did you not think of this? A girl like her might very well already be promised to someone else. We have no close ties to that family and cannot know of any such arrangements."

Daron did not speak, did not dare exclaim that he already knew that there was no such arrangement and of that he was completely certain.

"If there is such an arrangement in place, it cannot be broken," Mgro went on. It would deeply shame the promised family. It will not be done."

Daron did not speak. He wished his father to continue, to hear of any other objections he might have.

"Do you know her age?" Mgro asked.

Daron did not pretend to hesitate. "She has entered her fifteenth year."

He watched the men exchange glances for the first time. They then studied their cups, but Daron saw definite smiles on their faces. Yes, of course they knew. *Our boy is struck, in love,* they would be thinking.

"Daron, listen to me." Mgro put his palms flat on the table and leaned in.

"If you wish to marry, you will. But with this girl, it is not what you wish or what I wish. Although, at her age why she has not been betrothed yet if it were so, I do not know. The women will know." Mgro referred to Daron's aunt and grandmother.

"We will do what we can. If not this girl, then another," Mgro tried to finish tidily.

Now Daron put both palms on the table and leaned in slowly, just as his father had done.

"Hayrig," Daron quietly said, using the formal term for the second time. "This girl. It is to be *this girl.* Not another."

Three pairs of widened eyes settled on Daron. He knew it was out of character for him to speak this way, especially about a decision not his to make. No one breathed as Daron and Mgro locked eyes across the table. Daron knew he could very well be thrown out of the room at this moment and all hope of his father's help would be lost. But he had to know. Did his father fully understand and did he have his help, or would he have to go forward on his own?

Daron did not move as his father studied him, the strain on his face, the perspiration at his temples. Mgro slowly pulled a handkerchief from his pocket and dropped it near Daron's hands. He thought he saw his father's eyes soften and knew instantly what he was thinking.

"You take after your mother's side, my boy," Mgro had told him a dozen times. "Always carry a handkerchief."

His mother, too, had tended to perspire along the temples. That last day, the women could not dry her temples quickly enough. The labor had been normal, Daron had learned, but the afterbirth had not come. There were physicians in Moush, to the north, and several Armenian and American physicians and more to the east in Bitlis and Van, but they were too far away to help. Daron had just entered his fourth year. His grandmother and aunt had been mothers to him and his infant sister from that day on.

Daron knew Mgro was wishing she were here now.

"We will see, Daron." Mgro gave his answer kindly. "There are rules."

Daron nodded only, but he was relieved. "We will see" was the closest his father ever came to "Yes." Mgro would do his part, and so the first stone was turned.

CHAPTER 7

*R*affi wanted to whistle, but suppressed the urge. He was happiest when riding out on his horse, and their distance today from the villages made his mind wander away from his purpose. He reached into his pocket for another dried fig. A walnut came along as well.

He looked over his shoulder again while Meghr, his horse, trod on without any lead. He was a sure-footed mountain horse, sensible and calm. His coat was a reddish brown, always reminding Raffi of shades of glowing wood. Yeraz believed that Meghr's ancestors came from her native Karabagh, because she claimed that her grandfather had owned a small stable full of horses with Meghr's same sweet face.

Raffi did not argue much with his mother. Meghr, he knew, was a perfect mix of horse breeds and a fine saddle horse and he was most fortunate to have him.

Procuring more horses for the fedayees had been the sole reason for this journey. The information he had retrieved from a neighboring province guaranteed the gift of four steeds from a prosperous villager. Raffi would ensure their delivery at a later date.

He had now reached the tail end of his journey and would reach Salor late the next night.

Raffi remembered when the news had reached them that Sultan Abdul Hamid had been overthrown and the Young Turks had come into power. They were told that Turks and Christians had celebrated together for days in the capital. The Young Turks promised Armenians all over the Ottoman Empire that they would be treated as the citizens they were. This promise was to extend to the overtaxed and beaten in the faraway eastern provinces as well. The fedayees came down off their mountains as their leaders told them to believe in these new-thinking Young Turks.

That had been five years ago. Those who believed them had been fools.

Meghr drank from a stream and Raffi slipped off his back to stretch. He searched the cliffs for movement but thus far saw nothing threatening. On this journey he had passed camps of Kurds who had no quarrel with the Armenians. The children had stopped to stare at him, a few prepared to throw rocks, but had been called back by their elders. He had passed many villages as well. There were no lone farmhouses to be found along this way. Villages were formed around natural water sources and the homes were built close together for defense. Some of the villages were oases of beauty, green and lush with fruit orchards and fields of wheat and barley and corn. The landscape between villages, however, was dry, with rocky mountain cliffs overhanging the paths. Here, the air was cool and bright and Raffi enjoyed it, knowing that as he progressed higher to Sassoun, fog would be possible at any time.

Two falcons glided close overhead and Raffi admired the symmetrical shades and dabbings of brown and black under their wings. The sky beyond was blue and cloudless and the sweet smell of the dry grass filled him, at last, with a moment of peace.

From the day of his birth Raffi had begun absorbing the fact that his people were, if nothing else, tenacious. He often wondered if those of his people who finally left and emigrated to foreign countries to worship God and live without fear had found their lives acceptable. They did not live in homes that resembled small cages, perhaps, nor were their doors pounded upon in the dark night. The sight of uniforms no longer made them want to flee, and they were not called names in the streets by people mocking their religion. But what did they have now, Raffi wondered time and again, to make them feel joy?

They could no longer pull the ripe, dusty fruit off their own trees, could they? Or gather under a tree at harvest time with dozens of family members to eat their noon meal, teasing and laughing at the slower workers. And did they miss the icy mountain water that would be passed around at every meal, with the youngest drinking first, their eyes sparkling with mischief as they prolonged their moments of attention? Did they miss the echoes of the priests' songs and hymns resonating off the damp, moss-covered walls of their churches? And the tight, muscled grip of arms linked while they danced their circle dances, whistling, dipping, leaping in unison, while the smoke from the roasting meat soaked their hair and skin. And the children, all the children, running and playing around the skirts of the women, stopped at any time by any of the mothers or grandmothers and handed a dripping piece of kebab tightly wrapped in lavash bread. Or the sight of the orchards in the early spring, blossoming in shades of pink and white and green, and the young shepherds cursing tangled flocks, tripping and slapping their sticks at the uncaring animals. Did they miss that? Raffi did not know. Perhaps they did not need all that, but for him, anything else, anything but this, was unacceptable. He would not be driven out. He did not judge those who finally left of their own free will. Perhaps if he had a wife and children to protect, he would do the same for them. But, no, he would not be driven out.

Suddenly, Meghr's ears straightened, his head lifted and his nostrils widened. Raffi pulled back slightly on the reins to listen. At first there was nothing, and then he heard voices, chanting in Turkish. The chants were prayers and Raffi thought he heard many different voices. He allowed Meghr to walk again, slightly faster now. With any luck, he would pass them and disappear over the next hill before their prayers ended. They were off to his right, somewhere in a cluster of shade trees, facing Mecca, away from him. He could not believe his luck. He watched their arms raised and lowered, raised and lowered. They were gendarmes, and Raffi knew he did not pass unobserved. Twenty more paces and he urged Meghr on as fast as he dared. They could not gallop just now because of the noise and the suspicion it would cause.

Finally over the hill, Raffi let Meghr have his lead as quickly as was possible on the narrow, rocky ledges. There was no doubt that they would be followed, but Raffi was doing his best to make sure that they were caught in a village, with plenty of people around, so that the meeting might end in just a beating or a fine, instead of imprisonment or death.

Nearly an hour later, Raffi entered the village of Khoronk. Poplars, willows, and maple trees shaded the narrow road and a good-sized stream ran the length of it. Upstream, Turkish women conversed and washed dishes.

Raffi had felt rather than heard the gendarmes' pursuit up the mountain trail, and he felt no surprise now to see them finally come thundering in on their horses, yelling and shouting as soon as they spotted Raffi.

"You! Infidel!"

On foot now, slowly leading Meghr by the reins, Raffi inhaled deeply and forced himself to turn slowly, feigning surprise at the commotion.

There were three of them and they towered over Raffi in their saddles.

"What is your business here, giaour?" one demanded, branding him as the non-Muslim "faithless" person he was.

"I have no business here," Raffi answered meekly. "I was looking for water for my animal."

"Where have you come from and what is your name?" one demanded.

Raffi gave a false name and told them he had come from Diarbekir. One of the gendarmes demanded his identification papers.

As a boy, Raffi had been sent to a monastery in Moush to study and could read well. But now, he wanted the Turks to believe that he was illiterate, a common villager, and not worth their time. He squinted at his papers and handed them to the gendarmes upside down.

The papers were straightened, read, and thrown back at him.

"There is much spying in these parts," the same gendarme continued. "You are one of those troublemakers."

"No, Excellency, I am not. I went to visit relatives." Raffi tried hard to sound respectful.

"Give their names," another demanded.

"I would do so gladly, Excellencies," he started, again promoting their status many-fold, "but I do not want to waste your valuable time. Because I must admit that by the time I reached there, I was told that I was too late. They had gone to America." He drew out the pronunciation of the distant land in four rough syllables and laughed a little, shrugging, as if the relatives had emigrated to the moon.

"Give us your papers. You fit the description of a man we are looking for, a messenger from Diarbekir."

Raffi handed them his falsified papers.

"We saw you coming from the west, not the east," the first gendarme accused. "You were lying from the start."

By now, men and women alike had stopped all activity to listen to the exchange. And this was just what Raffi had hoped for.

"No, Excellency, you are mistaken, if you will forgive me for saying so. But I passed you as you prayed, and so you could not possibly be sure of which way I came. Unless," Raffi drew out the last syllable thinly, "unless, it is in your religion to gaze to the right and to the left as you worship, then I could accept that you saw from which direction I came." He shrugged again, as if leaving the decision completely in their hands. "For it is true, I know, that I passed as you were most devoutly praying," he finished humbly.

The Turks stared down, speechless. No devout Muslim would ever break concentration at prayers and observe passersby. They glanced at each other, lost for an answer. Raffi took this opportunity to bow his head to them to indicate a graceful end to the questioning and slip away.

"Stop, giaour!" the first Turk commanded again.

Raffi obeyed, biting the insides of his cheeks.

"Where do you think you are going?"

"To get water for my animal," Raffi repeated dumbly, appearing to be slightly exasperated now.

The crowd was silent no longer, Raffi realized. They were whispering to each other and backing away. Some were leaving altogether.

"What is happening?" one gendarme asked the other.

A woman who stood alone from the others spoke very quietly.

"They say there is smallpox to the west. I heard so today."

Raffi turned to see a young Muslim woman, covered from head to foot in colorful silk scarves and a woolen skirt and jacket of the finest quality. She was quite tall and slender. Only her eyes were left uncovered, and they were dark and slanted.

Raffi looked away quickly and made a slow show of wiping at a perspiring forehead and rubbing parched lips.

The gendarmes peered at Raffi differently suddenly, then in unison mercilessly yanked their reins so widely that Raffi was suddenly looking into the rumps of three large steeds.

"Leave here at once! Be on your way and do not let your horse drink anywhere. Go now!" they ordered and galloped off.

Raffi turned Meghr around as ordered and headed back out of the village the same way he had entered. The crowd scattered quickly and some of the women screamed at him to hurry. He felt rocks at his back. He turned to search one last time for the young woman. She was hurrying along with the crowd, leading a small child, but their eyes met briefly, and Raffi thought she smiled.

CHAPTER 8

The following night, Raffi's tall, thin frame passed through his father's courtyard. The front door swung open and he felt Vrej reach with both arms to help him remove his woolen coat. He slid his weary body onto a divan by the door.

Across the room he watched Yeraz take one rushed step toward him and suddenly halt. She clasped her hands tightly together and squeezed her eyes shut. Raffi watched her lips moving silently in prayer, and then, he too closed his eyes and wordlessly leaned his head back against the wall.

Anno considered Yeraz for a moment but decided she did not care to practice the same restraint. She hastened forward and pulled off Raffi's boots and socks. A neighbor had informed them that Raffi had been seen returning, and so she was prepared with a copper tub of warm water and soap.

Anno began washing his feet, gently at first, and when her brother still did not open his eyes to acknowledge her, she playfully tickled the bottom. Raffi pulled his foot back instinctively and flicked the top of her head sharply with his thumb and forefinger, never moving his head from its resting position.

"Ay!" she protested.

"Then behave," Raffi responded and opened his eyes briefly to smile at her.

As he did so, he paused. Even in his tired state he was caught unawares at how much her face had altered. He had expected to see the same round, shining face he had always known, and instead he saw delicate cheekbones where none had been visible before and large, brown, shadowed eyes looking back at him. Anno saw the surprise in his face and looked down.

"Have you been ill, Anno?" he asked.

Anno shook her head and hastily scrubbed at the top of his feet, careful not to show her face to him again.

Raffi noticed her agitation and the water she had tipped onto the floor.

"But you do not look well." His voice slow and hoarse with fatigue, he persisted. "When was I last here? Three weeks ago? Not even a month. You were not like this."

Anno was afraid. She lifted and dried her brother's feet and suddenly wanted only to hasten away with her tub of filmy water, away from the attention he had brought upon her and the questions he should not be asking.

"I shall bring your slippers," she mumbled, and with shaking hands she collected her bowl and moved away.

Raffi nearly spoke out loud after her, but closed his mouth again. He took in the room full of people who stood clustered close and had never taken their eyes off him.

"All went well," he said simply.

Raffi watched his father's shoulders relax and heard a low grunt of relief.

Raffi had not even told Vartan where he had gone or what his task had been. The fedayees were instructed to never tell. It was to protect both the fedayees themselves and the villagers in case they were captured. One could not tell what one did not know.

Yeraz hurriedly laid the low table with bread, yogurt, olives, and tomatoes and Vartan brought forward a cup of oghee.

Anno was forgotten.

CHAPTER 9

That evening, in Khoronk, the young Turkish woman stood before the town's chief official, her husband. Her vision was blurred from the powerful, knuckled slap he had given her, but she was still standing.

"I have brought a prostitute into my home! A prostitute who speaks to any man who passes! Did any other person on the street speak to those policemen but you? Man or woman?"

Derya looked up and tried to focus on his face. Just that morning she had wondered if it were possible to loathe this man more. His red velvet fez had tipped to one side and only partly covered his shiny baldness. His round face was red and spittle dripped from the sides of his mouth. His belly heaved up and down with his heavy, angry breaths and his velvet vest had fallen completely away from his bulging belly. Behind him, as far away as possible, stood his first wife, quaking against a wall.

It was hard to tell if he expected a response to his question. Thinking that ignoring him might be worse, Derya offered a quiet "No."

"Whore!" he screamed at her again and his fists pounded her to the floor this time. "You still speak then! You still have things to say! Well, let us see what you have to say when I am finished with you!"

He yanked her to her feet and gave one, two, three concentrated blows across her face and then he swung her around and gave her three more on her backside. She toppled forward onto the carpets. After that she did not know any longer if he used his fists or his feet, she only felt her body jerked and rolled on the carpets of his large sitting room and was distantly aware of glass and lamps falling all around her. She thought she could still hear Mehmet screaming curses at her, but by then everything was muffled by an angry humming in her ears. He ground her face down into the carpet and her wounds burned and bled into the rough wool. The last blows came between her shoulder blades and she gasped for air before losing consciousness.

After a long while, she thought, she awoke to the sound of breathing, raspy and short. Eventually, after deep concentration, she realized it was her own breath she heard and accepted that he had not killed her this time either. She was still belly down on the carpet where he had left her, and her head was slumped to one side. The pain came gradually from far away, and then it was so forceful that she started to weep but did not know if she was making a sound or not. She tried to open her eyes, but only one lid lifted. Was she alone? She could not move, but she tried to focus her vision with her one eye. She thought she saw something. A figure. A figure was creeping slowly closer and she knew it was her child, her son. And as he cowered nearer, she saw that his slanted eyes were now rounded with terror.

CHAPTER 10

Anno was no longer finding it difficult to rise in the early morning. Although the air had become very chilly now that autumn was ending, she was much too uneasy to sleep well anymore, and she welcomed any activity at all to take her thoughts away from Daron.

No one had come to her father's house to discuss their betrothal. Two months had passed since the day of Lucine's wedding and the scrapes on her arms were healed. Her long sleeves covered whatever slight scars remained.

She folded the family's bedding carefully and stacked it by a wall in the sleeping room, first her parents', then Vrej's, and lastly her own. Raffi's quilted woolen mattress and blanket were at the bottom of the pile; they had been left there for days now because he was not at home. She did not ask where he was or when he would return, because she would be silenced with cold stares from the elders if she did. She had tried once before and had practically sunk into the floor with the intensity of the warnings she had seen there.

Her mother had not removed Lucine's bedding, but had instead moved it aside where extra pillows and blankets were kept for cold nights or visitors.

"Anno! Where are you, girl?" Aunt Marie called out sharply. It was baking day and she had appeared at dawn to help Yeraz, just as

Yeraz would do in turn for Aunt Marie's household.

Anno peeked around the door to the front room. Her aunt's reddened and flour-dusted face looked back at her as she mechanically patted the last of the dough into plump, rounded discs. Anno looked away, surprised to discover how little guilt she felt at the reproach she saw there.

Yeraz had taken the freshest of the lavash from the top of the pile and placed it on the table for the men along with cheese and cups of tea.

Anno listened to their conversation as she braided her hair.

"Maratuk was crystal clear this morning," Uncle Hagop announced loudly. He was Vartan's father's brother and the oldest living member of their family.

On the days that Mount Maratuk was unobscured and vivid, Uncle Hagop let it be known proudly, almost as if he were personally responsible for it being just that way. Vartan and Vrej nodded but never looked up from their breakfast. All knew that this was the old man's way of relating the weather.

If it looked like rain, he would say quietly, "Maratuk is lost behind the clouds. I either glimpsed a peak just now or I did not. I am not sure." In the obscure winter months, he would shake his head sadly and murmur once, "Maratuk is not there." He would seem slightly bewildered on those days when the clouds covered the beloved mountain peaks for days on end. He would come inside from the cold and once again shake his head at the household. It was as if he had not lived in this village, in these highlands, for over seven decades at all and did not understand the pattern of the seasons. To start the day without taking in the wide stretch of the mountain's base and its long row of dipping and rising peaks always left him lost. Why should he not see it?

In the summer, when there was almost always a slight haze from behind which Maratuk stood, he might make several announcements during the day. "Maratuk was clear as a bell just an hour ago. Now it is gone. Let us see what will happen."

Fog, thick and fast-moving, was also common year-round and teased Uncle Hagop mercilessly. At the evening meal he might blaze accusingly, "Maratuk was shining this morning, each peak. Then, at noon, it all disappeared." He would pause to make sure that all present understood the full extent of this misfortune, that a day should begin with such promise of good weather for them all and then be unexpectedly cut short. Already worrying about the next morning, he would remove his fez and say, "We shall see about tomorrow."

"It will be a fine day for finishing up this field work, then," Vartan announced now, rising from his cushion, and Vrej fluidly did the same and began wrapping himself in coat and hat.

Including Uncle Hagop himself, the Vartanian men dispersed to begin the long day's work.

The entire village was joined together to thresh the wheat. Endless wagons full of straw were sorted from the grain and moved up and down the roads to be stored in the stables. The wheat was then either ground to flour or stored for various dishes to be enjoyed throughout the year.

Today, Anno would join the other women and children of different households to winnow the grain. The wheat would be laid thinly on large, clean cloths and hit with sticks to separate it from the husks. Then, with shovels, they would toss the grain and chaff into the air so that the chaff would fly off and the grain would fall neatly to the cloth.

Anno's hair was now neatly braided down her back and she had on a long, faded woolen jumper that covered her to mid-calf. She looked down to make sure that the baggy trousers underneath fell evenly at her ankles before joining the women to sit on the cushions the men had just vacated.

Aunt Marie wrapped thick slices of salted goat cheese into the warm lavash.

"Let the winnowing of the wheat be over soon," Yeraz sighed. "We are falling behind on storing the vegetables."

The rooftops were never bare this time of year. Tomatoes, sliced in half, were laid out there to dry. Figs, apples, apricots, plums, and pears were dried whole and halved. Cabbages and vegetables were pickled. Walnuts and hazelnuts were gathered now and stored in their shells. Mulberries were stored in one corner, waiting for Uncle Hagop to begin his distilling.

"Do you know," Aunt Marie started, "it is two years now that I have noticed the eggplants in the merchant's garden."

Anno choked but was able to keep the tea from spurting out of her mouth at this unexpected mention of Daron's family. Her cheeks burned and she kept her head lowered as she composed herself. Yeraz stopped her earthenware cup in midair and looked fully at her daughter.

Aunt Marie followed Yeraz's distracted stare to settle on her niece, and wishing to quickly regain Yeraz's full attention, she whipped out a cloth and dangled it directly under Anno's nose. Anno mumbled something and snatched it gratefully.

"They are not too fat. Rather long instead of fat and nearly perfect." Marie continued. "Last year I looked upon them and thought it luck, but no, it seems they are the same again this year. What do you think it is, Sister Yeraz?"

"I would like to see them too," Yeraz murmured, expertly pulling off only as much lavash as she intended to eat from the large round.

"I would like to see them as well, Mama," Anno's voice was even and contained. She knew this was a perfect and rare opportunity to actually go to Daron's home. From an early age she had loved to work in the vegetable garden and had shown a true understanding of what the vegetables needed to thrive. She had even tried growing flowers from bulbs here and there in their small courtyard to border the vegetables. So she hoped now that her request should not raise any suspicions. She chewed her bread slowly and waited.

"It must be a new seed then," Aunt Marie continued.

"From Van," Yeraz and Marie concluded together and smiled.

The merchant's wife had come from Van. He went there infrequently still.

"They will pick and dry them soon, Mama," Anno offered, a bit desperate now. "Shall we go today?"

"Today? The lavash has been baked and stacked as high as my head. Shall we leave it just that way? The wheat is to be winnowed and sorted today. Today, tomorrow and the day after that, my daughter. The potatoes, the turnips, the onions," she counted off on fingers not holding lavash, "must still be stored in jugs to be buried in the stable. And *then* the men will be hungry in the fields soon, waiting for their meal, while we still sit here and chat. How, my daughter, can we look at eggplants?" Yeraz implored, eyebrows fully arched.

"Then let us go now, quickly, look and get on with our work." Anno decided, and, rising, began to clear away the remaining breakfast.

Marie stared after Anno, amazed at the turn this conversation had taken. Anno was everyone's favorite and much indulged, but to decide on a morning visit during these desperately busy autumn days was unthinkable.

It was then Yeraz began to understand much that she had struggled to understand before. No, she knew this visit could not be about eggplants at all. This was about her daughter's quiet detachment of late, her restlessness and dark-circled eyes.

Yeraz thought of the merchant and his family. His daughter was young and sweet, Yeraz knew, but never a playmate of Anno's. But the merchant's son, or his nephews, were more of a possible age of interest. Now, she believed, she was closer to an answer. It was certainly a good time to go look at eggplants, after all.

"Marie, you come as well," Yeraz decided.

They scattered in different directions then, the older women donning head coverings before leaving the house. Anno, Yeraz noticed, was checking all angles of her face in a narrow mirror.

As they hurried down the lanes, greetings were returned every few yards. To the right and left of the road were flat-roofed homes clustered tightly together. They noted as much activity in the homes and on the roads as on the roofs.

An old woman seated under the shade of a hazel tree simultaneously churned her goatskin full of milk and rocked the grandchild strapped to her chest. She snapped angrily at a young boy pulling a cart full of straw too close for her liking. "Continue just this way and you will kick up enough dust under those wheels to choke the lice on your head as well as everyone else, you careless scamp!"

Mihran was already red-faced and hard at work repairing field tools as the sparks flew out about them. The waiting men loudly advised and directed his every move.

Anno glanced up at the sun worriedly. Were they too late, she wondered? Had Daron left for the fields already? They would not have passed him. His home was on the very bottom of this village road and on the other side began the orchards and then the grain fields beyond to where he would have headed. Or, worse than that, he could have left hours ago to tend his family's herd and would be somewhere in the ridges and knolls surrounding them.

To their left now was the church. Crumbling in places from the last attacks in 1894, the porous stone of its walls bore stains of a deep and permanent brown, the blood of the people slain there. But it still stood and served as the heart of the village.

A large, rectangular slab of walnut stood not far from the church door, and short wooden clubs hung at its side. Each Sunday the clubs were lifted and pounded against the walnut to call the villagers to church. Now, Anno watched them swing listlessly in the breeze. Was there anything more stubborn than a church? she wondered to herself.

They were almost at the end of the road now. Anno began to feel foolish. What were they doing marching up to Daron's home this way? She felt unclean suddenly. She turned to look at her mother, and Yeraz returned her look expressionlessly.

Anno's face heated and she quickly looked away.

She knows! Anno realized at that instant. Her sight clouded, but her legs continued to move forward mechanically. Ten paces later she looked at her mother again, but Yeraz's face was averted.

Behind a high, mud-covered brick wall was the entrance to Mgro's small courtyard and garden. Facing them was one door that opened up to a tiny store with room for four or five shelves of goods. Anno saw no one there and looked beyond to the stairs that led to his family's home. That too looked deserted. To the left of the store entrance, around the corner and away from view, were the doors to the stables. Could she perhaps stroll that way, she wondered? She looked down and it was there she saw, in the middle of the courtyard, the vegetable garden. There, shiny purple eggplant skins shone in the sun.

Anno could not remain still and moved toward the vegetables. Yeraz called out a good morning in the direction of the house. A covered head appeared and a woman returned her greeting. Then male voices were heard from around the far side of the vegetable garden where the stables were, and Daron and his cousin Kevork appeared pushing a heavily loaded cart.

Daron froze at the sight of Anno and they both, involuntarily, broke into wide, happy smiles. Then Anno noticed Daron's smile begin to fade and, following his gaze, turned to see Yeraz watching him.

Dismayed at how obvious they had been, Anno squatted suddenly and fingered a tomato vine. Her legs trembled beneath her and she dared not look up. A rush of relief enveloped her as she heard Daron's grandmother and aunt come into the garden, trailed by his young sister, Nairi.

The women begin to chatter at once and Anno saw eager hands, close to where she knelt, pluck repeatedly at the vines. As she noticed Marie's apron filling with an array of vegetables, she slowly stood again.

Daron began to make his way forward, past Anno, to Yeraz, who still stood watching him. Anno hugged herself as he came closer, her eyes moving from his face to her mother's.

He bowed his head as he wished Yeraz a good morning, and quickly after, good health as well. Then he turned away from Yeraz to walk back toward his cart. The smile had long left his face, but he stopped in front of Anno to murmur, "It is wonderful to see you again." He passed before she could answer.

Anno watched him leave, and there, on her face, Yeraz saw such sadness that she finally looked away.

CHAPTER 11

Anno expertly balanced a large wooden tray laden with the afternoon meal for the men in the fields. She stonily walked alongside other village girls doing the same.

Even from beneath the cloth, the delicious smells came to them of heaps of rounded balls of thickened yogurt mixed with boiled wheat and spearmint. The last of the large tomatoes, red and juicy, bounced next to green olives and jugs of yogurt thinned with cold spring water and flavored with dill. Lavash bread, folded into quarters, was placed at all edges of the trays.

Still stinging from the morning's humiliation, she kept herself apart from the girls around her. Yeraz now knew her secret. Anno was certain. And worse still, she had watched her young daughter fumble and force her way into Daron and his family's company. If they had been at all interested in having her as their hars, Anno imagined her mother scolding, then Daron's family should send someone to present themself in Vartan's garden one morning!

Anno did not notice that many of the girls she walked with had slowed their pace or changed direction altogether. She merely plodded ahead, hands still trembling, until it was time to stop and locate her father's particular whereabouts.

Immediately, she saw that something was wrong. Instead of

bending to their work all across the field, the men stood straight and watched as Vartan spoke to two Turkish gendarmes.

It did not often happen that any Turk came to Sassoun. They had no Turkish neighbors here. A peasant might wander in and out for trading, but rarely a gendarme.

Anno looked around her. She stood nearly alone. So close now, she could hear what was being said.

"But it is days now that he has not been seen." The gendarme directed his challenge to Vartan.

"Yes, it is true, Pasha. We have not seen him either because he is spending these last good weeks of weather sleeping with the flock. We have had trouble with their butchering and theft," Vartan answered conversationally.

So this was regarding Raffi's absence, Anno realized, and her legs weakened.

"As much trouble as that, ey?" the other gendarme prodded. "You Christians are stealing from each other now."

"No," Vartan answered evenly. "We only try to keep what is ours to begin with."

"Then your other son should be by his father's side if the flock is being looked after so thoroughly. I do not see him either." The Turk's eyes crinkled as he scanned the field again.

"And he shall return at any moment, Pasha. He never misses a meal." And with this unlikely promise, Vartan took the last few steps to where Anno stood rooted with their tray of food.

"We would be honored if you shared our meal with us until Vrej returns."

Face-to-face with Vartan now as he took the tray from her arms, Anno searched his face in alarm at this last lie. Her father's eyes narrowed at her and then he swung back toward the Turks, pointing them to a comfortable spot under the shade of a row of poplars.

Anno understood. Vrej was not due to come to the fields at all. In his older brother's absence, Vrej had taken over the care of the flock as these Turks suspected. Too lazy to climb the vast hills in search of Raffi to prove that indeed Vartan's story was a lie, they would gladly wait here until sundown if necessary for one of the brothers to make an appearance. Vrej must now be found on the hills, wherever he might have roamed, and stealthily brought to this spot, without delay.

Anno stared helplessly at her father's back as Vartan laid sheets of lavash in the gendarmes' hands. One was already tearing the bread into strips and chewing large mouthfuls, but the other one was still. He was studying Anno intently. Seeing this, she swung around, controlling the urge to run.

She knew what had to be done. When the Turks could see her no more, she would run to the hills and bring back Vrej.

She hurried through the village. Eyes ahead, the morning's events forgotten, all she could think was how she would locate her brother.

Well, she thought to herself. *I must get there first*. She wished she could run, but did not, for that would surely draw a crowd and many, many questions.

She looked for the open spaces left between the walls of the homes. She darted through one now and climbed the low slopes behind the village. Remembering her father's drained face, she did begin to run.

Minutes later, reaching an area where the land flattened briefly, she slowed to rest. Searching constantly, she knew that once she was able to find just one shepherd, she would be pointed in the right direction.

But here, the grass was still too dry for grazing. She must climb higher.

After many slips and falls, Anno glimpsed a flock. But looking for the shepherd, she saw no one. Moving closer still, focusing under tree trunks where they might lie resting, she still saw no one. She moved on. After another long distance of open space, she saw another flock of sheep and again searched in vain for a shepherd. Frustrated, and more than a little afraid that she would fail her family, she swung herself around in one full exasperated circle and began running in a new direction.

There! More sheep, and this time goats too, but *no shepherds*.

Light-headed with exhaustion, she called out in desperation. Her throat was dry and hardly a sound emerged. She dropped to her knees, and swallowing once, took a deep breath and screamed out Vrej's name. The sheep raised their heads in surprise in her direction and their mouthfuls hung unchewed.

Feeling alarmingly weak now and dizzy, Anno walked blindly toward a wide shade tree and slumped against its trunk. Bent and ready to slide to the ground, she was suddenly seized from behind and her nose and mouth were covered by a large hand as she was dragged down behind the trees.

Anno's legs kicked out. Her screams burned her throat, but she could make no sound at all, so firmly was the hand clamping down on her mouth. She tried to swing her body to the left and right, but the grasp on her only tightened. And then she heard a low voice speaking angrily in her ear.

"Do not," he said. "Do not." And he spoke in her own language!

Her entire body slackened in shock and her head fell back. The large hand slowly peeled itself off her face and Anno whirled around to look into Avo's face. Behind him she saw Daron and two other shepherds.

Astounded, she could only stare at them.

"Sister, listen," Avo whispered. "Did you see anyone on your way here?"

Anno still only stared.

"Did you *see* anyone?" he insisted.

Anno shook her head, eyes tearing now in relief.

"Why are you here?" Avo implored. His attempted whisper had become more a low growl.

Anno opened her mouth. She closed it again. She cleared her throat and tried again to speak. "Vrej. I need Vrej. Two gendarmes are sitting in our field and waiting there until he appears." She tried to keep her voice from breaking.

"What? Why Vrej?" they all asked at once.

"Baba told them that Raffi is not absent as they suspect. He said that he is shepherding and that Vrej is working in the fields as usual. And so, they will not leave until they see *Vrej*." This last came out more quickly as she reflected on how much time had already passed.

Her eyes rested on Daron. She had scarcely seen him all month and now it was twice in one day. The affection and sympathy she saw in his eyes did not help her fight for composure and brought her closer to tears.

She turned accusingly to Avo. "Why did you silence me that way? Why are you hiding like this?"

The younger shepherds let Avo speak. "There is trouble today. First one animal was slaughtered and left for us to find, and then a second. It is the Kurds. They are baiting us."

Daron pointed up to his left. "Vrej is just behind those rocks."

Avo shook his head. "He is angry. Getting him away from here is a good idea."

Almost before he had finished his sentence, Daron had stood up. "I will go to him now and send him on his way."

Avo nodded in agreement. "He can choose a faster path and return on his own. Tell him to go. Then you come back, Daron, and take my sister safely down the mountain. When you get to the village, bring help."

Daron disappeared. Avo and the two shepherds again turned their gaze toward the flocks.

Anno, trembling, settled cross-legged behind them on the grass and waited in silence.

Minutes later she ventured, "Were there many, brother?"

"No," he answered without turning. "But they were reckless. They want us to show ourselves and retaliate so they can make an example of us to the Turks." Crushed between the manipulations of the Turks and the Kurds, as always, his voice said.

Hearing rustling behind them, they looked around to see Daron jump down off one rock to a second and land next to them. Stretching out his arm, he lifted Anno to her feet and told them all, "Vrej is on his way and I shall be back with help."

While the trek up the hills had been so laborious and desperate, Anno felt as if she were practically flying on the way down. Daron had not spoken a word to her, but neither had he let go of her hand even once. He guided and pulled her expertly and slowed only to avoid injury. He often checked behind them as well, but finally Anno had to insist that they stop because her boots were so filled with pebbles that each step had become agony.

Not wanting to waste even seconds searching for a comfortable rock to lean against, she sat straight on the ground and began to unlace her right boot. Daron lifted her left to do the same and she stopped and stared at him. He gathered both her hands together and kissed them, laughing. "Soon I shall see much more of you than your feet, Anno."

Completely unable to move now after such a promise, she stared at him as he pulled off her boot and shook out the pebbles and dust. He cradled her foot in his lap and brushed off her wool sock as well. With a quick caress to the bottom of her foot, he replaced the boot and motioned for her to lace it while he moved to do the same to the other. When both boots were laced again he pulled her to her feet and held her to him.

"Do you know how I love you, Anno?" he asked.

She nodded only, embracing him even more desperately. Would their happiest moments always be so overshadowed with fear and helplessness?

They did not stop again until they reached the village. Daron warned Anno to stay away from her father's field and then they separated. Anno went straight to join the women for the winnowing, while Daron headed toward Headman Vartan.

He planned what should be done as he walked. If Vrej had made his appearance and the gendarmes had left, Daron would go straight to Vartan and carry out whatever instruction he had regarding the Kurds and their slaughtered sheep. If the gendarmes were still there, and he could not consult with Vartan, he would go to his father. Daron nearly halted on the spot as he remembered. He could not go to his father. Mgro had left for Van many days ago.

It was simple enough for Daron to see across the fields now that the barley stalks were mostly harvested. Intent on their work, villagers mumbled greetings as he passed. The few who would have liked to chat, Daron discouraged by looking away. It would do no good for everyone to know of the morning's incident with the Kurds. Practically everyone had sons or pesas in those hills.

Reaching the edge of Vartan's field, Daron stopped a great distance away.

The Turks were still there, but they were mounted. Vrej was there as well. Vartan was looking up at the horsemen as they still spoke. Abruptly they turned their horses around and trotted slowly away, the animals' hooves sinking heavily into the softly furrowed soil. Vartan stared after them and wiped his brow. Tired, he turned back toward his family. Vrej, angered and ashen, watched Daron approach and moved toward him.

Daron greeted Vartan respectfully, face-to-face with Anno's father for the first time in his life. Knowing it was hardly likely Vrej could have explained any of the problems with the Turks still present, Daron did so fully and quickly, giving the man no time to recover from his first shock of the day.

Vartan barely hesitated. He knew what should be done. Lifetimes of pacification had come and gone.

"You are the merchant's boy, are you not?"

Daron nodded.

Vartan put his right hand on Daron's shoulder and began his instructions. When finished, he watched Daron cross the field back to the village and did not allow himself to reflect on his decision.

CHAPTER 12

Mihran was mentally attempting to appropriate just one short minute of time to wipe his dripping brow when he felt a still shadow of a presence at the entrance to his forge. It puzzled him so he turned to face the distraction fully. It was Mgro's boy, Daron, and he was empty-handed.

Only broken farm tools or animal harnesses would bring agitated villagers rushing to his stall at midday and Daron was not rushing at him like the others. Mihran was opening his mouth to question the boy when he caught the expression in his eyes.

The two men waiting for their tools roared at him when he waved them away without completing their work. "Am I to blame if my mother-in-law insists on feeding me her pickled cabbage? There is a battle going on in my belly and I cannot be expected to end it here on this spot, can I?" He had roared right back at them and cleared the stall. They grumblingly retreated, faces harshened by the weather and the worry of passing a morning away from their crops.

"But this is foolish child's play." Mihran shook his head in frustration once Daron had told all. Nuzan Bey, the head of the Kurdish clan who never seemed to forego an opportunity to raid and plunder Salor, would never waste time with such subtleties strewn here and there as those discovered today.

Mihran shouted at his apprentice to mind the stall, and a short while later, Daron led Mihran up the grazing slopes to where the shepherds waited.

The young men sprang to their feet at the sight of the most powerfully built man in their village. And the one man they knew whose mother had been a Kurd.

They stood straight for the first time that day. Avo felt he could even smile a little when Mihran's bushy eyebrows separated in the middle as he took in the sight of them. The shepherds stood like soldiers waiting for orders as Mihran eyed them.

A substantial breeze had started blowing through the hills late that morning, cool and persistent. The only sound was the rustling of the oak tree they stood under. And a faint clucking noise.

Avo's eyes met Daron's for a wild second, and Daron looked quickly away.

Along with the clucking, there was now the faint sound of shuffling.

"What is that?" a younger shepherd demanded.

Mihran stepped in closer to the group and the clucking was all that could be heard now. He swung his body slightly to one side so that the boys could see a knapsack tied to his back, with rolling movements of protest inside causing the sack to bulge in places.

Mihran watched the young men's eyes suddenly dim. They looked to Daron for one last confirmation, and their spines seemed to curve in defeat. There would be no justice today, either, and any attempts to argue were futile, not with those great hens strapped to Mihran's back.

The shepherds watched the ironsmith's back until he disappeared around a ledge. The hens' squawks could be heard for many minutes longer and then, finally, there was just the rustling of the leaves.

"What was in that knapsack, Daron?" Avo asked.

"A jar of his best honey."

"And?" Avo persisted.

"His two best red hens. He said the honey was to remind Nuzan Bey who his mother had been. The hens were to remind him that there were things to be eaten other than lamb."

Avo wordlessly picked up his staff and moved toward his flock. The others did the same, moving slower than ever, as if their movements caused them bodily pain.

CHAPTER 13

*A*ram had not found the first two days of travel too tedious. He had left the region of Kars with a companion. But then they had parted ways and Aram had chosen to walk many of the miles to Sassoun at sporadic times of the day and night. He had crept through plains and grasslands in the dark, urging three skittish donkeys each step of the way. The hills and mountains he had rounded during the day, keeping hiding places within sight where possible. Traveling singly, it was easier to remain unseen, but almost impossible to defend himself and save his precious cargo if attacked.

It had bothered Raffi deeply that he would not accompany Aram for this trek, but his family had fallen under suspicion, and he had been forced to stay behind.

Aram's only luxury had been staring into the vivid night sky and allowing himself to think of Lucine. He pictured her as a girl, her head bent to needlework, her scent as she whirled around her father's small home, serving her brothers, the clear green of her eyes. He remembered how he and Raffi had returned that one day, after many weeks of absence, to find that she was betrothed and the date of marriage had been set. Yeraz had looked back into their stony faces, confused as to why her news had not brought forth joy. Aram had reacted first. He had kissed Yeraz's hand and congratulated her and the family. Lucine, standing somewhere close behind Yeraz, had become a blur. He had not been able to say anything more. Leaving the house, he had not seen Lucine again until her wedding day.

He would see her again, soon, he thought. He could content himself with just that. He wondered how she might have changed. Had her hair grown even longer? She was most likely working even harder than ever now, as the youngest bride to join the family. But she would be matriarch someday. And the Avedissians' large sheepfolds and hemp fields were well envied.

Dusk had fallen, and Aram secured and tightened the loads one last time before slapping the rump of the lead donkey. The guns made no sound as they swung to and fro in their sacks. Raffi had instructed Aram to roll and wrap them individually at the onset of his trek.

He followed a trail now that seemed to have been forged by a horse and wagon. There was no shortage of ditches and dips here, but the body of the wagon had shaved the grass so that they walked with relative ease in its wake. On either side of them, the tall grass formed twin walls of protection.

"Raffi, my brother," Aram had said before leaving Salor, "I shall bring in three donkey loads of weapons and ammunition. I shall bring in however many they say. But how will a tiny band of men such as ourselves, with nothing but the guns we can smuggle, protect our people from the whole of the Turkish army?"

"We will protect whoever we can, one load at a time," Raffi had answered.

Vrej's head snapped to the left. He had seen movement. He was certain of it. He desperately tried to still the animals. But the middle donkey startled and brayed. Aram peered through the grass to see three men turned in his direction.

Aram gave a low curse. He knew what had to be done. At all costs, they must not approach him and discover his load. He left the donkeys behind and moved toward the men. He prayed the donkeys would busy themselves pulling at the grass and not give themselves away.

The Turks were on foot and seemed as disheveled and worn as he was. Aram's mind worked furiously as he walked toward them. He decided to feign confusion and ask for directions. He carried nothing of any value and his pockets were empty. Perhaps the Muslims would lose interest in him straight away.

As he moved closer he realized how wrong he had been. All three men were drunk. But now they had seen him and he could not turn back.

"Giaour!" *Christian dog* was their greeting to him.

Aram stood glued to his spot on the road, expressionless and silent.

"What is your name?"

"What business have you on the road?"

Aram created short answers to their questions and tried to still his breathing. He watched them look him over, knowing they were assessing the quality of his jacket and shoes. Their eyes were blurred with drink, and dusk had deepened so quickly that they squinted at him. Aram knew he must try only to leave. At the first pause in their questioning, he ventured, "Well, I shall move on now to avoid the roads at dark." He started to turn away.

A large fist caught him on the arm and he whirled around to face the Turk who had struck him.

"Christian dog," he heard again from somewhere.

"Faithless dog. You learn nothing."

Outnumbered, Aram was dragged forward. He fought and kicked and scratched at their eyes and brought two Turks down with him. He heard himself shout just before his head was slammed hard against the dry dirt road.

His vision blurred but he felt his arms pinned above him. He fought and bucked as he felt his trousers pulled down to his ankles.

Powerless as the weight of the men held him in place, all he knew were his screams as one brought a blade down between his legs.

His eyes burned with pain and fury and he watched them cry out praises to Mohammed and swing the bloodied, jagged blade triumphantly in the air.

CHAPTER 14

Old Mariam sat cross-legged on the straw mats that covered the earthen floor. She rested her rounded back against the mud-brick wall in one far corner and blew into the chipped china cup. In her lap lay her two-month-old great-granddaughter, crying with discontent.

It always seemed as if the anise seed would never boil when there was a colicky baby present, Mariam thought to herself. Twin boys giggled and snuggled closer to Mariam's knees to watch their tiny cousin.

"Keep yourselves away from that teacup!" their father called to them sharply from the far side of the room.

Once the anise brew was ready, the baby was soon quieted and contentedly tucked into her cradle. Mariam cautiously began to unfold her legs, inches at a time, giving her muscles and joints time to respond. She listened to the silence.

The room was already dark. When the men had come in from the fields that day, their dark silhouettes were outlined against a quickly falling dusk. They would be needing to burn more candles now.

"Mama? Mama?"

Her head popped away from the wall as she realized that she was being called. There was a scurry and the front door opened just a crack at first and then all the way. Her daughters-in-law appeared from an inner room and smiled widely in pleasure when they saw that their visitors were women. Mgro's mother and his brother's wife stood in the shadows of the short hallway. Almost reluctantly, Mgro's brother Manuel followed.

Mariam's eyes narrowed slightly. Her son called out to his male guest to join him and Manuel eagerly disappeared into a smaller, smoke-filled room.

"Well, either help me up, one of you, or bring a candle along with those cushions," Mariam called out, finally.

The younger women helped Mariam slowly make her way toward the divan to sit near Mgro's mother, Nevart. The older women grasped and patted each other's hands in greeting, gripping each other for support as they eased their backsides onto the rug-covered plank.

"Prepare some tea for us, Hars," Mariam instructed the babe's mother, who sat a bit behind the women.

Nevart opened the conversation. "The days are short again. My bones feel the cold already." She removed the brown scarf that had enveloped her head and throat.

"Oh, but Mama, let us forget that for a moment." Naomi scooted to the edge of her cushion. "We have Old Mariam's attention, let me tell her about my dream!"

And without waiting for the customary permission, she plunged into her story. Mariam chuckled to herself. Nevart never did have the proper control over anyone in her family, least of all this energetic, lively bride who had come to her home almost nineteen years ago.

"Oh! I was shivering. The water was like the melted ice coming off the mountains!" And now, Naomi lowered her voice before continuing.

"And I was naked. Completely. Naked." She nodded once at Mariam, who was looking steadily into Naomi's eyes. "But not bathing properly," she added quickly. "Because the water was dirty! I was bathing in dirty water, Sister Mariam!"

Naomi's spine was as straight as a stake. She tried to read Mariam's thoughts but could not. "Is this bad or good? Or not so bad?" She coaxed meekly now, fearing Mariam's continued silence.

Mariam took a breath.

"I will tell you, dirty water is never good," she offered slowly. She never lied when asked to interpret a dream, but she often softened its delivery.

She watched the guests' expressions as they received this bad news. It did not matter to them that Naomi was the one who had the dream. Whatever was to happen would likely affect them all. When Mgro's wife had died in childbirth, they had all, immediately, acquired the full-time care of two small children, had they not? They waited, hardly breathing, for Mariam to continue.

"It does not matter whether you are bathing in the water or simply washing your hands in it. But," Mariam shrugged, "it is an inconvenience. The dirty water shows that your way will be murky. Clouded. It is an inconvenience. I cannot say that it is much more than that."

"Well," Nevart turned encouragingly to Naomi, "if that is all—"

"What life is not full of inconvenience?" Mariam interrupted. "That, and trouble will come whether you have had a dream such as this or not. Do not think much of it," and she leaned her heavy back against the wall once more. She had not liked what she had heard and wanted to erase the images coming to her.

Eager to cheer their friends, the younger women started chatting. Nevart lowered her voice to say, "Mariam, I have something of importance to ask you."

So, it has finally come, Mariam thought to herself. Since that day at the well, she had been waiting for something to occur. She was not surprised to have the first steps taken under her own roof. Her earliest life memories included Vartan's mother, her crystal blue eyes catching hers with mischief.

The tea was served. Mariam wrapped her hands around her cup.

Her fingers, no longer supple, slowly unwound and the rounded knuckles hugged the heat of its curve.

"We have come to speak for my grandson, Daron."

Mariam remained expressionless and Nevart continued.

"It is his father's and our family's wish that he be married. We have given much thought to headman Vartan's younger daughter, Anno, and believe they would be suitable for one another."

It is certainly not you who think them to be suitable, Mariam thought to herself. She studied the pattern of the rug she sat on for a moment while choosing her real response.

"Anno," she acknowledged aloud with slow nods and continued. "I am fond of that child. Although it is Lucine who most resembles her grandmother and carries her name, Anno is the one who carries her spirit."

Suddenly, it was as if her friend Lucine were beside her again, urging Mariam on.

They had been nearly eleven years old, hiding behind some prickly bushes while their neighbors washed their laundry in the river. The clean clothes were spread out on the bushes to dry. Just beyond their reach were two pairs of newly washed men's underdrawers.

"Snatch them, Mairo!" Lucine had hissed, always calling Mariam by her nickname.

They had snatched them both and then choked back their laughter for nearly a quarter of an hour while the poor woman who had laid them there silently searched for them. Confused, she had looked again through her pile of soiled clothes, then, she hoped, unobtrusively through her neighbors', and then back again toward the bushes. Unable to bring herself to actually ask aloud if anyone had seen her father-in-law's underdrawers, she had kept silent. And finally, Mariam and Lucine, afraid that they would soon wet their own underpants from the strain of suppressed hysterics, had escaped unseen back through the bushes to a clearing where they fell onto the crackled and leaf-covered ground in laughter.

A smile had come to Mariam's face with the memory of that afternoon, but she turned to see that Nevart had her arm extended toward her, offering her handkerchief. She warmly patted Mariam's hand, understanding where her friend's thoughts must have wandered. Mariam shook her head and pulled her own handkerchief out from under her sleeve. She blew her nose and looked fully at Nevart.

"Shall I be the go-between, then?" she asked pointedly.

"What? Well, yes." Nevart was startled by Mariam's sudden directness.

"Daron is a good boy, and from what we have understood from him, Anno would be agreeable as well. If, that is, her parents do not have," Nevart hesitated, "other plans for the girl."

"I, myself, do not know of any," Mariam offered. And remembering the day by the well again, she added, "I will go to speak to Yeraz soon." *Before those two do something truly foolish,* she thought only to herself.

CHAPTER 15

*A*nno had her arms wrapped around the roughened bellies of both water jugs. Her mother had given up trying to convince her to just fill one at a time.

"They are too heavy when full. If not tomorrow, then the next day you will be a bride, and what good will you be for childbearing with a weak back?" Yeraz used to say.

But Yeraz had stopped making references like that for some time now. Anno had pushed away the memory of her mother's expression that day by Daron's family's vegetable garden. Anno had received no scolding from Yeraz, but she felt her mother pitied her and was disappointed in her youngest daughter.

Anno hurried along the stream's edge. She searched ahead, hoping to catch sight of Lucine, and her face lit with joy when she saw her, slim and graceful, waving one arm above her head to catch Anno's attention.

Anno smiled as she hurried to reach her sister. Even when only collecting water, Lucine resembled a graceful dancer. She gently dropped her jugs to the ground and ran to embrace her. With squeals of happiness they wrapped their arms fully around each other and Anno buried her face in her sister's hair.

Many yards away, women chuckled at them, and one called out,

"Enough. It is already enough. Are there so many streams available to us that it seems such a miracle you find one another here each morning?"

When her goading was ignored, another called out, "Anno, girl, gather your jugs and stop this foolishness before something even larger than what I just saw crawls inside."

Lucine gasped at this and whirled away from Anno to retrieve the jugs. Chuckles came to them from the water's edge.

The sisters joined the others. Women's heads bobbed closely all around them as news and gossip were exchanged.

"Are my brothers well?" Lucine asked.

Anno was still attempting to situate herself on the moist soil so that she might trap the clearest surface water without overly dirtying her skirt and shoes. At a glance, she noticed that Lucine had already done so effortlessly, and by the way her arms were bent and fixed, she guessed her jug was nearly full.

"They are both well, although I hardly saw them this morning."

"Why is that?" Lucine asked, her full jug set on the ground and both arms raised to her head as she attempted to readjust her head-band and veil.

Anno squinted back at her and Lucine rolled her eyes upward as if to say, "It is a nuisance, and it is ugly, but it is unavoidable."

Turning back to her task, Anno answered, "I was in the stable, storing the preserves."

Anno rested her filled jug on the ground as well and fetched the empty one. Lucine bent slightly to steady them both.

"Have any visitors come to my father's house?" Lucine pressed.

For anyone within earshot, the girls hoped that it would sound as if Lucine was simply gathering the daily news of her father's home, but Anno knew that Lucine wanted to know more: whether Raffi was still considered a fugitive in the eyes of the Turkish police.

"No one has come at all, Lucine."

This last Anno said rather quietly, almost to herself, causing Lucine's eyes to fix on her. The sun shone brightly on Anno's dark brown hair. Shorter, finer strands had come loose from their braids, and they curled close to her face, a becoming contrast to Anno's eyes, honey-colored in the bright sun. Anno stood and turned, her mouth pursed and eyes heavy-lidded.

Lucine's confusion lasted only a moment. Her brothers were safe for the time being. Anno's momentary sadness had been for herself.

They walked back toward the houses. Lucine searched Anno's face again. Her own life had changed so suddenly. She was busy trying to know and understand Avo, trying to find her place and contribute to her new family and their household, so that she was in contact with her father's family in only the most basic way. Were they safe? Were they well? But whether they were happy was knowledge out of her reach. She was not at all aware of the extent of Anno's attachment to Daron, but she knew it had turned her little sister into someone older and sadder.

"Whether they come or do not, Anno, all will be well."

"No! It will not," she burst out.

Lucine stared at her sister in astonishment. Anno's teeth had clenched as she spoke and large teardrops rolled down her face.

Lucine did not understand when feelings such as these had developed. She herself was not even sure she would know Daron if she passed him on the road. She had thought this a childish attraction. She had certainly had them herself at Anno's age. But then Avo's family had come and she had forgotten, had she not?

"Anno, what are you thinking?" she demanded anxiously.

Elopements happened in their village. The families accepted these marriages and carried on to avoid more shame, but it had never happened in the Vartanian family. Lucine was not sure how her parents would bear such a thing.

"I do not know anything. How can I? I hardly see him. I hardly speak to him. It is as if it is only I alone in all this with my imaginings."

"Then why are you waiting for his family to come? Why do you think that will happen?"

"Because," she halted as Lucine reached forward with her free hand to wipe at her tears.

"Because he has told me he loves me." Anno's head fell forward and her body shook with all the loneliness and months of hidden feelings and hopes not realized.

"And, Lucine," Anno struggled to speak. "Lucine, I am afraid."

"Of course you are. I can see that," Lucine retorted.

"No. No." Anno shook her head. "There is something else."

Lucine tightened her hold on the water jug.

"I think someone saw us already. Old Mariam."

Lucine gasped. "When? What did she see?"

"We went to meet at the well." Anno hung her head again. "On your wedding day."

Anger rose in Lucine. "Walk, Anno," she commanded. Too many stares had come their way already. "Do not drop the jugs. It is lucky for you that Sister Mariam has remained silent about this for so long, but if she has seen you, she will not remain silent forever."

Anno had no answer. She knew what her sister said was true.

"How was it when you went to sort the herbs? Did she seem disappointed in you?"

Anno shook her head guiltily. "I did not go."

Lucine gave a sound of exasperation. "But, Anno. That was unwise. I am sure she was expecting you."

For several years now, just before winter arrived, Anno had rushed to Old Mariam's side to help her crush and store that year's collection of herbs and grasses. From the first, Mariam's worn, experienced hands had painstakingly guided Anno's smooth, eager ones. She had taught Anno to recognize every herb and its uses and how to prepare and store them with the least amount of waste.

Mariam would converse only lightly as they worked. She had admonished Anno at the first that their careful preservation and division of these herbs would someday help in the healing of their own neighbors and must be carried out with the utmost care. If Anno had done something incorrectly, Mariam would wordlessly reach out and redirect her hands. A short nod was Anno's only reward. And then, when all work was completed, they would sit back on a cushion and drink sweetened tea and a special pastry that Mariam had put aside for that day.

"Oh, Lucine, I wish I had gone. I wanted to, but I did not think she would want me."

"She is like our grandmother, Anno. She might have helped you."

Avo's family's home was just yards away now. Lucine tipped the water jug into her cupped hand and wiped Anno's face from brow to chin with the icy water, then hastily dried the drops with the edge of her sleeve.

"Do nothing foolish, Anno. I shall ask around and see what I can learn about his family. But you must do nothing foolish."

Anno nodded tiredly.

"Give me your word," Lucine demanded.

"I give you my word," Anno repeated dully and turned down the road. Lucine watched her sister's back and listened to the crunch of rocks beneath her boots for a moment longer before entering her husband's home.

CHAPTER 16

Anno walked unseeingly. The water jugs nearly slipped from her hold once, but she was able to catch them and continued to grip them weakly.

She heard her name called but did not turn, not caring to be seen with swollen nose and eyes. She concentrated on moving while hugging the jugs that had grown too heavy for her.

"Anno, *kiz*," the voice called again. *Anno, girl*. She knew that voice. She slowed her steps and searched to see where it came from.

It was not hard to spot Turgay. Her head covering sat lopsided as always on her snowy white hair, a startling contrast against her stark black garb.

Anno set the jugs down. She never had the heart to make a quick escape from Turgay. She joined her on the edge of the tree stump where she sat.

Turgay blinked up at Anno. "Is she coming?"

Old Turgay had borne four children, who had then produced a true dozen grandchildren, and then great-grandchildren in still multiples of that. Their home was in the Kurdish camp on the other side of the river from where Anno collected water daily. It was not possible to cross the river without a soaking, but in a few places, the river narrowed and large stones and boulders were laid in a row to serve as a bridge.

Turgay had first been seen wandering through Salor almost five years earlier. Hands outstretched and always weeping, she would approach men and women alike and plead with them, in Kurdish, to help her. She stood no more than four feet tall, and her still fair skin was folded in deep lines. Her filmy brown eyes, perpetually troubled, were quick to twinkle at the slightest kindness.

At first, the villagers were wary of her presence. They returned her greetings when it could not be avoided, but skirted by quickly, wanting to avoid any knowledge of her should something happen and her people come searching. But eventually, the older women of the village began to stop and listen to her pleas, and they remembered. They pieced together clues from her mutterings and, round-eyed, clapped their hands to their mouths in shock at the realization that Old Turgay was, in fact, one of their own. They clung to each other and to Turgay as they remembered.

Tiny and fair, in her fourth or fifth year, she was noticed by a passing Kurd. He slyly followed Turgay's mother, on her way to the baker, balancing a tall load on her head with her tiny daughter skipping along behind. Turgay's mother had noticed the Kurd on horseback from the start and knew she was being followed. When the horse's snort sounded too near, she turned in time to see the Kurd lean over and lift Turgay to him by her arm. Turgay remembered her mother's screams for the rest of her life, but the memory of her face gradually faded.

Living just across the river, she was raised as the daughter of a Kurdish family. She was made to forget her true family and her true identity. Now, as old age weakened her mind, she lost her reasoning and discretion for great chunks of time and would break free to seek what was taken from her as a child. Her mother.

Anno had been the exact same height as Turgay when she had first seen her. Turgay's cries for her mother had broken Anno's heart, so she had pulled the old woman to her own home and presented her to Yeraz. It was just days before Easter and trays of chorek topped with sesame seed lay cooling everywhere. Yeraz knew of Turgay and had pulled her close to the fire and pressed a warm braided loaf into her hands. The woman had stared at it as if it were a bar of solid gold, pressed her face to it in remembrance and wept, with the suffering of a lifetime cutting forth each sob.

Later that day, Vartan had taken her back to the river. She had crossed to the other side easily enough, but then turned and looked stubbornly back at him. Vartan had been forced to cross over as well and gently coax her home. He had come face-to-face with Turgay's eldest son, who clasped his mother to him in relief. Neither man spoke a word, but their eyes met and Vartan saw knowledge reflected there, and sadness, and fear.

"No, Turgay. I do not think your mother is coming just now."

Turgay accepted Anno's words trustingly. Their shoulders slumped and they drew comfort from one another for long minutes.

Eventually, Anno stood and went to retrieve the water jugs. She had already decided that she would not leave Turgay behind.

"Come, Turgay Dade. Hold on to my apron and let us go home. My mother will be waiting and we shall have a cold drink of this water and a bit of something to eat together."

CHAPTER 17

*V*rej peeled the outer leaves off a neatly cut chunk of cabbage, folded them into his mouth and noisily crunched his large mouthful.

Raffi leaned against the door frame and watched his younger brother. Vrej suddenly took in the silence of the room and lifted his head to see Raffi standing there, holding both their caps. He raised his cabbage wedge invitingly in Raffi's direction, but his brother only chuckled and shook his head.

They heard the sounds of the clubs calling them to church. "You should be thinking of communion today instead of cabbages," Raffi admonished.

"When you decide to take communion, then that is the exact same day that I shall as well," Vrej answered and popped the last leaf into his mouth.

Since Raffi's absences had been questioned by the gendarmes, he had remained in Salor, attending to his family's crops and livestock and openly appearing at village activities. Now, as they walked together, the brothers watched the sway of skirts ahead of them, the wide, muted skirts of the older women and the brighter-colored ones of the young.

There was so much Vrej wanted to ask Raffi. For instance, where was Aram? His absence had stretched to weeks now and Vrej wanted to know where he had been sent. He wanted to know why Raffi was always so tense and why, no matter how their mother tried, he would not eat enough to put the lost flesh back on his bones. And why were so many of the village dogs taken in at night when the weather was not yet frigid? But knowing better than to ask, he said instead, "I believe our mother is fashioning a fez for that big head of yours."

At this unexpected absurdity, Raffi laughed out loud, and the sound warmed Vrej so much that he joined in.

A fez was a gesture of fashion, Turkish in origin and adopted by all the Turks' subjects, much like the thick upturned moustaches of the day. Yet, Raffi could no more wear a fez than drop to his knees and raise his arms to Allah.

Behind them, Lucine walked with Avo, her hand on his arm. Raffi turned to look at his sister, at the dark purple of her long dress and veil, at the silver linked belt shiny and fitted around her waist, and then back to the worry in her eyes.

"Is Anno with our mother?' she asked them.

Vrej shrugged.

Lucine searched the road. She was always worried now about Anno's whereabouts. Raffi was watching her, she knew, but she dared not say anything just yet.

ANNO WAS ALONE, roaming the cemetery behind the church. She decided that she would lean here against one of the gravestones for just a moment longer, in the rare sun, and then head to church. It did not seem possible to fill her lungs in the dark of the night, but here she could, again and again.

Her eyes traveled to the church dome and then down to the high, narrow windows framed by stone carvings that allowed only slivers of amber sunlight to fall on heads bowed in prayer. At Easter, only a quarter of the village would be able to squeeze inside its walls.

Anno's eyes fell on a spot on the north wall and she remembered.

She and Takoush had merely entered their eighth year. Raffi had found them on their hands and knees beneath that wall, digging their small fingers into the base of a crumbling tufa stone block. They had told Raffi that they were looking for gold coins buried beneath the church, left by their ancestors.

He had dusted them off and sent Takoush home. As he and Anno walked side by side, she had asked, "Brother, why does our church have holes in its walls? Why does it have pieces breaking everywhere?"

"Because it is almost sixteen hundred years old, Anno."

Her eyes had widened at the incomprehensible number.

"Our great, great, great, great, grandfathers built it that long ago. It is very old and so it crumbles," he had explained.

"And the Turks *let* them build it?" Her voice dropped as she asked. Even at so young an age, she had perceived that they lived with strict limitations on their freedoms.

"The Turks were not here then to stop them," Raffi answered her.

"Where were they that they did not see?"

Raffi wondered how to explain.

"Anno, do you see where the sun rises every day behind that end of the church?" Raffi pointed to the east.

Anno nodded.

"In that direction, far, far, *far* away there is a land where the Turks' great-great-great grandfathers were born. That is where they were when we built this church, where their real home is."

Anno was silent, but for only a moment. "Has Baba seen where they came from?"

"No. None of us have seen it. It is very far away. The Turks' ancestors traveled for seasons and years over great rivers and mountains to reach here. And when they arrived, they did not look like us. They had very black, very straight hair and slanted dark eyes. When they came, they looked like *their* grandfathers."

She scooted to the side to kick a stone as they walked, moving it only a few feet and coating her shoe in a new layer of dust. "Do you not wish that they had never come, Brother?" she asked softly. "That they had stayed where they were born?"

"I do wish it, Anno," he answered, just as softly. "I wish it every day."

THERE WERE JUST a few minutes left to her, she knew, before the church services would begin, and later the cemetery would fill as many others would slowly weave their way through the gravestones to find the resting places of their loved ones.

Utterly alone, Anno leaned her head against the great smooth stone that marked her grandparents' grave. Nearby was Vartan's brother's grave. All three had died during the massacres of 1894.

Anno mechanically crossed herself and, with palms loosely joined, recited a prayer. Then she sank to the ground beside the large headstone and sobbed.

The chance to unleash her emotions unobserved was so rare that each time she brought her head up, thinking her tears were surely spent, something triggered more sorrow and she wept again. She was not so careless as to make herself heard by any of the other early comers, but leaned into the sun-warmed stone and, resting her head against her forearms, let her tears be absorbed into its gray pores.

She wept for herself, for the smell of Daron's hair and skin, and for the deep hollows beneath Raffi's eyes. And for the evenings spent waiting for Daron's family to appear at her father's door, and the meaning she took from their never coming.

Suddenly Anno sucked in her breath. She heard footsteps.

"Ann! Anno!"

She tried to still her tears.

"Oh! You are tiring me, Anno!" the voice scolded, closer now, and Anno tipped her head sideways.

"Takoush, I need your handkerchief."

"Lucine is searching for you!"

"I think I dropped mine somewhere."

"Do you know what is happening?" Takoush pulled Anno to her feet and wiped at her face impatiently with her own handkerchief. She hugged her hard and whispered in her ear.

"Aram is coming home. He has been seen."

Takoush's eyes sparkled and Anno squeezed her hard in return.

"I am so glad," she whispered back sincerely.

CHAPTER 18

*T*he shepherds had strained their eyes and stretched their necks for days now. Aram's return was overdue. Then at last, shortly after the moon slipped down below the horizon, a solitary figure was spotted. Heavily clothed and bent, he prodded his donkeys along with a thick staff.

One young shepherd, having placed himself at the peak of a high, balded slope, looked out over acres of rocky hills and treetops. Raffi had given him field glasses and he used them, discreetly, under the cover of stone ledges or behind wide trunks. A herder grasping field glasses would bring forth jeopardizing questions from passing Muslims.

The rocks and slopes were matching shades of muted browns and mauves. Aram was seen for a moment at a time only to disappear again while he made his way slowly along the shelter of the ridges and through their shadows.

Once certain that the traveler was indeed Aram and no one else, the young shepherd had painstakingly secured the field glasses inside his coat and, with a large accompaniment of careening and bouncing rocks, leapt up from his squatting position and scrambled down the hillside.

He longed to call out the news to the shepherds on the knolls, but did not dare. With only a nod and a glad wave he slid by. One stood as he passed and stared into the long trail of dust that had been kicked up in his friend's wake. He thought it lingered and hung there an unusual amount of time, as if to taunt him that he would not be the one to carry the good news back to the village.

Aram waited just outside the village, under the protection of a large willow. He would not enter the village until many hours past dark. The dogs would have been taken in again by then and most would be asleep. Aram's donkeys were still and spent beneath their load. Storage space underneath the dirt floor of a home was deep and waiting. The guns and ammunition would be stored there only briefly and then moved out again as needed.

He had run out of cigarettes long ago. While he waited, if he could have chosen between a hot meal and a cigarette, he would have chosen the latter.

It had taken days for the throbbing in his groin to subside enough for him to walk. Then he had washed himself with the bit of oghee he had brought along.

They had slashed away his foreskin. It would heal. At least, the wound itself would. But his body still shook with rage and humiliation.

He decided to move into the village in another hour. And he decided he would tell no one the reason for his delay.

THE NEXT EVENING, Aram placed himself strategically near Avo's father's house. Villagers greeted him warmly. A baker slipped away from his ovens with a warm loaf in his apron, pressed it into Aram's hands and squeezed his shoulders in welcome. Beginning to feel self-conscious, Aram considered leaving, but then he saw Lucine. She was emerging from the coppersmith's carrying an old pot that had likely already been mended a handful of times. A trace of a smile formed on his face and he moved toward her. He stretched out his arms in greeting. He would hug her and kiss her hands. Had he not done just that so many times when they were children? He would carry the pot home for her and steal extra time at her side.

A wide, joyous smile lit Lucine's face at the sight of Aram and her steps lifted and quickened. Her long apron curled and flipped sideways from the breeze and Aram's eyes followed the movement down to an unmistakably rounded belly.

CHAPTER 19

*M*ariam had asked her younger son, Haig, to accompany her on this Sunday evening visit. He was short and stocky like his mother. His muscled chest seemed constrained beneath his tightened coat, and his arms, instead of resting at his sides, were bent at the elbow and held inches away from his ribs. He appeared ready to leap to battle at a moment's notice, but by nature he was more inclined toward firm handshakes and warm embraces.

Haig had been born just months earlier than Vartan. Their mothers nursed them side by side under the shade of great walnut trees, and they were baptized within days of each other, but they were each other's antithesis from birth. Haig's appetite for milk and bread was boundless, Vartan's indifferent. Haig's interest in people and objects would throw him forward palms outstretched for the first dozen years of his life, while Vartan observed and noted details from a distance. Haig's laugh was loud and open, while Vartan's indication of pleasure was a gentle smile and a warmth around his eyes. Haig would toss and catch a scythe recklessly for his own amusement, while Vartan would turn the pages of a rare newspaper tirelessly until its contents were memorized. They complemented and balanced each other's lives improbably, but the keystone to their devotion was laid in 1894, days after Raffi's birth.

Freedom fighters led the people in their own defense, but the end was near and their losses devastating. Young girls and women still ceaselessly refilled gun cartridges for their men who were standing for the final battle.

Yeraz, too, had remained behind for as long as Vartan allowed. Until that early morning when Vartan had pulled her out of her slumber and ordered her and their entire household of women and girls away, up the long and arid mountainside.

Short days later, Vartan had been grazed in the temple and Haig had dragged him into the thickness of the forest. He had washed the wound with the last precious drops of oghee from his flask and had left, for how long Vartan did not know. When he woke, the flask was lying on his chest, filled with water. The blood from his head had soaked down his cheeks into his high collar and he was alone.

There was a buzzing in his ear. He lay still and determined that it was not in his ear, but near it. Flies. He reached up tentatively, found his cheek, and flapped his hand at them. His hand came away with blood, thick and clinging between his fingers. He wiped his hand on his trousers. He listened again. Silence. Where were the screams? Where were the galloping horsemen overtaking the fleeing? He could smell the smoke well enough. They had laid fire to everything—fields, rooftops, stables, women's skirts.

His trembling hands tried to lift the flask to his mouth and he felt the liquid slip onto his lower lip. He licked at its coolness and tasted a good amount of blood and grit instead.

The air was too still. He could hear nothing. He fought against the urge to close his eyes. He opened them again and turned his head from side to side. He tried to bend his legs. He would search for survivors. He would start up the mountain and find his wife, his mother, his sister. Where was Haig? He slept again.

He heard laughter. He sniffed the air for the smell of baking lavash. The layers of pine needles and leaves were his warm wool mattress and the laughter was his father's.

He sniffed harder and woke himself. His bleary gaze met the night sky. The leaves and branches were shades of green and brown and darkness and he had only dreamed the laughter and the bread and the closeness of his family. But there, he heard it again. He felt it was close, but harsher now. There were grunts. Vartan stopped breathing, his eyes and ears strained to understand. The ground rustled and he heard a low groan. *A groan of pleasure?* It was unmistakable. Something, leaves perhaps, rustled again but with a whispery rhythm. He froze. He knew he was listening to the sound of a man taking his pleasure.

Vartan's teeth clenched. He had witnessed enough rape these last days to know what he was hearing now. It perplexed him that he did not hear any protest or struggle, but he did not want to be found lying under a tree defenseless once the bastard had re-fastened his shalvar.

The groans were loud and free and Vartan rolled to his side gently and sat up. His vision blurred and he took deep breaths to fight the nausea. He heard loud Turkish cursing and a slap. He thought he heard a whimper, something high-pitched. He struggled to his knees. He must have the advantage of surprise. He was too weak to fight anyone. His gun, useless, had been dropped somewhere. But his sword was hanging off his belt. He staggered closer to the sounds, still coming in rhythm. Several feet away, he saw the back of a man, in military coat, trouserless, kneeling atop something. Vartan tried to focus, but he was having difficulty. Unthinking, he stepped closer. The soldier was so large. Was that merely his own shadow moving beneath him? Just his own shadow? Vartan crept closer still, watching the broad back of the military coat rock backward and forward. Close enough now so that he could take in what was on the ground, straddled between his massive bare legs, Vartan saw a girl. Her clothing was torn in half away from her pale body, creating a dark frame against her nakedness. Peering at her flat undeveloped chest and thin arms, Vartan sucked in his breath in revulsion. This was a child, aged nine or ten at the most. And he saw the reason why he had heard no sounds of protest. Her nose and mouth were wrapped and muffled tightly with a scarf. Only her eyes were left uncovered, and they were tightly shut.

Vartan strode forward quickly and dug his sword into the back of the soldier's neck. The tinkling of the medals stilled as his back arched in pain, and double-fisted, Vartan dug the sword in further. His strength spent, he fell to his knees and waited. The Turk pitched forward and Vartan grabbed a fist full of hair and thrust him sideways, off the child. He watched the soldier convulse and once the blood flowed from his mouth, Vartan crept forward on his knees. He cradled the child's upper body in the crook of his left arm and pulled her free.

Her lower body was smeared with so much blood that Vartan, sickened, scrambled to cover her. He fumbled with the scarf and unwound it several times before her nose and mouth were exposed. He could not tell if she was dead or alive, and he did not have the will to find out. He gathered her close, and with her head still cradled against his chest, he sagged down onto one elbow and closed his eyes.

ONCE HAIG HAD filled the flask of water for Vartan, he had taken great gulps from the stream himself. He had walked for a long distance upriver, to a place where he saw no more bodies floating on the surface and the water flowed reasonably clear.

He had been climbing now, for hours, and knowing he was near, he did not search for another water source anywhere. Although his head pounded and his tongue felt rough and dry, his legs moved on.

He remembered walking beneath the cover of low-flying vultures and spying Yeraz seated beneath an elongated slab of boulder, jutting out of the side of the hill. Its layers were visible in shades of slate and gray and it provided a perfect roof over her head. In the shadows, her breasts were bared, and one breast was hidden completely from view by the head of a suckling infant.

Haig led their way down the mountain back to their smoldering village with Yeraz lifted high in his arms, resting only to ensure that the long trail of women and children still followed.

CHAPTER 20

*M*ariam left Haig inside the garden. Vartan sat there beneath the brittle, yellowed leaves of the gnarled grapevine that stretched across the garden wall and spilled over its sides.

From the opposite end of the yard, Uncle Hagop's voice, raised and indignant, came to her.

"Vrej, boy, why did you not choose the taller stalks?"

"There were no stalks taller than these," Vrej answered calmly, twisting hemp fibers across his thigh.

Mariam saw them, seated side by side, with a huge pile of stripped stalks near their feet. She watched Uncle Hagop attempt to roll the delicate fibers with his large, fumbling hands. The fibers slipped and unraveled across his leg. Next to him, Vrej was serenely rolling yet another length of fine rope.

Mariam chuckled and entered the house.

Anno faced Yeraz and waved a white pillowcase frustratedly in the air. Her face was flushed and her hair untidy.

"But Mama, I do not *want* a pillowcase such as this. I do not care whether I sleep on an embroidered..."

"I do not know where this girl's mind is but it is not on improving her skills!" Aunt Marie's voice rang out.

Yeraz took the pillowcase from Anno's hand and inspected the tiny stitches.

"Now, Anno, I taught you this design myself years ago. You can do much better work than this." She handed the case back to her daughter.

Mariam watched Anno and thought the girl looked defeated.

"Go wash your face and start again," Yeraz directed.

But Anno had turned away. She had seen Mariam and the pillow-case dropped to the floor. Aunt Marie bent in annoyance to retrieve it.

Before Marie could add to the scolding, Old Mariam hastily made her greetings and moved across the room as if she had witnessed no altercation at all.

She had brought a plate of halvah with her, knowing it to be Vartan's favorite sweet. Yeraz sighed with relief at her presence.

Mariam turned back to look into Anno's guarded face. *At least the child did not bolt from the room at the sight of me,* Mariam thought.

"Come, let us sit, Sister Mariam." Yeraz invited, "away from the draft of the door."

Mariam clapped her hands once and suddenly announced, "Yeraz, Marie, Anno, we have things to discuss."

Anno's heart sunk at her words. *Old Mariam has finally come to tell all she knows,* she thought. *There will be no hope left now.*

"Let us begin, and then the men shall join us, if they wish," Mariam continued as she eased herself onto a fluffed cushion, looking pointedly at Anno.

Anno knew it could be nothing else. She would not be specifically included in any other such discussion with these women. She never had before! Her eyes fleeted from one face to the other.

"Anno?" Yeraz scolded lightly. Her mother was motioning for her to help assemble a table of refreshments for their guest.

Anno turned mechanically to where her mother pointed and still did not move.

Yeraz sighed and quickly made the preparations herself. Large raisins, newly dried and darkly golden, were laid in small plates on a quickly assembled table. Young walnuts, their meats cleaned and free of their hard shells, were also placed close within reach of all to be seated.

The tea came and the cups were filled, leaving nothing more to forestall the conversation, except Anno, who still stood.

Mariam reached for a generous palm full of raisins and seemed to concentrate heavily on choosing just the right size and amount of walnut meats for accompaniment. She absorbed the tension in the room from the first but expected Yeraz to take control when she was ready.

"My daughter, we are waiting for you," Anno heard.

Anno's legs finally brought her to the table's edge, where she sank fluidly to the bare floor beside Mariam. She kept her head bowed.

Mariam drew a deep breath and chose her words carefully.

"It was my pleasure to receive visitors to my hearth just ten days ago," she began. "They are well known to me, and to you also." This last she directed to Yeraz only. "The visitors were the women of the merchant's family, Nevart and Naomi."

Yeraz thought she heard Anno exhale. Mariam, she noticed, was averting her gaze from the girl from the first, and Anno continued to stare into the triangle of her cross-legged lap.

"It was, for me, a joyous visit, and I will now tell you why. And, I hope, if it is God's will, that once I have told it, it will be a source of joy for your family as well."

Joyous? Minuscule hairs covering Anno's body tingled and froze on end.

Mariam paused to allow Yeraz time to absorb the news thus far. Marie pulled herself nearer the table still. Her large, dark eyes flitted from Yeraz's thoughtful face to Mariam's tranquil one.

Anno had lifted her chin imperceptibly, but enough to peer sideways at Mariam, to glean some hint of what was to unfold. But the old woman was using every ounce of self-control to appear neutral, as was her role, so she did not dare to convey even the slightest bit of comfort, though she ached to do so. Instead she continued calmly. "I was told that it is the family's wish that Daron, Mgro's one and only son, be married."

Mariam paused once again, but only long enough for Yeraz, who had lifted her cup to her mouth, to slowly return it to the table. She was nervous, Mariam knew, and so the old friend continued to go forth slowly.

"Daron has entered his eighteenth year. He was schooled, here in the village, until the age of twelve, and with his father's consent, after that, devoted himself wholly to the work and livelihood of his family. He had, however, Nevart was proud to say, displayed a quick understanding of mathematics. And, he has displayed a great deal of interest in his father's trade of merchantry.

"And now," Mariam allowed herself a shadow of a smile, "I come to the purpose of my visit today."

Yeraz's face was unreadable.

"It is the Markarian family's wish that Daron's wife be our Anno."

Yeraz clutched her teacup with both palms. The tea had grown cold, the halvah had begun to cling to its plate like glue, and her neck stung with tension while listening to Mariam eloquently choose the words for her proposal.

She was glad this moment had come. She was glad for her daughter, and relieved as well. She studied Anno across the tiny table and watched her rigid spine slacken. Her eyes were still downcast and Yeraz waited for her to lift her head. Where were her quick happy movements? How had she turned so inward, so guarded?

Anno, inches from her mother, inches from Old Mariam, had heard, had heard the miraculous words. Now, she only wished to throw herself at her mother's feet and beg, *beg* her to consent! In almost all things her father had the last word, but not this.

Anno's face lifted and she met her mother's eyes.

Yeraz took in so much at once: the beseeching, deep-set eyes that were rarely dry any more, nostrils flared as if there were never enough air, and lips, bitterly red and swollen. There was no longer any child-like fullness there, and the contours of her bones offered a vivid impression of the woman she would soon be.

Yeraz would prolong this no longer. Let the customary steps be taken, and quickly, she decided. She had no desire to watch her youngest child wane before her eyes. She herself had resisted the urge to act unwisely more than once these past months, since the day she had witnessed Anno's desperation in Daron's family's vegetable garden. Unless they were to learn that the boy came from a family of thieves and murderers, she would push this alliance forward.

She glanced round the table and saw all eyes resting on her. Marie had already opened her mouth once only to shut it again. Let them wait, Yeraz thought. She needed to appear to be thinking. She nibbled the end of a long, plump raisin. It was crucial that Vartan and her sons not know of Anno's familiarity with Daron.

Yeraz cringed inwardly at the disastrous aftermath that would bring. Better to not ask Anno if she were agreeable. Better to not take chances of letting her speak at all. Anno would simply have to endure a bit longer, Yeraz decided. She would proceed as tradition had taught them, and daughters were simply not promised in marriage at the first asking. The second asking would do.

"This is unexpected, Sister Mariam," Yeraz began. "We have just begun to dry our tears since our Lucine became a bride."

Marie watched Anno.

"That is understandable," Mariam acquiesced quietly. Anno's legs were trembling near her own and Mariam stretched stealthily under the table and placed a warm, firm hand on her knee. To her surprise, Anno clutched her hand immediately and squeezed it tight. Mariam was taken aback, given the distance Anno had placed between them of late.

Anno held Old Mariam's hand and did not release it.

"And now our Anno has caught the eye of a family from our vil-

lage and we must consider that she leave her father's hearth as well."
At this, Yeraz smiled deeply at her daughter. It was a smile of warmth
and sadness in one, and tears slid from Anno's eyes as she realized, at
last, that her mother would give her blessing. No one else mattered if
Yeraz had decided.

"Tell us, Sister Mariam, what do you think? Is this a suitable
match for the granddaughter of your beloved friend? What would my
mother-in-law say of this family, this boy, if she were alive today?"
Yeraz asked, looking at Marie, who approving greatly the mention of
her mother, nodded heartily at Yeraz.

Anno no longer heard. She knew that this questioning was expected so that the go-between return to the boy's family with the impression that consent was not given easily, that their daughter was too
precious to them.

"I believe it is time your father and brother join us as well, Anno.
Let us hear of any objections they may have."

Anno's legs unfolded with difficulty. She stood and took uneven
steps toward the front door. The sleeves of her cotton blouse fell well
above her slim wrists and her skirt would have exposed a bit too much
of her ankles if they had not been covered with snug socks. She was
close enough to call out to her father but had never done so in her
life. No one had. She reached his side and waited. His last cigarette
tip lay smoldering by his shoe and he was leaning forward, elbows on
his knees, listening to Haig's explanation of the running of a motor.
He tipped his head up and pulled playfully at the tips of her fingers as
an indication for her to speak. Anno relayed her mother's message for
them to join the women inside.

Vartan twisted around and craned his neck to look back into the
house at the serious group seated at the tiny table. He looked back
quizzically at Haig as well.

"What is this, then?" he asked of his friend. Haig shrugged his
shoulders as if in ignorance, but could not help looking uncomfortable.

Vrej was no longer in the garden, and at Yeraz's insistence, Haig stopped a boy on the road and sent him on his way to locate him. She wished Vrej present to hear this discussion. Raffi had left the village again, four nights earlier.

The men settled themselves easily into the room. Anno stood close to the door that led to the sleeping room, her hands clasped loosely at her back, as if she were merely an observer and not the purpose of the visit at all.

Mariam began again, but his time she spoke with more enthusiasm. If Yeraz, as the mother, had had any objections or doubts, the men would have never become involved. Now they had moved on to the next stage, and Mariam wished greatly to be the bearer of good news to Nevart and Mgro. For, as Anno was committed to Daron, she knew, she had seen, Daron was committed to Anno.

"…and so, it is the heartfelt wish of the Markarian family that they may have Anno…"

"No." Vartan's voice was even, emotionless, almost as if he were rejecting a piece of bread or second cup of tea.

Mariam and Yeraz stared at him. Had they heard correctly? Surely they had not? They exchanged glances.

"What have you said, Vartan?" Mariam pressed, convincing herself she had misunderstood. She was old and misheard often.

"No. Not that family. I cannot give my daughter to that family."

There, again. Anno heard her father speak again. Not emotion-ridden words, exclaimed and repented later, nor words born of anxiety or sentimentality. These words were spoken with certainty, spoken with knowledge, and directed, pointedly, to his wife.

Yeraz blinked in astonishment.

"But, why, Vartan?" she implored, her voice made small.

More gently, now, he asked, "Does it matter so much? Will our Anno become an old maid, do you think? There are so many more lads in the village." He wished to end this conversation.

Unmoved at his attempt at lightness, unable to look at Anno, Yeraz kept her gaze, disapproving and probing and unsatisfied, fixed on her husband.

Uncomfortable now, not having expected Yeraz's insistence, he began to notice that Mariam was scowling at him. And in the shadows, he saw Anno. Her arms seemed glued behind her back and her legs were braced as if to keep herself from falling. Her eyes pierced his.

All this brought a slow, unwanted understanding, and he asked the one question no one had asked before. "Anno, my daughter, do you *want* this boy?"

A voice, urgent and loud, called from the road "Sister Mariam! Sister Mariam!" Rushed and heavy steps approached Vartan's door.

"Is Sister Mariam here?" A neighbor, his eyes enormous with fear, stood in the doorway. "Please, come! She is not well...my wife!"

It had grown dark inside and, engrossed in conversation, no one had cared to move to light candles. All started at the intrusion. Mariam acted first. She scooted her bulk from her flattened cushion and, taking Yeraz's arm, motioned for her to follow.

The men rose heavily from the room. When Yeraz looked over at Anno, she had disappeared.

Vrej had practically reached home, only to be met on the road by Vartan and the other men. As he searched their faces in confusion, they turned him back in the direction he had come.

"How could you let this get so far?" Vartan controlled the pitch of his voice, but the words were ground out.

"My brother," Haig answered, "I knew of it not five minutes before my mother started out the door. I knew it would not be welcome news, and that is why I joined her."

Vartan's sharply tossed head was his only answer. They were climbing the gently winding road toward Mariam's home and the conversation would not continue there.

CHAPTER 21

Anno's fury overcame any good sense left to her these last months. She bounded down and around the houses lining the twisted road. Her path was dark and if Anno had not known each stone, each dip, each turn by heart, she would surely have faltered or tumbled by now, but as it was, her legs strode as long and purposefully as her skirt allowed and her eyes stared straight ahead, seeing nothing.

The night had turned cold and damp and there was hardly a person out. The few left were hurrying toward home and shelter. Doors were shut tight and the small, high windows gave no clue as to how time was passed indoors. Had Anno turned her head to look, she could not have told what was taking place inside the rooms of even one single home. Passing the stables, she could smell the hay and earth and the smoky, dense hides of the animals.

Her ears rang and her vision was clouded with emotion. She felt as if she had been tossed back and forth for an eternity. And for what, she challenged, to no one but the solid walls she fleetingly passed. For *all of them* to agree, on a whim, if Daron were the proper husband for her? Well, they did not know anything, Anno decided. Not of him or his family.

She felt the cold grip her neck.

"Not that family," her father had said. That statement, she knew, was not born of a whim. Everyone had been surprised by it, had they not? Anno turned a sharp corner and reached out to lean against the corner of the building for support. Her weight on one arm, she turned her face skyward and tried to remember her mother's reaction. Yeraz and Mariam had both been in agreement. Yeraz was giving her consent. Mariam had no intention of speaking of her and Daron's meeting. All was to be well and then her father, *her father*, had said the most unexpected thing. It had shocked everyone.

Anno strode forward once again. She would wait and yearn and hope no longer. She would go to Daron, now, and let him hear of what had happened, and if there was truly a reason why they could not marry, then she would know of it. She decided more as she began to run. If necessary, they would run away and be married in a different village.

"Anno, kiz," she heard her name whispered, raspily.

Anno's steps faltered, but ignoring the sound as if it were imagined, she hurried on.

"Anno, girl," the voice beckoned again.

Anno stopped now, looking right and left in searching recognition.

"I am here. Right here," the voice called softly, as if to guide and lure.

Anno focused on a small shape huddled into the corner of a high garden wall just yards away from the church square. She stepped closer. "Turgay Dade?"

"Anno, child, won't you help me?" Long black sleeves stretched toward her.

Reluctantly, she took the old woman's hands. The bent fingers twisted through her smooth ones.

"Anno, child. Anno. Anno," she crooned and tears flowed abundantly to her eyes. "My mother, is she coming?"

Anno stamped her foot now in frustration. The mist had turned into a steady rain and she knew she could never leave Old Turgay outside, alone, in the wet and cold. She must be led back to the river now and encouraged to return to her sons.

Anno searched the roads and then the square, hoping to catch sight of someone else who might take Turgay. A boy, perhaps. She was struck, suddenly, at the complete emptiness around her.

"Anno, girl. Take me home. My mother is crying. I can hear her crying."

"I will take you home, Dade," Anno conceded. She did not understand Kurdish well and had no practice in speaking it. Her words were thought out before she spoke.

"Let us fix your head covering first." Anno reached down, pulled the covering back onto Turgay's head and secured it the best she could.

"We must walk quickly, Turgay Dade, or you will get sick." This last Anno gave in warning because Turgay often refused to move forward when she sensed she was being coaxed over the stream before she was ready.

Anno led Turgay down toward a smaller square, where three lanes met at once. There, only the branches of trees topping the garden walls shifted and it was as if the wind sloughed through the air in warning. Anno shivered and glanced down at Turgay. The old woman, for once, had nothing to say. She merely peered back at Anno trustingly.

The moon, three-quarters round, cast its shadows as Anno led Turgay on.

They reached the basket weaver's shop and turned onto the flatland that separated the village from the river. They walked heedfully forward, arm in arm, leaving the safety of the village homes further and further behind. Anno's legs became weighted as she sensed the full extent of their helpless exposure. Turgay, in her fatigue, was pulling down heavily on Anno's side, but she seemed oblivious to the close presence of danger that they had placed themselves in, moving in the open grasses after nightfall. Wolves and brown bears were prevalent always, but it was the striped hyena Anno feared most. Her head moved to the right and left, trying to block the reappearing vision of its wide jaws and nail-like teeth.

Anno knew they would need to walk directly along the banks of the river in order to spot the crossing points. She heard the lap of the water, but did not hurry toward it. For one, she was examining each bulge, each shadowy protrusion for movement. Also, Turgay had guessed where they were headed and Anno was reduced to tugging her ahead in miniature steps.

Turgay had started weeping again in anticipation. Her shoulders shuddered, but her tears had been trained, it seemed, to fall soundlessly. Her anguish had long been borne alone.

Staring ahead into the darkness, Anno considered turning back. She was unsure how long they would have to search for a safe path across the stream. She was not certain where the crossings lay and she did not expect any help from the old woman. But they were closer to the crossing, Anno knew, than the distance to her father's house.

It would be wiser, she decided, to hurry toward the bank without any further thoughts of hyenas. Once Turgay passed to the other side, Anno would run the distance home. She would seek out Daron tomorrow. It would be madness to present herself at Mgro's door after this. She would find a way then.

The raindrops, probing and constant, had seeped and soaked between the fibers of their clothing. The smell of sodden wool was familiar and it comforted Anno. As they reached the bank and turned upstream along it, Anno coaxed gently, "You are almost home now, Dade. Once we see the row of fat, smooth stones, you can pass over them and straight to your family."

At the water's edge, the cold seeped through the soles of Anno's shoes. She knew Turgay was not even looking in the direction of the water, and Anno puffed in frustration. As she had feared, Turgay would offer no help at all.

Desperation rising, she hurried Turgay along a bit roughly, and when the old woman did not even raise her eyes in objection, Anno released her hold with shame.

Several feet upstream, Anno thought she saw the water's flow alter. She left Turgay and ran ahead. There, unmistakably, five flat boulders lay stubbornly in the path of the current. Their surface was so wide that Turgay could dance across if she wished. Excitedly, Anno ran back.

"Dade, you shall soon be home with your grandchildren. You should be glad to warm your back by the fire."

The rain pelted their bodies now and the marshy land was hard to cross. With no room to walk side by side, Anno walked backwards, holding both of Turgay's hands in hers. Once they had reached the boulders, she bent to hug the old woman good-bye.

"Good night, Dade. You hurry home to your mattress and I shall hurry home to mine."

Anno's teeth were chattering now. In flight, she had taken no coat. Her dress had soaked through, and the coarse, wet cotton of her thin blouse lay against her skin like a cloying, icy sheet.

Anno urged Turgay toward the first boulder. Turgay did not move.

"Turgay Dade, do not stand here. Your shoes will be soaked. Get up on the rock."

Turgay stood frozen, staring down at her feet.

Anno changed tactics while trying to keep the panic out of her voice.

"Dade, will you come visit us again tomorrow?"

Only Turgay's head covering moved. Thin and dripping, it fluttered heavily and folded on itself.

Anno studied it and was consumed by a deep shame. She was struck by the enormity of what she was doing to Turgay, at once a quick contrast of childlike goodness and sage adult, keenly aware of the cruelty and trickery of all people. And trickery was just what

Anno was practicing, costumed as a good deed, upon this person who had been yearning for just one thing all her life.

Anno sank to her haunches and buried her head against her knees. She could move no more. She could make no more decisions, not for herself nor for anyone else. Decisions were being made for her, and for Turgay, and it was best to stop trying so hard. She closed her eyes and listened to the rush of the water, her warm breath cloaking her icy hands. Drops of rain rolled down her neck.

Seeing Anno bring herself to a level lower than Turgay, the old woman shifted her eyes to study her. She did not understand what had happened. For some time the two figures stood by the water's edge and lost themselves to its splash and scurry.

"*Barakata kiz,*" a girl child who brings luck, Turgay tried, voice nervous. This was what she had called her since that first Easter, when Anno had taken Turgay home to Yeraz.

Anno heard but did not move.

"Anno, do not leave me."

She heard the fear now in Old Turgay's voice.

"I will not leave you," Anno raised her head tiredly. "But, Dade, I cannot take you to your mother."

She rose to face Turgay, and gentling her voice, as though one could cushion the thrust of a spear, she spoke the truth to the child Turgay, ripped from her mother's side just yesterday.

"Your mother, Turgay, is no longer here." Anno's voice broke and her jaw quivered. "She died soon after you were taken from her."

The moonlight had long been hidden behind the crush of clouds, but Anno was able to look clearly into Turgay's eyes. Something glinted there.

"She did not want to live in this world without you any more than you wanted to live without her."

Anno had not given any consideration to how Turgay would respond to the truth of her words. The need to say them and to have them known was more valuable, more humane, and a lifetime late in coming.

Turgay's folded eyelids seemed to drop lower around the edges of once large, deep-set eyes. Unblinkingly, she stared at Anno, but Anno knew she was seeing again, for the millionth time, the pulling, the tearing, the jerks and screams of the Kurdish horseman and her defenseless mother. With a long exhale of defeat, she spoke in a whisper. "No, she did not want to live either." And she turned her body in the direction of the Kurdish camp.

Both women shivered. Turgay was fully in the present now and staring stonily before her. "Run home, child. Return to your sweet mother. If God decides that I should continue to live this life and see another Easter, perhaps I might share another piece of chorek with you and your family."

Turgay had said God, *Asdvadz*, as her mother had taught her. She had not said *Xuda*. It had taken one long, concentrated beating from the Kurd for the tiny Arev to become Turgay, and Asdvadz to become Xuda, until today.

Anno stared wide-eyed and tried to speak, but Turgay did not need a response. She turned to finally cross the stream.

What they both saw made them freeze in disbelief. The stream had risen so rapidly that only the very tips of the boulders peeped out at them, the rest submerged in wild swirls and surges of water. The water seemed to be frothing and racing its way to empty into the Sassoun River.

Anno's hands went to her forehead. Further upstream, the banks would be still wider apart and she would not know how to locate the crossings in the dark even if the stream had not risen. She frantically reassessed the only crossing known to her and found it had vanished.

Turgay had also been rapidly weighing the situation before them and had decided that lingering at the water's banks any longer was folly. She grasped the muddied hem of her skirt and pulled it up past her knees, revealing short, bent legs again covered in black. As Anno realized what she intended, she cried out in protest, but Turgay had already taken one step forward. Anno's hands stretched out to pull her back, but the old woman waved her away.

"Run home, Anno. Run home," she called back over the rush of the water. "May your mother forgive me."

Anno clutched her head as she watched Turgay's slow, steady progress. After the first two steps, she began gripping the boulders for support instead of trying to walk along their slippery backs. Now she was submerged waist-deep in the current, struggling against the water's force.

There remained almost ten feet of crossing for Turgay to reach safety and had even a viper appeared at Anno's feet, she would not have left her spot. She dared not call out. She knew the woman was using every ounce of concentration to reach safety.

The rain fell in mocking dances, vertically, then diagonally, and Anno's eyes stung and blurred.

Turgay took one more step and her body lifted out of the water an entire foot's length. Anno realized she must be standing on a rock. She held her breath, waiting for Turgay to move on. How much longer would the woman's strength last, she wondered? Had anyone thought to give her bread today? Anno's neck and shoulders ached from the strain of helplessness. She was lightheaded herself.

Turgay remained unmoving, perched on her rock. Anno tipped her head back and opened her mouth to catch the rainwater. A few drops slipped down her throat and she looked again to see if Turgay had moved forward.

Anno blinked in confusion. Her head whipped to the left and right. Turgay had disappeared.

Anno's heart pounded in her ears. She opened her mouth to call out and could make no sound. She plunged into the water and re-coiled at its iciness. On the banks, the cold had numbed her feet, but her calves and thighs tightened now with shock. Her hands reached into the water, her arms stretching out blindly into its depths. Flailing emptily, she stepped deeper into the current and saw, just an arm's length away, Turgay's white head emerge. Stumbling and scraping against the stream's bottom she grabbed at Turgay and pulled her head out of the water. The old woman's eyes shot open and Anno lost no time in dragging her body the last few feet toward the far side of the bank. Beneath her feet, sand and rocks shifted and dislodged. Anno tripped and slipped, heavily unbalanced, almost safely to the edge when, ready to collapse herself, she trod heavily on the sharp edge of a rock. The rock turned instantly under her weight and, together with Turgay, Anno crashed sideways into the water. The impact of her temple against a boulder was the last thing she knew.

CHAPTER 22

"We have a girl baby. Call the baby's father..." Mariam's voice trailed wearily. She searched the room for Yeraz.

Yeraz was controlling an urge to scream as loudly as the babe's mother had this last hour. Instead, she pulled close to Old Mariam and ground out each word. "Anno ran from the house. I must go see that she has returned."

She left Old Mariam as she was burying the umbilical cord near the front door. It was a tradition strictly followed, to ensure that the child would never travel far from the hearth.

Twisting a large shawl tightly around her head and shoulders, Yeraz stepped out onto the lane. She had not noticed the change in weather, and the rain surprised her. Her anxiety rising, she moved quickly.

She found her home dark and empty. She had already known that Anno would not be there. But where could she have gone? Yeraz considered the possibilities. Could she possibly have run to Daron? Remembering the stricken look on her face at Vartan's denouncement, Yeraz knew it was likely she had. Her breath came hard as she imagined the merchant's face, all their faces, upon seeing Anno at their door, at night and alone. How had everything unraveled so?

Why had Vartan said, "Not that family?" What did he know about them that was so serious, that Yeraz had no knowledge of, nor

Mariam, for that matter? Vartan was a tolerant man. His flexibility and goodwill had gained him this position as village leader over and over. What was it then that even he would not tolerate?

Yeraz looked behind her. She was as alone as she felt herself to be. She allowed herself to run.

As she pushed open Mariam's heavy front door, Vartan rose to his feet at the sight of her. She loosened her shawl and attempted to still her breath.

"Our neighbors have a girl child…" she started, but her voice broke. Her eyes filled and she gasped, "Anno is not at home! She has been gone this last hour and more."

A dreadful silence ensued.

"The babe came so fast. I could not get word to you." This last was almost inaudible and directed to no one. All present knew that Vartan had refused the Markarian clan's proposal.

Vrej stood now with the men. "She must have gone to Lucine," he offered, then quickly contradicted himself. "No. No. She would feel more comfortable with Takoush. Girl talk is what she will be after."

He looked around, hoping for support for his simple solution to a problem that seemed so grave. But the men's eyes remained on Yeraz. They sensed there was more to be said.

Yeraz knew that time wasted would work against them. There was no room for secrecy any longer. She tried to draw a deep breath, and looking straight into Vartan's eyes, spoke as if there was no one else in the room. "You should know, Anno wanted this marriage very much."

Vartan's eyes narrowed. Yeraz saw and knew that this would be as impossible as she suspected.

"She has been waiting months now for Daron's family to take some step toward arranging their union. But she never expected *your* reaction today. In short, she may have gone to Lucine or Takoush, but she may have gone straight to Daron."

Vartan found he could not move. Haig found himself wishing for the first time in his life that he paid more attention to his wife's talk. His older brother was watching him a bit accusingly. And Vrej found himself unimpressed with his parents' separate concerns. So little Anno had found and chosen a husband for herself right under their noses. Was that so awful? He would wait for these slow movers no longer. The night was dark and wet and Anno should be found, wherever she might have chosen to go.

"I will go straight to Takoush. If she is not there, I will go to Lucine. I feel certain I will find her." Vrej had already opened the door and stood with his hand on the frame.

"You will meet us in the church square in twenty minutes," Vartan spoke. "If she is in neither of those places, then *I* will go to see Mgro."

"You will not go alone," Haig and his brother spoke in unison, having studied his suppressed wrath. They understood how quickly these circumstances could turn to feuding.

Vrej's running feet could be heard no more and the men pulled on their coats and hats. Yeraz had still not moved from her spot inside the door, and she imploringly watched Vartan for some sign of encouragement or warmth as he passed her. He did not even look her way.

Haig's wife, unable to ignore her desperation, laid a wide arm across her shoulders, and it was Yeraz's undoing. She turned into the other woman's arms and shook with sobs of dread.

The walk to the church square was a silent one. Even Uncle Hagop seemed to have no advice to give. Vartan was calculating and recalculating a situation that could have no positive outcome. If she were found safe with either Lucine or Takoush, there would still be two entire families who would know of this night's business. If she were not found there, but with Daron, then they would have to marry. That was, if they had not already run away together, somewhere, for just that reason. Vartan did not have much faith in Mgro's morality to try to restrain them.

Then he thought of Yeraz. What of her part in all this? Why had she not shared her knowledge with him? That pierced him almost as much as his daughter's name linked with the Markarians'.

He glanced sideways at Haig, who had studied him constantly all night and now finally spoke. "If I had a daughter, I would be more concerned that she may be accosted this night at one luckless turn, by a snake. Or a Kurd," Haig spat, equally cold-blooded avenues to a lingering agony and death. "And I would be relieved to find her in the home of anyone who cared for her, instead of *that*."

Once in the church square, the four men climbed the red and black tufa stone steps to back close into the frame and shadows of the church door, avoiding the steady pour of rain.

The smell here of the dampened wooden door and the porous tufa beneath his feet brought memories to Vartan of Sundays, so many Sundays. Anno's spongelike baby fingers buried deep in his moustache as he held her against him while they walked along the twisting lanes to the church square. Yeraz would pretend to not notice that Anno's care had been left to the father. Anno toppled his fez and ate bits of bread from his fingers and still he would keep her with him. He did not call out that she was a distraction, a disturbance to be removed. Yeraz would turn away and allow them their love.

Later, as Anno grew, he would extend his index finger and together they would walk the roads. Vartan steered her away from the wagon ruts, the stones, and the deepest hoofprints to safer, smoother paths. Then, was she perhaps in her eighth year, as they stood side by side inside the confinements of the church's walls? He faced the altar, his eyes on Father Sarkis and his mind on the waning health of their best hen. He noticed Anno's body arched, her head tipped back to look up into the dome. Her mouth had fallen open and she was still inching her head backward to get a better view when she lost her balance. Her arms swung wildly to prevent a fall, and that was when her gaze met his. Vartan could have laughed out loud at her antics and her near escape. Anno saw, clearly, the crinkles at the corners of his eyes and beamed at him with pure, conspiratorial joy.

Vartan cleared his throat now, at the memories and the fear lodged there.

Vrej ran into the church square, sprinting as fast as he had started out, and sprang up the steps. His head was bare and his coarse hair was pushed off his forehead. He blinked the rain from his eyes to focus uneasily on the dark faces watching him from the shadows. The intensity of their gazes was searing, and he shook his head once before speaking, his throat grating the words, not from exertion, but from dread.

"Takoush has not seen Anno at all today. Neither has Lucine. Avo is taking Lucine to be with our mother now."

A deep and dirty oath regarding the woman who had borne Mgro ground out of Vartan's throat. He lunged down the steps and the rest followed him closely, through the church square and down the hill to the edge of the village, to Mgro's door.

ANNO'S HEAD STRUCK the boulder and her cheek scraped along its curve until she fell face downward in the rising stream.

Turgay, long accustomed to a role as mute spectator to the passage of the days of her own life, watched Anno's head disappear and her clothes billow and swell. Steadied for the moment, she steeled herself, her soul, for another incomprehensible loss. Then, Anno's head lifted, lifted and lowered. Turgay's body became a wheel, thrust in motion. Reaching Anno's side, she lifted her head out of the water and pulled her, at last, to the far side of the stream.

Deluged, Anno and Turgay lay unmoving on the ever-softening bank, as the temperature on their mountain plunged.

CHAPTER 23

Mgro's door did not open at once. No one expected it would.

Vartan rapped again and eventually Mgro's voice, gruff and suspicious, could be heard through the door.

"Who is there?"

Vartan gave his name. The sounds of the large key forced through its turns came to them, and the door swung open. Mgro stepped back to make room for them to enter, his face puzzled and his dark eyes searching. These were not frequent visitors to his home, and certainly not at this time of night. And judging from Vartan's face, the man was barely containing himself. Something was gravely wrong.

When still no one spoke, Mgro waved his arm in the direction of the stairs, and they all ascended. Once in the front room, they began searching all its corners, ignoring the startled faces of Mgro's family.

Nevart stared from her corner beneath a candle, her silvery hair let down and loosely braided. She pulled her shawl tighter around her and leaned forward anxiously. Her granddaughter, Nairi, close to her side, dropped her doll and bit her lip as she watched the men. Manuel and Naomi stood close together and their faces mirrored the same look of bewilderment and concern. Daron scrambled out of an adjoining room with his shirt hanging loose and open-collared over his pants.

All five men's eyes settled on him, and finally, Mgro's voice boomed. "For the love of God, what has happened?"

In all the years since Mgro's wife's death, Vartan had not entered this home. He had never had reason to. Yeraz had, he was certain. Now, the utterly tranquil and ordinary scene they had intruded upon unsettled him.

He did not remove his eyes from Daron. The young man was muscular around the shoulders as all the village men would be, but he had not developed their slouch yet. He appeared to be strong, and as Vartan remembered, alert. Much like Vrej, he looked ready to leap forth, but common sense held him back. Another young man, Manuel's son, he assumed, appeared and stood close to Daron's side.

Daron's black eyes locked with Vartan's and did not drop to the floor. Finally, Vartan spoke. "We are searching for Anno."

Had the room not been so deadly silent, perhaps not all would have heard, so reluctant was Vartan to even speak the words. But as it were, all did hear. Nevart heaved herself to her feet and all took anxious steps closer.

Mgro opened his large, empty hands and shrugged his shoulders. His forehead now heavily lined, he implored, "But why here?"

Daron, his feet already thrust into leather boots, stepped closer, past his father even. "*Why?* Why do you not know where Anno is?"

Vartan suddenly wished mightily that Anno had been found here. Even here, however upset she might be.

Daron was fully aware of how many eyes were on him. Anno's father, her brother, Mariam's sons. He did not care. They would not be here looking for her if they had not exhausted all other hope. What they knew and what they thought bothered him no more. Anno was missing and he thought he could hurl himself at any one of them now, with furious release.

Vartan, accepting that the time for discretion and half-truths was over and that holding back information could only diminish hopes of Anno's recovery, explained fully and simply the reason for Anno's anguish and then her departure.

"When?" Daron nearly growled. "When did she leave?"

"A good two hours ago," Vartan said and turned to Haig. They started down the stairs, making plans for a larger search. Vartan turned his back on a household scrambling for coats and lanterns and one pair of black eyes filled with censure and fear.

News of Anno's disappearance made its way to a dozen households. Sixty men and boys gathered in the church square with lanterns flickering and bodies wrapped against the cold and the rain. They were separated into four groups and sent in four different directions, told to return in one hour. If she had not been found by then, more people would be gathered. The details of her disappearance were not clear, and though they speculated furiously, they trod on, all expertly scanning and searching Salor and its surroundings.

Daron joined none of these groups. He could be told what to do no longer. Instead, he concentrated on the workings of Anno's mind and heart as he knew them. Having heard that her father would not allow their marriage, and the reason why not yet known or discussed, she had fled. She had not gone to Lucine or Takoush. Why had she not come to him? Her rejection of him renewed itself in his thoughts over and over until he stopped walking. His steps had been aimless as it were, just a restless, agonizing motion. While possibilities of her whereabouts rushed through his head, Kevork hovered close. He was suffocating with inactivity, horrified at the endless rolls of fog that at times even blocked his view of Daron, just paces away.

"Anno moves with purpose," Daron began. Kevork strained to hear. "If she has been gone these last two hours, she may have set out before the rain began."

Kevork burst forth, "Daron, the girl is not crazy, is she? She cannot be out in this rain! She must have sheltered somewhere."

Daron faced Kevork and continued to voice his thoughts out loud, slowly and calmly, as if they were not standing in a gray, frigid cocoon. "If she did not go to anyone, then she might have gone to the willow."

Kevork tilted his head, trying to accept this possibility. This very old, beloved tree was just behind the village homes, on a short plain upstream from where water was collected. It was known as "the sweethearts' tree," as betrothed couples met there, in open view of passersby, to converse and become acquainted with one another.

Anno had scoffed at this, saying she would not wait to be betrothed to lay her cheek against its rough trunk and watch the stream glimmer through its swaying, pinnated leaves, like a curtain.

"Also, the stream. Any water, really. She enjoyed sitting by the water."

"But, Daron, not in this rain!" Kevork protested.

"There was no rain when she started out, was there? And if nothing had happened to her, she might have returned home by now, do you not think? Something has happened to her, or she is so upset..." Daron's mind raced.

They were walking swiftly now.

"Where else?" Kevork persisted.

"The orchard, but not now, of course. The churchyard."

They were moving uphill.

"We will start at the willow and end in the churchyard. She may be by the stream where it pools. She may be there," Daron called back, his walk already turning into a run.

They left the village roads immediately. It would be the quickest way to the shelter of the willow. Slipping through an opening between the homes, they leapt out onto the surrounding steppe.

Their boots were quickly caked with reddened soil as they leapt from mound to rock. At one point, they leapt onto the low, flat roof of a one-room shelter with its back built into the side of a hill, saving minutes of time by going over rather than around it. They were soon by the willow.

From a distance it was plain to see that no one was there. Nevertheless, Daron slowed his run and walked the last remaining steps inside the shelter of its branches. He stared straight up through the leaves to the blackness beyond it and exhaled at this first failure. Then he turned to Kevork. His cousin raised his lantern to better see Daron's face. He lowered it again quickly and waved toward the stream. "Come! Where is that section of the stream? It pools, you said?"

Again they ran, across the short plain to the banks of the stream. They saw immediately how the water had risen and then they ran again, more slowly now, outside its uneven ridge. They traveled downstream to an area where the land flattened abruptly and the water's flow slowed as the natural walls of the stream widened and rounded. In the summer the girls loved to remove their shoes here and wade in its twinkling coolness. Now, the two men only stared into its ugly, muddied depths.

Their soaked heads fell forward with yet another defeat.

"Daron," Kevork spoke softly, very near his side. The growing absurdity of searching for someone in the open air, in this downpour, made him ask. "Daron, listen. Do you think, she would have tried to just," he faltered and began again. "I must ask. Do you think she would have tried to just kill herself?"

Daron's head snapped around. "No!" he shouted.

"Are you certain? She would not do that?" Kevork persisted.

"She would not do that! *To me!*"

Kevork was silenced. A relationship like this was beyond his understanding. Anno was almost a stranger to him.

The rain had thickened the air, making it pungent and spicy. Daron found it hard to breathe suddenly. Could she be dead somewhere? He must think. The churchyard was still a possibility. He had not understood the peace Anno felt by the gravestones, but he had accepted it. Could she have fallen there? Tripped on one of the stones in the dark? Perhaps she had been so close to them all along and they had not known?

"The churchyard, then, Kevork?"

They turned away from the rush of water.

Three hundred paces downstream, Turgay and Anno lay cradled against the yielding bank. Their bodies had ceased their hard trembling, and now waves of warmth lulled them into unconsciousness.

NEVART HAD DRESSED and stood leaning heavily against their open door, peering into the street for someone to appear with news. The men had been gone for less than an hour, but it seemed more.

No one voiced their utmost fear. No sane person wandered in this rain and fog for hours. She was either dead or hurt or taken.

Naomi had helped Daron and Kevork with their coats and then had backed into a corner of the house, where she sat on her haunches, unmoving and wide-eyed with disbelief. Mgro's daughter, Nairi, was staring at her strangely. Naomi knew she should go stand with Nevart by the door where news would reach them first, but she could only stare at the walls and remember her dream, again, coming to her so vividly. She clenched her teeth. Cold, muddy water was washing over her naked skin. She was not immersed in the water, but her hair was wet and twisted around her neck.

Her left hand lifted and pressed against her mouth. It felt so close, but she was here, here in this corner on the dry floor staring at dry walls. What had Mariam said? Dreams of dirty water were *never* good.

She rose and crossed the room. Again she clenched her teeth. She thought surely they would crack. They chattered so loudly in her ears. Down the stairs and she saw Nevart standing alone. She murmured only that she would return and continued out the door. She passed the flooded rows of vegetables and the high garden wall to the left and walked uphill to the church square. Nevart had cried out after her. Perhaps because she had not understood what Naomi said, or perhaps because Naomi had left without permission, or perhaps because she had not taken a cloak or head covering. It did not matter, because her dream told her of this night, and she must find someone who would listen to her.

Tiny flames of light flickered as she approached the square. The rain had all but stopped. She searched their faces and saw them solemn and lined. Anno had not been found, then.

She asked for Mgro or Manuel, for Kevork, for Daron. They had not been seen. Heads shook slowly. Even Naomi's father-in-law was out searching.

Naomi walked as far as the churchyard and then turned back. Perhaps she should find Mariam. She would be an ally and not think her foolish.

Now the hour of searching was nearly up, and Naomi noticed men straggling back to the church square, heads shaking. At the sound of footsteps behind her, Naomi turned. Kevork and Daron were emerging from between the headstones and descending the incline of the graveyard.

"What news?" Daron asked, his eyes hollow.

"None. Yet." Naomi took both his wrists. "Daron, my son, please listen. I beg you."

Blankly, he watched her.

"Did you search the stream?" she asked.

Kevork glanced at Daron, who did not answer. "At some points, yes," Kevork supplied.

Naomi turned to him and held his eyes with a seriousness that he rarely saw. "You must search the stream. She is there. I feel it." Her hands squeezed Daron's wrists uncomfortably.

"Believe me." She looked back at Daron now. "I know what I am saying."

Daron felt as if a stranger were speaking to him. There was no trace of his light-hearted aunt. Her face was colorless and harsh.

"If you do not go, then I shall."

She did not say that it was a dream, real and persistent, that made her insist. And they did not ask.

Both nodded back at Naomi. They would search the length of the stream. Many times.

Kevork clapped a hand on Daron's back and choosing to move methodically, they retraced their steps past the flatland and up the knolls back to the pool, to continue their way downstream past all the lengths of water they had missed.

Naomi heard the voices in the square. Her back was to them but their words carried.

"...useless in this mud and rain."

"I never recovered from my cough last spring..."

"In this fog I can see about as well as my blind grandmother..."

"I tried to check the bottom of a well, but could not see further than the length of my arm."

Shivering, she moved away from earshot.

The fog had coated the moon in layers so that now its light was nearly extinguished. Daron and Kevork could not move as quickly as before. Globules of rain spattered and trickled off leaves and branches twofold in weight onto their numbed faces and shoulders. Reaching the pool, they trod ankle-deep along its melting ridge. They peered deep into its depth this time, instead of only around it.

"Your mother has seen another dream," Daron said.

"Yes," Kevork admitted.

And we are desperate and helpless enough to act on a vision, a dream, they both thought. Well, they had to search somewhere next. Let it be this stream.

"How far along do you think we should continue, Daron?"

Almost a mile more and they would meet the rush of the Sassoun River.

"To the end," Daron answered.

Up ahead, the ridge of the stream's bank, on the far side, rose unusually. Daron ignored it. They were looking everywhere at once, to the right and the left of them, and in the water. They searched anywhere their limited vision allowed. Eventually, they neared the unusual rise, and standing almost straight across from it, Daron froze as he focused on its shape.

Kevork stopped as well and followed Daron's gaze. They both cried out and bounded into the water in wide-armed, disbelieving rushes of hope and discovery. They plunged themselves fully and gratefully into the same icy water that short hours ago Anno and Turgay had tried so tragically to cross over.

"Anno! Anno!" Daron cried out her name repeatedly, thunderously at first—and then once he reached her side, it became almost a moan as he pulled her still and weighted body to him, her limbs flaccid, her eyes closed.

Kevork pulled Turgay, unconscious as well, out of the water and laid her flat on the bank. Daron frantically bent his ear to Anno's mouth, searching for life and calling her name. Kevork looked over his shoulder toward the Kurdish camp and saw no movement.

Daron's head reared. "There it is! A pulse in her throat."

With one mighty thrust he stood on his feet in the rushing current with Anno cradled high in his arms. Water spilled off her body like a waterfall. He sank with his first step and straightened himself with the next and Kevork watched him forge ahead with long cautious strides.

Kevork followed closely behind with Turgay in his arms. He was stunned by her leaden weight, but thought she was most probably lighter than Anno, her bones hollowed and slighter with age. But then there were the layers and layers of clothing she wore, soaked and dragging.

Daron climbed the other bank of the stream on his knees. Once clear of the ridge he felt he could run with Anno, straight to warmth and shelter. He turned once to see that Kevork followed and then never looked back again.

He did not allow himself to dwell on her lifeless face. Her head bobbed and rocked limply and he thought he could easily fling Turgay's body into the nearest pit with satisfaction and pleasure. It did not take much deciphering to realize she was the cause of all this heartache. He could see that Anno's temple was bloodied red even in the shadows.

For the third time that night Daron and Kevork passed through the churchyard. As Daron passed Anno's grandparents' stone, he sent a short prayer to them. "Please. Please, not her."

Daron and Kevork burst into the square and a stifled shriek arose from Naomi at the sight of them. Heads swung in alarm at the sound and a great rush of bodies moved toward them.

"Is she alive?"

"Who is that with her? Old Turgay?"

"They are soaked through. Are they alive?"

"Where were they?"

"Anno is alive," Kevork answered once. He did not respond to questions about Turgay, because in truth, he did not know.

As it became obvious that Daron was taking Anno straight to her father's home, many offers were made to help carry her. He did not slow his pace and he did not respond.

"Where is Headman Vartan?" he called back to the trail of people behind him.

"He is being called."

Still neither Anno nor Turgay stirred.

Suddenly, Vartan and Haig appeared, running toward them from a side lane. Only then did Daron slow his steps. Vartan's large, trembling hands cupped Anno's face and he stared up at Daron in terror.

"She is alive," he answered gently, praying it was still true. Vartan's arms shot out for his daughter and for a tiny fraction in time, Daron and Vartan held Anno together, and then, reluctantly, Daron released her.

Vartan waited for Daron to take his eyes from Anno's face, and with one toss of his head, motioned for him to follow.

Kevork still carried Turgay, and Daron fell into step alongside him, leading the long trail of villagers. He searched once for Naomi, but she was not there.

Nearly home, Yeraz burst toward them, her headpiece billowing like wings, her shoes tossing gravelly stones into the air. She came arms outstretched but was struck at once by Anno's utter stillness and halted several feet away. She clamped both hands across her mouth as strangulated sobs erupted from her throat.

"No! Yeraz! She is alive!" Vartan shouted.

Yeraz sucked in air, disbelieving, and swung back toward home. She pulled her skirts high above her knees and stretched her thick, stockinged calves to new extremes as she cried out directions.

CHAPTER 24

A rush of bitter mountain air lashed each corner of the front room. The toneer's steady but weak flow of warmth was no match for the onslaught of drenched bodies that proceeded through the door. No sooner had they exclaimed over Anno and the wound to her temple than Kevork entered bearing another body. All rushed forward to see who it was and, upon recognizing Turgay, began to piece together what they believed might have been the events of the night.

Mariam sprang into action like a woman of twenty years. She helped Vartan lay Anno gently on a straw mat and motioned for Kevork to lay Turgay down as well. She and Yeraz immediately began to peel off Anno's shoes and clothes. Lucine pulled her wet hair off her neck and slapped her face gently, calling her name. The villagers dispersed, pleading to be called if help were needed. Kevork, feeling awkward, left as well. Daron did not follow. He turned his back and faced a dark wall that flickered now with his swollen shadow.

Anno's garments seemed fused together, but Yeraz and Lucine tore at them fiendishly and Anno was soon lifted off the mat onto a mattress. Mariam had already warmed its surface by applying rows of flat, rounded stones heated at the fire.

Haig had remained at Turgay's side for long minutes, but could find no sign of life left in her. Unlike Anno's, her expression seemed content, almost as if she were already warmed.

Uncle Hagop shuffled forward and, eyes brimming, made the sign of the cross above her forehead. He whispered, "God be with you now, little sister."

Vrej came through the door at last. His cheeks were flaming red and he smelled of pines and wind. They realized he had been searching the forest at night for Anno, and Yeraz did not let herself think of the danger he too had been in.

He took in the entire scene before him. Anno looked as though she were sleeping; she was swathed heavily, like a newborn, while her chest was being rubbed with warm oil. Her temple, he saw, was deeply cut. Not far from her, Turgay lay, wet and tiny, on her straw mat.

Vrej took off his coat and boots, and his eyes roamed the room. Aunt Marie was busy at the fireplace hoisting a large pot. The men were gathered around the toneer, still wearing their half-soaked clothes. His eyes rested on Daron. He, too, had been pulled close to the toneer. Vrej had been told on his way home that Daron and Kevork had found Anno and Turgay, but considering the circumstances he was surprised to see Daron here, still, in their home.

Vrej went and stood by him.

Lucine pulled Anno's hair out from under her and spread it out to dry.

"Turgay is dead?" Vrej asked of no one in particular. Grunts were his only answer.

"Tell us now, Daron, where you found them," Vartan finally asked.

Daron told them how he and Kevork had searched. He was too tired to explain to them about Aunt Naomi and her dream. He did not understand it himself and was not prepared to endure their looks or questions.

He crossed the room wordlessly and stood over Anno. He bent to touch her hand and thought she felt a bit warmer. Chunks of moss clung to her hair. He knelt, and his eyes, on a level now with Yeraz and Mariam, were sunken and vacant.

Anno was covered to her chin. Her mouth was slightly opened and he watched her breaths, slow and shallow. Mariam saw his eyes well. Unprepared to bear the pain there, and the fear, she snapped at him. "Go near the toneer, boy! Take off those shoes and those socks. Lucine, get some hot tea inside these men. Have we not seen enough today?"

Mariam, he knew, was making it understood that he would stay.

Vrej built up the toneer's fire, Anno's specific chore, and it sparked and spread a welcome scorching heat.

Had Anno opened her eyes just then, she would have seen Daron seated cross-legged between Vrej and Uncle Hagop, watching her. He was holding a steaming cup of tea, but a cup of oghee was being pushed at him as well by Uncle Hagop. As it was, she did not stir.

"Why has no one come in search of her?" Marie hissed to the women. "Is she not their mother, after all? Leaving her to wander in this rain! Did they *want* her dead?"

Yeraz exhaled. She felt as if her chest would burst with fear. Fear for her daughter, whose temple blazed as she battled whatever unknown ailment was upon her due to her exposure. And fear of how the Kurds would choose to interpret the causes of Turgay's death and where they would choose to lay the blame.

At midnight, Vartan and Haig reached an agreement. At first light, they would cross the stream to the Kurdish camp and locate Turgay's family. They would be told the entire truth of how their mother and Anno were discovered. Daron had remembered, later, noticing the large row of boulders close to where Anno and Turgay lay. It was quite obvious that while crossing to deliver Turgay home, the two had fallen. They would be told that Anno lay unconscious. Turgay did not survive.

It would be done at first light, so that Turgay's body would be buried the same day as her death.

"Let us shroud her," Yeraz said from Anno's side.

It was left to Yeraz and Marie to prepare the shroud for Turgay, while Mariam produced an untiring line of heated stones to place around Anno's body.

Yeraz produced the white cotton cloth, and Marie set to work stitching the edges. Turgay's family could do what they wished once she was with them again.

"Shall we wash her, then, Sister Mariam?" Marie asked as she worked.

Mariam nodded. "We shall not ignore their rules. At least they cannot say we did not respect their ways."

Vrej held up a blanket and behind it the women washed Turgay. Their backs and arms ached, but they did not stop until even her hair was brushed, freeing it of the river's traces. She had no veil with which to cover her head. They did not dwell on where it had been lost. They braided and coiled her hair neatly and put her own wet clothes back on her. At last, she lay cleaned and shielded in white.

SEVERAL HOURS OF darkness remained. Anno's temple was bandaged and all agreed that her color was better. The toneer's fire was kept hot and strong, rapidly burning the discs of dung and hay that had been prepared for their long winter confinement.

As Daron watched Anno, a more distinct picture of her lying in the river came to him. It was no longer a stream by the time he and Kevork had arrived. The rushing current was licking and bouncing off her body, and eventually it would have risen until it drowned her. He, like Yeraz, continuously exhaled to relieve the pressure on his chest.

Vartan's gaze was on him always. He had not been asked to leave, and that was a type of victory. But Daron did not presume and he did not assert himself in the least. Merely being in the same room with Anno must be enough. He did not move from his place on the floor again. He tried to be invisible.

Lucine's old mattress was drawn out and pulled close to Anno's. She spoke into her sister's ear as incessantly as the string of heated stones was brought to her bedside, hoping to draw her out of her unconscious world. Vrej soon joined her, appropriating a generous corner of Lucine's mattress for himself.

Leaning into Anno's ear, he threatened. If she did not awaken soon, he would begin snipping the ends of her hair, he warned. He would do this bit by bit until she did awaken and he did not care if she soon resembled a little boy. He even scrambled off to find Yeraz's sewing basket and returned to snap the scissors widely next to her face. Lucine swatted him away, but then, both gasped as Anno's head made its first restless movement.

Lucine squealed and everyone in the room jolted upright. They waited.

They heard a cough, faint and ineffective. They watched. Underneath the layers of blankets, Anno's arms moved.

Mariam's lips tightened. She would waste no time. Seated on the hard floor, she bent her legs and set herself into a sideways rocking motion. She swung herself to the left and brought herself to her knees, her upper body resting on her knuckles. She drew a breath and waited for someone to rush over to help, as someone always did. It was Vrej. He pulled her to her feet. Not waiting for her back to straighten, she partially addressed the floor.

"My dear, she will awaken soon. I shall go bring my grasses."

They all watched the door close behind Old Mariam with dread. What was it she suspected?

Anno's head tossed. Voices coaxed her to consciousness. Again, her cough, barely audible, her eyes screwed against the pain. Her arms struggled against the heavy covers and fought their way out, pale and slim and bare. Daron saw her shoulders for the first time, the upward sweep of her collarbones where they met the twin cups of her shoulders.

He shrunk back.

Needing to move, he tossed more discs in to fuel the toneer.

Anno's eyes opened in confusion and clutched at the wide binding on her head. Too quick, she tugged it off. Groans of protest, and laughter, and claps of relief as she concentrated on the faces peering down at her. Yeraz demanded more cloth as Anno's temple bled again.

Daron moved in closer, as close as he dared, and came abruptly eye to eye with Vartan. He dropped his gaze, but only slightly. He would leave now if told to, but Vartan said nothing. He only moved away and went to kneel between his daughters, pulling Anno's blankets tenderly but fully to her chin.

CHAPTER 25

*L*anguid shafts of sunlight dawned over the ridges of Mt. Maratuk. The clouds rollicked densely by in the same shades of chalk and silver as the thick fog that met the ground beneath Uncle Hagop's boots, whose goatskin had thinned and molded itself closely to his feet.

Uncle Hagop's eyes, grainy and wilted, had not seen a pillow that night. Nor had any of the other men. He had plodded to the door, as was his self-appointed morning task, to gaze at his mountain and give his forecast. But this morning, although Anno coughed and wheezed valiantly in her corner, there was death in the house.

It was first light now and time to deliver the news. Turgay must be buried by sundown.

Several pairs of eyes lifted as he closed the door and turned back into the room. He could not forecast this day.

"How are you to do this, then?" he asked of Vartan.

Vartan gazed at his uncle and wondered at the way his whole being seemed to hang. His thick, scraggly brows shaded downturned eyes. His drooping moustache covered a grim, downturned mouth. Then there were the shoulders bent from an existence of worry and toil and yielding.

He is the mirror of myself, Vartan thought, *of us all.*

"Leave that to us," he answered gently. "Haig and I shall go slowly."

Yeraz's hand shook as she spooned warm tea into Anno's mouth. Marie took the spoon and cup from her hand.

Mariam had retrieved dried hollyhock and other grasses from their containers in the grain room. It struck her that it was the same hollyhock she had gathered the afternoon of Lucine's wedding, when Anno had flung herself into that old well. She fingered it incredulously and raised her eyes upward. "My God, let Your plan be for the good."

Anno's temperature had risen steadily these past four hours.

Yeraz could be of no help to Vartan and Haig in this day's task, but she would spare nothing to help Anno back to health. And that included forgetfulness regarding Daron's presence, until this morning's sunrise.

Yeraz had no doubt that Anno was aware of him. Her eyes had followed him several times, before closing against the fever. Each time, she had seemed to question whether he was really there, doubting her own wakeful state. Yeraz did not have to turn to know that behind her, Daron's eyes locked with Anno's. She could feel their black depths calling to her daughter. She could see Anno struggle to respond, then melt back into herself.

Vartan's eyes passed over the long, rectangular room. The flickers from the candles and oil lamps, not yet extinguished, showed Yeraz's silhouette, bending and straightening near their youngest child. Lucine slept rock-like, on her side, her mouth fallen slightly open as if to speak. Mariam had propped herself against a wall behind Yeraz, facing Anno. Her head dipped to one side and her snores deepened.

Vrej ached to accompany his father, but knew it was an impossibility. Vartan would not expose his son. Daron, in turn, watched Vartan and Haig.

"It is like this when you allow them to elect you village leader," Haig commented, pulling on his coat. "Otherwise, we could have thrown this task on someone else's shoulders by now."

Vartan grunted. He again heard the telling sound of apricot seeds tossed into a hat as votes were collected. Again, he accepted the position of diplomat, peacemaker, negotiator.

He called Daron. "I wish to know where you found them. The exact spot. You remember it?"

"Yes," Daron answered simply. He could never forget it.

"Then let us go."

Bowed against the cold and the anticipation of the task before them, Vartan, Haig and Daron did not care to take in the newly washed walls and roofs of the houses to the left and right of them. Nor did they lift their faces to the shrubs and trees winking in the morning light, vital and freed at last of the dragging layers of dust and sap.

The rain had ceased completely and their lungs exhaled great white clouds as they strode sharply toward the church square, with Daron a scarce step ahead of Vartan and Haig. The lanes, filled with puddles formed by the ruts and imprints left by animals and wagons, made it impossible to walk a straight line. Daron walked along the edges of the lane, sure-footed and alert.

He is like my own two sons, Vartan admitted to himself. And then, frustrated, he remembered Mgro.

They were no longer alone once they neared the square. Craftsmen and shepherds were busied already and quickly gathered around Vartan, asking after Anno and Turgay. Seeing Haig at his side was a common thing, but they eyed Daron curiously. Vartan pushed by quickly, an old tactic of his to minimize panic and rumor, and the villagers felt strangely optimistic watching them all walk away, although they could not say why.

They trod across the same flatland Anno had coaxed Turgay over. The men realized where Daron was leading them. It was not at all the way he and Kevork had traveled the night before, but it was the quickest way.

All the stream's crossings were precisely known to the men. Minute and detailed knowledge of their land had been one particular reason for their salvation. Following Daron, they realized that Anno had headed to the crossing that was closest to the village, and the narrowest. Soon they heard the full, bursting rush of the current. At its narrowest, the stream rose and overflowed with ferocity. Topping the ridges of its banks, the three stared down into the water and Daron pointed to where Anno and Turgay had lain. The boulders were submerged and lost, and the water still frothed and thrust its way to the river beyond.

Gone was the smell of sweet, dry grass and dust. The earth had at last filled its spiny, thirsty cracks. This, now, was the face of their winter, and it had always been welcome and familiar. But now, they only saw the depth and breadth of the water, with their Anno drowning in it.

Haig's arm reached out and he clapped Daron heavily on his shoulders. "However did you find them, boy?" He shook his head in disbelief. "Long life to you."

Daron did not know the answer to this himself. It was just as well that he was not expected to answer. Vartan's eyes were on him with a warmth he had seen turned only on the headman's own family members.

"Now go home. We shall do the rest."

It was not the dry, final dismissal Daron had been expecting from Vartan this past night.

Daron closed his mouth against the urge to speak. It was not the time to question. He would have gladly plunged into the icy water again if it meant that he could accompany them across to the Kurdish camp, if it meant that he would be allowed to speak, to ask, *why* had he been rejected? He had begun to hope that he would be allowed once they had come this far. Instead, he dropped his eyes again before his elders.

"I shall go then. God be with you." Daron falteringly turned. Steps away, he stopped and watched Vartan and Haig travel upstream until they disappeared from sight. He knew where they were going. About a quarter-mile away was a crossing that had been formed decades ago by their own people. The stream did not narrow there as much as the crossing Anno had chosen. Instead, boulders of all sizes were settled one atop the other, so high that they topped the surface of the water even in the deepest of winter and weakened the river's flow. The crossing was called "the waist of the stream."

It would have been an ideal place for the women to do their laundry, and had been, until years ago, before Anno was born. Several women of the same clan had gathered to do their washing when they were stung by scorpions that nested there in the dozens. All the women had died over a span of a few days, and since then, that spot had been allowed to become overgrown with brush, never to be used again.

Vartan and Haig located this bridge of rocks and passed over it quickly. Their boots, having only begun to dry, were soaked again thoroughly, but they continued on, paying no heed.

They walked a full mile and more and caught sight of the mud huts under a quickly clearing sky. They had always lived peacefully beside this Kurdish tribe. Perhaps, at the time of Turgay's kidnapping, it was the Sassountzis' sincere wish to keep their relations peaceful, and so unusually close was their proximity that no one had intervened for her return. Vartan and Haig did not know. They did not question the judgment of those who came before them.

The Kurds' camp was quiet. It was most probably time for their morning prayer. Vartan and Haig did not go near until they saw a sign of movement. Shouts and calls were heard, and then the men moved forward.

Vartan remembered vaguely in which direction they should head. They walked past the curious eyes, gave their morning greetings and asked for Turgay's family. They could feel fingers pointing and deep stares. They hardly lifted their heads and looked hard at the ground when they saw the skirts of a woman.

There was no mosque or town square, just a collection of huts. Haig, following close behind Vartan, was relieved to see him slow. All the dwellings were alike, with the roofs cone-shaped to let in light and let smoke out. Smoke drifted out the peak of this hut now.

They could hear voices from inside, speaking too quickly for them to understand. Men spoke at once. Vartan and Haig could only catch stray words. No one saw them standing outside, as they stood a good distance from the door. They were reluctant to enter and reluctant to give their news, so still they hesitated. The men's voices lowered and stopped. Vartan cleared his throat.

"*S'ara hava kherbe,*" he ventured a good morning in Kurdish.

A like reply came from inside and the hut flap was drawn wide. A young man stood there, of about thirty years. His head wrapping was coiled and completely covered his head, but his thick moustache, free of gray, was a gleaming black that matched his brows and eyes.

"We have come to speak to Arsad, if it is possible," Vartan said, asking for Turgay's oldest son.

The young man's eyes traveled in detail over the Armenians. Queries came from inside the dark dwelling.

"Would you tell him that Mixtar Vartan asks for him?"

The man turned around and called out.

Arsad appeared but his son did not move far away.

"Arsad," Vartan greeted him. "We have come to speak of your mother."

Something of relief flickered in Arsad's eyes. His head was uncovered and shafts of gray had grown in his brown hair and beard that Vartan did not remember seeing at their last meeting. A brightly designed wide woolen vest reached below his knees to meet woolen boots.

Arsad called over his shoulder and then motioned for Haig and Vartan to enter. He would prefer for them all to discuss Turgay in private away from his neighbors' eyes and ears. They stepped into a room emptied of women and children. Half a dozen men of different ages seated on carpets looked expectantly back at them. No introductions were made. They all knew who Vartan was, and their mother had been missing all night.

Seeing their solemn faces, Vartan spoke immediately.

"Yesterday, at sunset, the rain had begun to fall, if you recall. The women of our household were busy with the delivery of a baby, so it was some time later that we discovered our youngest daughter, a child, was not at home. Concerned for her well-being, about sixty men searched for her within our village and around it."

The Kurds were as still as statues.

"We do not know what occurred precisely, but one to two hours later, my daughter and your respected mother, Turgay, were found in the stream. It seems they had crossed the river to the opposite bank but got no further. We believe my daughter was leading Turgay Dade back here. To her family."

The Kurds moved now, exchanging looks, and gasps came from beyond where the women listened.

Vartan continued. "Once found, they were both carried to my home, but Turgay Dade was no longer alive."

The men murmured to each other, but it was of no importance what their reactions might be. Vartan and Haig watched Arsad.

He blinked several times. His eyes, too, were bloodshot and his skin colorless from a sleepless night.

"And your daughter?" Arsad asked tonelessly.

"Our daughter awakens now and then, but lies next to your mother with a rising fever," Vartan answered, his voice equally toneless.

The rustles and cries from the storage room grew. Vartan and Arsad's eyes never left each other's faces. Vartan's face showed no trace of guilt and he offered no apologies. Turgay's wanderings had nearly been the cause of Anno's death; they might still be. And this entire Kurdish clan would have preferred their mother wander all night alone rather than risk her cries and yearnings being heard in their camp.

Vartan's disgust grew as he stood. Haig, anxious to move on, spoke. "We believe she passed just hours ago, four or five at the most. We came at first light to call you, as you can see."

"Yes. Yes." Arsad shook himself. He spoke to the men watching him. There was much to do.

His son, who had greeted them at the door, and another man with similar features rose to dress in coats of shaggy fur while Arsad wrapped his head. The man who might have been Turgay's husband was not there. Vartan wondered if he had died, but did not ask.

Once outside the hut, Vartan and Haig followed Arsad and his two sons through the village. Seeing the two Christians, the neighbors asked Arsad in passing if all was well. To this he replied truthfully. "It seems not. We must prepare for a burial. It is for my mother." He would divert their many questions when they returned with her body.

They walked in silence the distance to the stream. Vartan believed that if his sons were not present, Arsad would have burst forth with questions. The man's discomfort was close to the surface. *Let him live with his questions,* Vartan thought. He had already guessed at most of the answers. He wondered if it would be easier now, with Turgay's death, for them to live with their sin.

By now, all of Salor knew of Turgay's death and none were surprised to watch her family march through the lanes with Vartan and Haig. They cleared a wide path at their approach.

Mgro and Daron had placed themselves at the end of the high road past Vartan's house, before the road rolled to the right and then out of sight. They studied Arsad's face, trying to anticipate what trouble he might bring.

Vartan pushed open his front door. His rough hands caressed the planks as if to draw warmth and reassurance from their strength. Was he bringing more grief to his own hearth or just helping to lay an old, broken woman into a peace-filled grave?

The front room was still warmer than it would have ever been at this time of the year, at this time of day. Only Yeraz and Mariam appeared to have remained. Their bodies were bent as if to shield Anno, whose rasping breaths could be heard from several feet away.

Vartan stepped aside to hold the door wide open for the Kurds to enter.

Yeraz stood, but Mariam did not. She inched herself closer to Anno and her eyes were cold as Arsad moved toward Turgay. His sons did the same. They took no notice of their surroundings, but only dropped to the floor at Turgay's side.

Arsad lifted the shroud and saw that his mother lay cleaned and groomed. Her skin was ashen. He held the white cloth in a tight fist. He thought, still, she might move and turn her eyes on him once again, pained and pleading. He waited. His sons watched him warily. Finally, Arsad took his mother's hand to his chest. He inhaled deeply and then released air, fraught with regret. He would spend his remaining lifetime trying to extinguish the truth.

"We shall take her home now." His voice rattled as he spoke to Vartan.

"Then I shall arrange a bier, if you will allow it," Haig offered, his hand already on the door.

Arsad did not refuse. Haig slipped his large shoulders through the door, allowing only a wisp of a draft to enter.

Arsad moved around Turgay to peer at Anno. She was awake now and turned glassy eyes to meet him. She had been aware of his presence despite the wall Mariam had tried to erect with the width of her own body. Her lips were parted and she took shallow, painful breaths. Tears slid out of her eyes and down past her uninjured temple.

"We do not know how long they lay in that icy water," Vartan said, at his side now.

Arsad moved closer still to Anno. "It has become our good fortune as well as yours that your home has been blessed with such a brave daughter as she."

Vartan did not answer. If that was how he would choose to look upon Anno's actions, it was acceptable to him. It was what he would have wished for, since it was the truth.

"Our mother did not die lost and alone in some forgotten corner as we had feared."

Anno strained to see Turgay, but the view was blocked by the old woman's grandsons, still absorbing the reality of their grandmother's passing. Tears flowed from her eyes freely now.

"Have you all you need for her care?" Arsad asked.

"Yes. Everything," was Mariam's curt reply. But this was pneumonia and what cure did either of them have?

Anno wheezed deep into her lungs.

"Let us pray that is so," he said only.

Haig had returned with a bier. The coffin maker, who also crafted small pieces of furniture and fine barrels, had been pulled away from his breakfast, short minutes ago, by Haig himself. Having once retrieved the bier, Haig had carried it, high over his head, back to Vartan's door.

Arsad's sons lifted Turgay easily. As her body rose, her long white hair streamed down, hushing all with a startlingly intimate image of the woman.

Anno's coughing deepened. She understood that all her attempts had only amounted to Turgay's death.

Mariam, rising only in respect as the dead was removed, swung back to pull Anno to a sitting position as the coughing brought on a panic of suffocation. The sound pierced them all.

Vartan and Haig left to accompany the bier procession as far as the stream.

Yeraz sprang forward. She pushed open the front door and the back door leading to the stable, letting a bitterly vigorous wind blow through all the rooms of the house. She hugged her body against the cold and waited. The angel of death must enter and take Turgay's soul.

Hours passed into darkness again.

CHAPTER 26

At first, Yeraz had struggled to believe that Anno would suffer a bout of fever and chills only. She was healthy and young. She would toss and complain about her confinement soon. But then the fourth day passed and the fifth dawned. Her lungs were infected.

Old Mariam's heavy sigh filled the room. Yeraz knew she was watching them.

She and Vartan had pulled Anno to a sitting position, but her arms fell rag-like to her sides. Vartan held her up effortlessly, cradling her back against his chest. Her head hung forward as she coughed. Yeraz knelt close to her side, a bowl held to her chin, until finally, Anno filled it with a blood-tinged mucus. Vartan then slowly lowered her back onto her pile of pillows.

Mariam turned back to the fire to continue her stirring. For days now it seemed Mariam had never stopped her stirring.

A rope had been pulled from one short end of the room to the other and Anno's bedclothes hung on them, along with thin undergarments. Yeraz scrubbed and rinsed them each day and wrung them almost ruthlessly, as if she would squeeze the infection away.

The toneer's flame was never allowed to weaken and candles eerily lit each corner of the room.

Yeraz turned to one window and her eyes met blackness, staid and lingering.

Outside, the frosty air swirled over the village roofs and floated its way down the twisted lane to the last still and darkened house.

Inside it, Daron lay on his back with his arms over his head staring at the lead-colored ceiling. His thoughts were with Anno, always. He had seen her that day. He was admitted each day for one brief visit. He did not kneel or touch her. Her chest and shoulders ached and a small fold had formed between her eyes. Her lips were a bright, parched red and her face and neck glistened with a blend of oils and perspiration. A deep-colored tea was about to be forced between her lips as he watched. She had been lifted off her pillow and her eyes opened. She saw him and an abyssal series of coughs began that produced blood and left her nearly unconscious again, with pain and, he feared, surrender.

It was a week since the night Vartan had pounded on their door searching for Anno, and still Daron and his family did not know what had taken place before she went missing.

Daron felt his chest sinking into itself a bit more each day at the unalterable helpless state that was his and Anno's life.

CHAPTER 27

*V*artan was not accustomed to the sensation of guilt that was now with him always. Anxiety, trepidation, and often fear, yes, but not guilt. It sat between his ribs and bore deepest when he tried to rest. It had been with him twelve days now, because that was the very damned day when mention of Mgro and his boy had invaded his home. It was true, he argued with himself, that Mgro's boy found Anno and carried her home to them. But she would not have been out that accursed night anyway, if it had not been for their attempts at familiarity and union between their two families.

Vartan was not able to distance himself from Anno. This was unlike him and unlike their customs: The fathers commanded, directed. They steered the children this way and that with a look, an arched eyebrow, a nod, never a caress and rarely a conversation. But, now, he found himself to be Anno's nurse. He knew Yeraz and Mariam were watching him. He knew, also, that if either one could muster the strength, the heart, the moment of privacy, they would implore him. "Why? Why not that family for our Anno? What do you know of them that could be worse than *this*?"

Anno hardly opened her eyes now. It was enough that she kept breathing, kept swallowing the liquids that would soothe her chest and fever. It was two days now and she had gotten no worse and no better.

CHAPTER 28

*U*ncle Hagop blinked painfully into the bright winter sky. Maratuk's snowcapped ridges rose and fell vividly against a background of bouncing clouds. With the added reflection of a newly fallen layer of snow, his eyes watered as they struggled to adjust after the murky shades of the room within.

He had pulled his mattress to the front room. Here was infinitely better for all, he declared. Lying at the opposite end of the room from Anno, he found himself closest to the chimney fire and could be the first to make the women know when they had let Anno's teas and broth boil too long. He was needed here. Anyone could see that.

He was heedful, too, to no longer crack open the door when observing Mt. Maratuk. The draft was not good for Anno. He now stepped fully over the threshold and stood shivering outside a firmly closed door.

It was a singularly clear morning. It baffled him. Were they to be subjected to a dry winter, with water shortages to add to all their problems? There would be more opinions about this later in the morning, with the men who gathered in the church square. He would use this very subject to ward off their questions about Anno and Turgay. He hmmphed in disgust at the needling he had received these past days. No different than a lot of old women was what they were.

Yeraz stood near a rough wooden plank that served as a shelf for their cups and plates, not far from the chimney fire. Anno seemed to be sleeping, her rasping breath a bit slower and deeper than when she was awake. She and Mariam were alone in the room for the moment. The empty cup Yeraz held slipped from her hand and fell to the floor. Mariam looked up from her place on a stool near the toneer. Both their gazes fixed on the cup and neither moved.

Head hung, Yeraz spoke. "God has favored us, Sister Mariam."

Mariam, unsure as to her meaning, did not answer.

Yeraz's body swayed forward and her arms leaned against the shelf for support, upsetting more cups.

"Until now, he has favored us. We have not had to mourn the passing of a child."

Now Mariam understood. The child mortality on their secluded mountain was high. And massacres targeted the young no less mercilessly than the able-bodied men.

Mariam, herself, had never seen a doctor. She had heard of them and their skills but had never benefited from one. She had her grasses and her herbs and her experience and left the rest to God, because it was what there was.

"Nothing has changed, my sweet. Anno is neither a child nor an old woman. You will not lose her. She has the strength to overcome this."

"I feel she does not care to." Yeraz's voice was muffled, partly because she faced the wall and partly because she had begun to weep.

Mariam did not answer this last, because she also saw an absence of spirit in Anno. Certainly she pulled away from the pain, but she seemed to treat it as a sensation only, not as something trying to take her life. It did not seem to matter whether she filled her lungs with air or not; whether she was lifted to dispel the mucus that would choke her or not.

"When are we to discover what all this is about, then?"

Mariam twisted her weary bulk at the hips to look back at Uncle Hagop, standing once again inside the room. He was making his own best effort to not bellow his question, but have it received instead.

Yeraz, once certain he had not woken Anno, turned to face him. His bushy eyebrows had fused again and his mouth opened and closed as if to speak, a further sign of his agitation.

Mariam watched his large knuckled hands hanging at his sides. His fingertips were stained a deep reddish brown from whichever latest task he had put himself to.

"And your words are spoken correctly, my brother," Mariam answered as if speaking to his hands. Then she tipped her head backwards to address him fully. "My brother, today we must understand what this objection of Vartan's is. Why he continues to watch Anno suffer, watch us *all* suffer, and think he has good reason."

Yeraz's eyes filled again. "There is nothing left of her but bones now."

Uncle Hagop began to upset things in corners as he searched before locating his cane camouflaged against the spoke of the spinning wheel. He did not require it for balance, but rather for effect.

"Then this morning none of us shall attend church. It will be good to not stand next to that foul-smelling wool dyer! Not today!"

"And let someone summon Haig." Mariam rose and spoke lowly to Uncle Hagop. The old man disappeared into the maze of rooms, slapping his cane as he went. Both women dropped their weighted heads onto their hands.

Vartan did not regularly attend church. He made an early appearance in the church square to meet the people and be made aware of disputes among them. That morning, however, Haig drew him back home. He found himself sitting cross-legged on a thinning, uncomfortable cushion facing Mariam and Yeraz, with Haig at his side.

Vrej was told to assume Anno's care for now, but his ears strained to catch each word spoken. His father's head was bent as he fingered his wooden tobacco box with his initials carved on the lid. He ran his thumb over its curves.

"We are listening, Vartan."

He raised his eyes to meet Yeraz's and saw again Mariam's perpetual frown in his direction. Then he nodded, accepting that it was time to reveal what he knew. "I shall speak, then, if this is what you ask. If you insist on knowing what it is, why it is that I cannot give my daughter to that family."

He reflected for a moment before beginning. "It was two years ago." A quick glance at Haig, who tipped his head sideways, made him start again. "More. It was three years ago, to be sure, we noticed Mgro was making frequent trips to Van. Three seasons of the year we would hear of him either leaving or just returning."

"He went to see his wife's people?" Yeraz offered.

Vartan looked at her as if she had not even spoken and continued. "He would, of course, be gone for good lengths of time. It is days of walking just getting back and forth."

Vrej listened openly from across the room where Anno lay sleeping.

"We noticed his brother, father, never spoke of his whereabouts, never wanted to answer the simplest question, and were never too willing to even mention his name."

Yeraz wrung her hands and Mariam's chin lifted higher in defense, against what, she did not know.

"He did not bring much back with him to trade or sell. We waited for him to produce seeds, saplings, grain, jewelry, cakes of detergent from Lake Van at least. Nothing. There was nothing to explain these long, frequent trips away from his land and his family." Vartan shrugged. "It did not take long for our lads to notice either." He referred to the freedom fighters, always wary of informants. "They told me they would trail him. It was simple, really. He had no idea he was being trailed. From the moment he started down our mountain until he reached Van, he was watched." Vartan shook his head in disgust.

"Then?" Mariam insisted.

"Well, he did not go to his wife's village. He did not even pass through it. He went elsewhere. To Sufla. He stayed in a *han*. He visited the bazaars infrequently. He appeared to have no friends to see. He did almost no trading. He did only one thing. Regularly. He visited a woman."

Yeraz's eyebrows arched and Mariam's hands finally stilled. In his corner, Vrej moved not a muscle.

"This woman made her living, for herself and for her mother, as a seamstress."

Since Van's textiles were famous and the villages were full of tailors and of course seamstresses, the women still did not understand.

"In that house, there was no husband, no father, no brother, no uncle." Vartan counted off his fingers, pushing down on each to its limit. He paused no more, eager to be done with the telling. "The man trekked that entire distance, month after month, for her only." He threw up his hands. "He was trailed back here, again, almost to his doorstep, when our lads stopped him. They say he told them, outright, he was in love with the woman. He was a man, and should he feel it made sense, one day, he would marry her and bring her to his hearth.

"They told him that he was a fool. Any woman alone, with no male relative of any kind, who does not bear children, who lives with an older woman she calls her mother, does certainly not sit at home with her needle and thread waiting for only him to appear. You go back and forth all you care to, until your legs buckle, if you like, they told him, but our advice to you is to think again about bringing her home to sleep next to your mother.

"He, of course, found his way home and then back to her again, more times than I know of." Vartan stopped.

When, at some time, he probably returned with the eggplant seeds, Yeraz thought to herself dully, unable to speak a word.

"This woman," Mariam tapped her knee sharply, "what is she?"

"Assyrian and Armenian both, she claimed," Vartan answered.

"And for the next customer she would be a Turk or a Jew or a Greek, as would be preferred," Haig added.

They sat in silence for some time now. Yeraz rose only once as Anno stirred, to help Vrej spoon clear water into her mouth. She rubbed some oil on her lips and smoothed the hair from her temples. Her lids had not fully lifted for days now and they concealed eyes as opaque as glass. Yeraz returned to Mariam's side.

"So the man is a fool. Or let us say, he did a foolish thing." Mariam attempted to speak lightly but was cut short.

"There is more," Vartan said. "This woman's neighbors wanted her away from there and from their sight. The Turks, the Armenians, the Assyrians, I am not sure which. So one afternoon, Mgro arrived to see that she had been attacked. She did not know by whom. She was in a state where she could hardly speak and hardly move. Mgro wanted to bring her here, to Salor, for her safety."

Yeraz's hand pressed against her mouth. Vrej, always unsure of Anno's state of wakefulness, was anxious that she not hear what was being said and equally anxious that he should miss none of it. His eyes flew from his sister's face to his father's.

"To his home?" Mariam demanded.

"And the rest, I do not know. Either she did not want to come or perhaps Mgro's family discovered what was taking place. I cannot say. But the woman, as far as we know, was never seen again in Van. And I ask you, how should I give our Anno to that family, to live under the same roof as a man who has no judgment and no morals?"

Vartan and Haig lit cigarettes in aggravated gestures. Vartan gave one long exhale of release before allowing himself to look at Yeraz.

"My son, give me one as well," Mariam asked wearily. The last cigarette she had held between her fingers had been rolled and lit by her husband, in amusement, some ten years ago. She hoped this one would help the kneading pain in the back of her skull.

She drew the smoke deep into her lungs and thought. "Who was she? Someone was protecting her."

"Van consists of more than two thousand villages, foreign consuls, hospitals, and missions. In a place that size, only the guilty know," Haig answered.

"I, for one, do not care a bit for the comings and goings of this man who cannot keep his shalvar fastened," Yeraz pushed herself to her feet. "I only care about seeing my daughter back as she was."

A tap on the door made her pause. Searching the blank faces around her, she called out to ask who was there.

"It is Mihran, Sister Yeraz."

The door was pulled open, and the large man stood before her. He held a small jar containing a dark brown liquid in his roughened hands. His voice was barely above a whisper. "I have a unique bit of honey here for your Anno. It will soothe her throat."

Later, it was unclear to Yeraz whether it was truly Mihran's "unique honey" that helped Anno, or her own resolve.

At first, all remained unchanged. Anno's fever neither broke nor rose. Her aches neither worsened nor diminished. She wheezed and sucked open-mouthed for air, but her expulsions lessened. Her breathing grew easier and her skin no longer appeared scorched. Her eyes opened more fully, and she passed entire days without having her damp clothes removed from her body. She sat for small spaces of time and consumed larger amounts of liquid and broth. Lucine, grown even larger, hurried down the lane on Avo's arm. Even Takoush was summoned for visits and talked of the coming New Year and things they should eat and her new needlework. She did not speak of the two new betrothals that had been announced. Together with Lucine, they washed Anno's hair amid splashes and soakings that Yeraz did not scold over. Then Takoush braided Anno's hair elaborately, much as they used to do as children, and Anno's face smoothed for the first time in months.

Daron no longer made his daily visits. When it became apparent that Anno was out of danger, Vartan went to Mgro's house to share the news with them. He was, in truth, very grateful to Daron and Kevork for finding Anno and Turgay that night. He admitted it to them, himself, for the first time, as Mgro's entire family waited for him to continue, to add some grain of hope for their Daron. Vartan had concluded only by saying that Daron no longer needed to make his way through the freezing snow to see Anno each day. She was well and her family would see to it that she remained so.

CHAPTER 29

It was late December, and it would not, after all, be a dry winter as Uncle Hagop had feared. Rain, hail, fog, and snow took their toll on the massive rounded mountain slopes and plains. The rivers and streams swelled impossibly and flashed past oaks and pines, firs and cedar. Myrtles and juniper sat complacently beneath pillows of snow, and the foxes and bears blinked in confusion at the shimmering lights of day and again buried their noses in their voluminous fur.

The sheepfolds were checked and guarded regularly for fear of Kurds not satisfied with their collection of weeks before, and for hungry foxes and wolves. Livestock that was left to the villagers and not killed for their own consumption was passing the winter in the stables.

Anno sat around the toneer with her family. The winter lavash, now cracker-like, had been pulled from its pile and sprinkled with water so that it would again soften. It was being used in place of spoons to scoop the bulgur pilaf with traces of lamb's meat set before them. There were boiled chickpeas and greens and the ever-present yogurt as well.

Old Mariam had returned to her own home three weeks past, and many times Anno thought to ask when she would visit, but never formed the words. She knew that the woman had helped save her life, and she clearly remembered her cheerful eyes and firm hand stilling her limbs the day she had brought the news of Daron's family's wish for marriage. Mariam had been her friend all along, and Anno had avoided her at every turn. She ached to think how wrong she had been to have shunned her, as strong and loving as she was. And the hours they might have passed together and the comfort Anno might have received there.

Anno had asked about Turgay almost as soon as her confused mind had separated past from present, reality from dreams. Her mother had only been steps away, as she always seemed to be. Anno had tried her voice for the first time. It seemed as if the fire in her chest would not allow her to speak. But she had spoken clearly at once, and it seemed it was well heard.

The men were gone from the house. Yeraz had been mending socks, and they fell to her lap. She crossed the room and reached uneasily for Anno's hands. Relieved to finally answer this dreaded question, Yeraz spoke slowly. She had practiced the answer in her mind numerous times already. "You and Turgay fell into the stream that night, my daughter. Do you remember?"

Anno nodded, already feeling the burning behind her eyes.

"She was too old and too tired to survive that cold, my sweet. She died peacefully, there, in your brave arms."

Anno's jaw trembled and she tried to speak. "I...I do not remember."

It was a plea. Yeraz knew she wanted to know more. She deserved to know it all and Yeraz had decided to hold nothing back if Anno should ask.

"It was raining that night. Do you remember? The neighbor came calling us for help."

Yeraz wanted to see if Anno would remember that much, and from the square gaze she was given in return, she knew the girl did not.

"We searched for you. We were very frightened. Many, many neighbors searched with us. No one knew that you were with Turgay."

Yeraz had to stop to wipe her own stream of tears. Anno stared back dry-eyed.

"I could not leave her in the rain, Mama. There was no one else." She did not speak in her own defense. She stated a fact.

"They found you and brought you home," Yeraz went on. "Turgay's family was given the news that same morning. Your father and Uncle Haig went to their camp to tell them. Her son came here, himself, to take his mother home. Do you remember him?"

Anno, unsure, did not answer.

"They were decent. They were grateful for your bravery. Grateful that their mother did not die alone in some cold corner."

Anno clearly remembered the cold. Had it been the stream's cold or the rain or the wind? Turgay's trusting hand was in hers. The truth of her mother's death long ago had finally been admitted. Old eyes had stared at her from a broken, childlike body.

She swallowed back the pain and asked, "Did Baba find us?"

Yeraz shook her head and pressed her handkerchief against her trembling mouth.

Anno's eyes widened. "Who?"

Yeraz dropped her hands. Her white, swollen lips moved. "Daron. Daron and Kevork."

Anno felt her chest constrict. She felt air escaping from her throat. She tried to still herself. She *knew* she had remembered. There was one more thing she must ask. "Did he come? Here? To see me, here?"

Yeraz nodded, openly crying now. She would not torment her daughter anymore. She must give her the whole truth and watch the light in her eyes extinguish once more, God help her.

"He came every day, until we were sure you would recover." Yeraz did not allow herself to stop. "Then, your father went to thank him for all he had done and tell him that he need not come anymore."

Hope had raised Anno off the pillows. Her eyelids had lifted fully for the first time in weeks and her eyes had bored into her mother's.

Now, her body fell back and she turned away, away from the room and all those in it, and her body shuddered and keened.

Now, Anno did not know how she would chew her mouthful of food. Under watchful eyes she had rolled the bread, filled it and placed it in her mouth. It tasted to her like tree bark. Her mouth full, her eyes hollow and strange, she stared back at no one.

It was night again, and, it seemed, always dark. The knock at the door made everyone start. The same old fear gripped them, and the tap came again—gentle taps in quick succession. Vrej was on his feet and crossing the room in quick leaps.

A second's hesitation and Raffi's familiar face was made out beneath a thick growth of beard. Cries of joy went up and he was pulled into a tangle of arms.

Yeraz wanted to stand but could not move. Her nerves, she found, could not endure much more. She sat in her place and controlled her trembling. Anno, after a moment of thought, rose to spit out her mouthful of tree bark into an earthen pot filled with waste. She leaned against a wall and watched her brother. A slow, impossible gladness began to spread inside her.

Raffi searched the room, peering past the bodies that clasped him, pressed his arms, and tugged at his coat. To his surprise, he made out his mother, sitting curiously apart from the turmoil of his welcome. He thought it odd, and he strained for a closer look. The others fell away and let him stroll purposefully to her side. Behind Yeraz, in an unlit corner, Raffi sensed a presence, a thin, angular girl. He did not take the time to look. He cared, more than anything else, to lift his mother to him and hear her rare, adoring laugh.

Raffi's rough hands pulled Yeraz to him, and she did laugh, and cry for an unusually long while into the collar of his shirt. Raffi indulged her and himself with this long-dreamed-of moment. He wrapped his arms tightly around her and rested his chin on the top of her head as he took in the familiar room. It was difficult, because there were even fewer candles lit than usual. He remembered again the unknown girl somewhere behind him. He twisted his neck for another look. She stepped forward.

"Raffi?"

The voice was... He gasped. "My God! Anno!" He searched her face again to be certain. It was her eyes he recognized.

"Oh, Anno." He thought to touch her but his hand dropped away. It seemed as if a touch would pain her. The collar of her dress gaped around her willowy neck and seemed to hang on folds of air below. Her face, gaunt and absent, stared back at him.

Anno did not need to see the horror in Raffi's eyes to know. She was ugly now. So ugly. There used to be an irregular square of mirror in her sleeping room, but it had gone missing, so she had not been able to look at herself. At night, though, her fingertips ran disbelievingly over chains of sharp bones veiled by a papery layer of flesh, from her hips to her jaws.

Unable to bear Anno's distress, Vrej moved closer. "Our Anno has been ill, Raffi, as you can see. But it was a result of bravery and selflessness."

Raffi's arms had fallen away from Yeraz. He had stepped back from Anno and his mother both, his eyes whipping back and forth between them, and he now turned to Vrej, further perplexed. Anno looked like the villagers suffering from thirst and starvation that he fought so hard to help. It appeared as if she had been involved in her own private battle while he was gone.

"Tell me," he burst out. "What has happened here?"

Anno's curled fingertips hung listlessly past the edge of her wide sleeves. Raffi tentatively touched them with his own, and when she did not recoil, he drew her to an empty cushion at the table. She was grateful for the extremely dim room. Their remaining candles and oil were being used with complete frugality since so much of their supply had been prematurely burned during her illness.

The embers of the toneer beneath the wooden tray that held the food kept the meal lukewarm while Raffi washed. He came and sat himself close to Anno. She felt awkward and self-conscious at his pointed attention.

"Eat a bit first, my son, then we shall tell you all that has happened. Let your body enjoy some nutrition, something other than dry bread."

All waited to see Raffi take pleasure from a warm meal. Surprised, they saw him instead fill a dainty piece of lavash with only yogurt and hand it to Anno.

Her fingers grasped it and she looked back at him.

"You eat so that I can eat too," he coaxed gently.

Anno slowly chewed her bit of food and Raffi turned to satisfy his own stomach amid sniffles and sighs of relief.

"You have not brought Meghr," Vartan noted.

"No. I shall only stay the night and I could slip in and out more easily on foot."

Yeraz closed her eyes in disappointment. But even this short glimpse of her son was a godsend. Her mind moved ahead. She had a precious container of coffee she would bring out tomorrow with his morning meal. Perhaps he would enjoy a thorough washing, as well, before he slept. She would arrange it.

Anno had already been handed two bites full of lavash with yogurt and now Raffi decided to fill some with a bit of chickpeas and greens. She sighed back at him but could not refuse his wink. He was hurrying with his own food and the family did the same, knowing he was uneasy.

When their last bites had been consumed, cigarettes were rolled and the table was cleared. Anno remained unmoving on her same cushion and stared at the bare cloth before her. She had been on her feet a handful of days now but was not allowed to work. She folded her hands and spoke to no one.

Raffi took his time to study each man in the family. There was something wrong here, something strained. They acted almost as if they were preparing for some sort of defense. And why did no one go near Anno, or call to her? This was no ordinary illness she suffered. Her whole person was altered. He would wait no more.

"You must tell me what has been happening in my absence," he spoke out firmly.

Uncle Hagop, their most eager storyteller, only stared at his hands.

Raffi sat next to Vartan, with an unhampered vision of Anno.

"Hayrig, I am listening," Raffi prompted.

Vartan began with the neighbor's delivery pains and then Anno's discovered absence. He told of the frantic search in the frigid rain. He told of her and Turgay's discovery by two village lads. He told of Turgay's death and Arsad's carrying her home.

"There have been no further visits from Arsad or his family? No authorities?" Raffi leaned forward.

"No." Vartan's answer was firm.

Were they afraid that the repercussions of this death were not over? Raffi wondered to himself. Perhaps that was the reason for this tension.

"Do you have reason to believe they will still return?" he asked.

"No." Vartan's head shook. "I believe they wish to forget us and their mother's last years of rantings and wanderings."

"Good," Raffi answered, but was still not finished.

Vrej massaged his stockinged feet and watched Raffi thinking. He was intensely relieved that his brother had come. Perhaps he could draw his father out. Perhaps he could change his mind, or Anno's. He feared for his sister.

"Well, I would say it is a miracle those lads found you at all, Anno. In the stream." Raffi's head shook in admiration. "Who were they?"

He looked back at his father, his uncle. Still Yeraz concentrated on her work, eyes anywhere but in his direction. Only Vrej never dropped his gaze from him, but there was disquiet even there.

"Who were they? How did they manage it?" The answer to his question should be simple, Raffi thought. Why did no one answer? Was this where the problem lay?

"It was the merchant's boy. And his brother's boy as well," Uncle Hagop answered impatiently.

Raffi studied his father. Why had he not spoken these lads' names? Had they not done him the greatest service? Vrej's eyes urged him on. Anno was like a statue.

"I know them, of course. Daron and Kevork? Brave boys. I shall certainly go and embrace them both, tomorrow."

"There is no need. I have thanked them myself," Vartan spoke.

"Would you object, Hayrig, to my thanking them as well? They saved our Anno's life." He persisted with his questions but kept his voice even and respectful. He knew Vartan was indulging him, but he had to tread carefully to learn more. Their home had taken on an unrecognizable gloaming quality and he could not tolerate it.

"I believe there is no need," Vartan answered shortly.

His father would speak no further in Anno's presence, Vrej knew.

Just before dawn, Vrej's deep sleep was disturbed. Someone had kicked his shin. Thinking it just carelessness, he ignored it and tried to roll away.

"Vrej, get up," Raffi commanded near his ear.

Vrej did so in one quick movement, his blankets still clinging to one shoulder. He followed Raffi out of the sleeping room, past Uncle Hagop snoring by the toneer beneath layers of colorful blankets, into the narrow grain room.

"Now, let me hear the truth. All of it," Raffi hissed. He was as alert and clear-spoken as if it were noon.

"I want to. I am glad you woke me." Vrej cleared his throat. They slid to the floor and huddled closely together.

"Anno ran out into the night because Old Mariam brought news that Daron's family wished Daron and Anno to marry."

Vrej saw Raffi's eyes glint, even in the darkness.

"She did not want him?" he asked.

"Oh, no," Vrej contradicted. "She wants him very much, but Hayrig refuses."

"Why?"

Vrej could not speak quickly enough. He was desperate to unburden himself and wished desperately for the situation to change for Anno's good.

Raffi did not move or interrupt once as Vrej told in detail all Vartan had related to them. But his mind was racing.

"And Hayrig thinks Mgro is immoral and will not let Anno marry into his family," Vrej concluded.

"And that is why Anno looks like a corpse and does not care to recover?" Raffi looked to Vrej to see if he was right. His brother nodded.

"But, no," Raffi shook his head. He gripped his brother's shoulders. "Hayrig has been misinformed, Vrej. Purposely."

"It is not only Hayrig who knows of Mgro's doings. Uncle Haig knows of it as well," Vrej insisted. Their father knew secrets and details of many, many families. They consulted him, he helped, he reasoned and then kept that knowledge to himself. He was well trusted to do so.

"There is more to it than this." Raffi was thinking aloud.

"Who was the go-between, you said? Sister Mariam?"

Vrej nodded. "And Uncle Haig came as well."

"And they were refused. Does Anno know why?"

Vrej had wondered that same thing many times.

"I believe she did not hear anything at the telling. And now, I do not think she asks."

"And did Mariam tell Mgro why they were refused?"

Vrej raised his arms in exasperation.

"No one speaks of it."

Raffi motioned for him to lower his voice and asked, "Mariam has never returned here, even once, since Anno's recovery was certain?"

Vrej shook his head.

"And who would, in all decency, talk of marriage with someone who barely lives anyway?" Raffi concluded to himself. "Vrej, I shall tell you the real story of the merchant's travels, and then I shall see if I cannot have this whole misunderstanding put in order before I leave. I cannot leave Anno behind in this state."

The brothers did not sleep again that night. At sunrise, Raffi filled a bowl of water for himself, and locating his father's razor, began to shave away all traces of moustache and beard.

Vrej waited for Anno to rise and took her with him to feed the goats and cows in the stables. He handed her the braided field grasses to distribute and he fetched the heavy buckets of barley. She leaned her shoulder heavily into a cow's neck as it pulled the dried grasses from her hands and chewed.

Vartan sniffed the air at the smell of coffee and looked in Raffi's direction. His presence had lifted everyone's spirits, and he would leave them again, so soon, to their scarcities and their dark walls. But, he thought guiltily, what did the freedom fighters have in their high mountain perches? At least they could fill their son with some hot meals, grateful for his trouble to come to see them.

The fog made it impossible for any rays to brighten the room, but nevertheless, all were more cheerful than they had been in weeks. Uncle Hagop opened the door to locate Maratuk and closed it again with not a single comment, not wishing to dampen anyone's mood.

Yeraz had taken dried apricots and plums from storage and dropped them into boiling water. They plumped magically, almost like fresh fruit again, and were an extra delicacy for them to enjoy with their goat cheese and lavash.

Anno now sat beside Vrej at the table and did her best to finish her apricot with bites of salty cheese.

"I believe I shall go and see Sister Mariam," Raffi commented.

All nodded.

"And Lucine," Yeraz added.

"And then Lucine as well," he continued conversationally. "It will not take long."

"Did you know that our Lucine is expecting a child?" Vartan asked him.

"Yes." Raffi paused. "Someone...Aram saw her and told me."

Vartan nodded, pleased.

Once outside, Raffi pulled his coat closed tighter still. Old Mariam's threshold was as familiar to Raffi as his own. She had been a grandmother to him in every way, sharing long stories of Vartan's mother, Lucine, all throughout his childhood. He knew she had fought for Lucine's granddaughter's life with nothing but a few herbs and grasses and a refusal to surrender.

He called her name through the heavy door before her older son swung it open from the inside. His reception here was much like in his father's home and he was almost pushed to the table to eat again, but instead, he insisted on a few words alone with Mariam.

She cleared the front room of everyone save her sons with one swing of her body and Raffi almost laughed out loud at the result. He lost no time asking what he needed to know.

It was as he suspected. Mariam had neither gone to Mgro's house with Vartan's refusal, nor had they asked her to persist further in any way. Mariam shrugged. "I do not know why they are leaving it at this. It is not the time for Mgro to exercise pride and stubbornness. Let him hear why his son has been refused."

Raffi was nodding in satisfaction. "I am going to leave the telling of it to Mgro, but the tale you believe of him to be true, is not. The facts have been hidden to protect him, his family, and our village.

What I need from you is a chance to let him tell you all how it really was, and why. And this must be today."

"Well, then, let it be now," Haig decided and reached for his coat. "I shall bring Mgro here and you shall bring your father." Haig walked out pulling a well-stretched woolen cap down to the base of his thick neck.

Mariam looked at Raffi sadly.

"How is Anno these days, my son?"

He shook his head in bewilderment.

"Lucine was just married. There was Vrej still to be paired off. I never even thought of Anno. She was still a scampering child in my eyes. But look at the courage she possesses." He paused. "And the love. They should not be denied each other. There is *no* reason."

Mariam patted his shoulder encouragingly.

"Go bring your father, then. And I hope that you are right. His reasons stifled us all."

Raffi returned the same way he had come, only to find more people on the road than there had been earlier. Their figures emerged eerily through the fog. His presence brought questions to their lips but he smiled at them reassuringly. He said that he had come to see Anno for himself, hearing of her illness.

Vartan, he found, had left the house to go to the sheepfold. Raffi plowed through muddied snow to find him. Many others were there as well counting heads and examining the feed.

Raffi knew to be straightforward from the first. It was the only way Vartan would consider Raffi's wish to have him meet with Mgro. He drew him away from the other men. "Hayrig, Vrej told me of your objection to Daron and why."

Raffi was subjected to Vartan's one-eyed squint of annoyance. "Do not pursue this, Raffi. It is over," his father warned him.

Raffi shook his head. "But you do not know the truth. When we enter the fedayee ranks, no questions are asked as to where we come from or where our family lives. It is so that in case of capture, we do not give away information about each other. You know this. You know that even family names are not asked. So, when some time ago I heard the story of a merchant who traveled to Van, in our aid, I was not told that that person came from this village."

Vartan's eyes narrowed.

"It did not take long for me to discover who this person was, Hayrig. You have neither the complete nor the correct reasons for Mgro's presence in Van. You must hear the truth from him. He deserves that you do not believe the lies you have been told. He is waiting for you. He is with Uncle Haig."

Raffi held his breath. His father was a stubborn, proud mountaineer, as was his father before him, as were all his neighbors, as his youngest daughter was proving to be as well. But Raffi's news had unsettled him. Vartan's face angered.

"I was given this information by one of the fedayees *himself*, Raffi. I did not create this story."

"You were told whatever was necessary to ensure that further speculation and interest cease concerning Mgro's trips. You were not told the truth."

"And why would I, in this one instance, *not* be told the truth? How am I to believe that? What purpose would it serve, if what you say is true?" Vartan scoffed at him. His eyes roamed back in the direction of the sheep.

"You see me standing here?" he swung back to face his son. "*I* am the one person in this village who knows things, many things, about almost every family and I am trusted to keep them secret. And I do, do I not?"

Raffi nodded.

"And now, this one time, you expect me to accept that I was not trusted for some reason, and that my own daughter nearly died because of that?"

"Hayrig, why would I lie to you?" Raffi beseeched.

His father's fury was palpable. "Do you realize what our family has had to endure, Raffi?"

"Yes. I see it. And if you had lost your daughter this past month, I would have lost my sister." Raffi, beginning to fear that he would fail Anno, felt himself raise his voice.

Again Vartan turned away.

"The decisions made and orders given to us are not always the wisest, Hayrig," Raffi's voice dulled. He thought he had seen doubt appear on his father's face. "Let us think of Anno, Hayrig." His voice was gentle. "Let us put all this behind us."

Vartan sighed deep into his chest.

"You are angry and bitter," Raffi went on, "but you must accept that it is directed at the wrong person. Mgro was doing what he was asked to do by the fedayees. And at the time, it was more important for us all to obtain the ammunition needed, than think of Mgro himself or his family, or his neighbors."

Vartan grappled with Raffi's words. His pride had been torn at. Their hearts nearly broken. Slowly, he began to wonder if he could have been wrong.

Raffi placed a hand on his father's shoulder.

Mgro was not difficult to find. He was in the stable with his brother trying to separate two bad-tempered oxen and tie them far from each other. Haig joined in the struggle, and when the animals were subdued he asked Mgro to come with him. Headman Vartan had learned that Mgro had a story to tell him.

Mgro scowled at Haig. The oxen had already agitated him and he did not want to hear Vartan's name. Was it not enough that he had to witness Daron's misery day and night?

"What are you talking about? Say what you mean," he demanded.

"My mother acted as go-between for your son and Anno some time ago, did she not?" Haig asked.

"What of it? We have their answer. The whole village knows of their answer." Mgro fumbled in his pockets, frowning further as his cold, stiff fingers came out empty. "Manuel, where is that tobacco?" he asked of his brother, still bent at securing the second ox.

"Mgro, listen to me. You have a right to know why you were refused. Why have you not asked? Does Daron not deserve to know?" Haig questioned, hoping that he might relent for his son's sake.

"I have no intention of asking. It does not matter. His reasons are his own. I will not beg *anyone* to consider my family to be good enough for them." His voice had reached those indoors by now, Haig was certain. Perhaps Daron would hear and come to help change his father's mind.

As if reading his thoughts, Mgro swung back at Haig and pointed a thick finger in his face. "And neither will my son!"

Haig was losing patience. If Mgro had been a smaller man he would have simply dragged him the distance up the hill. But he was not small, and then there was Manuel to consider as well.

"You are asking me to do what you would not even do yourself!" Mgro continued. "I understand well the type of friendship you have with our village leader and that is fine, but you and I are friends as well and here you are treating me like a donkey." Mgro's head shook in disgust.

Something occurred to Haig suddenly. "My brother, I am not asking you to go to Vartan's home. I know that would be difficult. You have a right to your pride. I meant for you to come to mine. My mother has had a large part in all this, and she too deserves to know if Vartan's reasons for refusing your son are just, as you see it."

Mgro seemed to consider Haig's words.

"Also, there is one thing you do not know. Raffi has come home for one night, and he is eager that you come and speak to his father. This entire meeting was his wish to begin with."

At this Mgro's forehead cleared. Widely. "Raffi is here?" he asked with interest, his voice quieted.

Haig did not understand it, but seeing the change in Mgro, he pushed on. "Yes. But he will leave shortly. He is waiting now, only for you."

Mgro rubbed the stubble on his chin. He ran his fingers over his rough cheeks and smoothed his moustache while he considered this bit of information.

Haig watched him, wishing he had mentioned Raffi's presence from the start, amazed that it made such a difference to the man.

"So, this meeting is Raffi's wish, you say." Mgro thought out loud. Haig noticed that Manuel was looking their way now as well, for the first time. The brothers exchanged glances.

Mgro turned his back on Haig and stared down at the stilled hooves of the oxen. Then he turned back again and shrugged his shoulders at Haig. "Let us go, then."

Haig's chest heaved with relief and he hurriedly pulled his cap back on.

Old Mariam's household was further inconvenienced that day as the men gathered in her silent and empty front room.

Mgro greeted Raffi warmly with a trace of a smile in his eyes that had not appeared there for weeks. Raffi hastily stepped aside to let him pay his regards to his father. Vartan's place of status and respect should not be overlooked now at the beginning of this most sensitive meeting.

They greeted each other stiffly, and Raffi spoke quickly. "Brother Mgro, I will let you know why we have disturbed you this morning. There has been discussion among us, of your trips, your frequent trips to and from Van these last years. I believe you can be quite safe in telling all the truth and details of those trips now. It is necessary that my father, especially, know of the reasons. It would bring great relief and new understanding between our families if you would."

Mgro had assumed his expressionless merchant's façade. His eyes had roamed from face to face as Raffi spoke, but he was, in truth, dumbfounded to be called, after all this time, to recount those months, those dangerous risk-taking months to that woman's...that woman. He looked again at Vartan more closely and saw doubt there. Ahhh. Mgro almost smiled with understanding. He felt himself rising to a challenge.

"Is this finally about my son and your daughter, then, Mukhtar Vartan?" He did not wait for an answer. "I understand much now"— he held up his hand—"and I believe for Daron and my family's sake, and for your daughter's, you had better hear what I have to tell."

He inhaled deeply and reluctantly spoke with dull eyes pointed at the carpet he sat on. "You remember, we trusted the Young Turks in 1908. Our leaders told us we would have rights now and to have patience." He paused and looked at Raffi. "Although not everyone trusted them, did they, my boy?

"Most of the fedayees' best fighters went back to their villages and built themselves homes and finally married in an attempt to have the life they deserved. But many saw that we were, as always tricked. We were still just Christians.

"It became evident that it would again be necessary to defend our villages, and so we needed to acquire guns and ammunition. They were coming in from across the eastern border and stored in Van."

All were silent, and Mgro continued. "I was approached one night. I will not give names here. We understand that. I was approached. There had been discussion concerning me, it seemed. I was a merchant. I was known to travel to Van to make a living. I had no wife. If I were to be seen entering a lone woman's house, who would there be to tell? Mine would be the face people saw coming and going. It was decided."

Mgro remembered how angered he had been that they had used his wife's death to their advantage. "I needed to travel lightly and quickly. One or two of our lads began to travel a distance behind me in case I was stopped on the roads and there was trouble." He looked intently at Vartan for the first time. "Raffi himself trailed me more than a time or two from here to Van, did you know that, Mukhtar Vartan?"

Vartan's chin lifted, as if he had received a blow. Beside him, Mariam gasped softly.

Mgro only nodded, barely concealing his satisfaction at Vartan's shock.

"Many fine, brave lads like Raffi protected me. And the deliveries."

Mgro dropped his eyes again to continue.

"There was a woman in Sufla. Her house lay conveniently to the east of open fields on the edge of a less traveled road. The guns and ammunition were stored beneath that house. They were smuggled in at night, of course. I would warn her of its delivery and I would see it safely stored. I would pay her and leave."

Haig and Mariam had paled.

Vartan felt himself perspire, in shame, in the chilly room. Should he have not known, from the first, that Raffi would never speak to him of anything but the truth?

"This woman was a spy. It was how she was allowed to remain, a lone woman, among the Muslims. But then she began to work with the fedayees as well. I was never quite sure who worked that out for us. I was never told. She was paid for the information she supplied to us, and for her assistance. She was entirely discreet in every way."

Raffi nodded but did not provide any enlightenment in this regard, because he knew nothing more.

"Of course, in the end, she was driven out. The Muslims must have discovered which way her loyalties leaned. I was glad she was not killed. She was a good woman. Our fedayees got her away. I do not know where or when.

"After that, they decided that my face would be recognized if they sent me elsewhere, if I were to help further, and so my travels ended."

"What was this woman?" Mariam asked.

"She never said, but if I were to guess, I would say Assyrian. Her family, her menfolk, had been killed by the Turks as well. They are as Christian as we are, after all. I believe that is why she was willing to do what she did."

A long silence followed. Haig brought oghee and the cups slipped and spun from his agitated hands.

Vartan was astonished at how fully he had believed the story told to him, fully fabricated to protect Mgro's life, but not the man or his family. He trembled at how close his daughter had come to death, the needless grief they had suffered, as a result of it.

"We had not understood each other well, had we, Mukhtar Vartan?" Mgro asked stonily.

Vartan looked at Raffi, his own son, who had risked his life to protect the deeds of the very man Vartan had scoffed at and dismissed as immoral. He pulled his eyes away from him and turned to Mgro. He knew, he felt every word he had heard from him to be the truth.

With difficulty, Vartan cleared his throat. "We had not understood each other in the least, my brother."

Mgro shrugged. "You believed the story you were meant to believe, for my protection. I should have considered that, knowing how our people like to talk, that just because my travels had ceased, the memories and the stories regarding them might have, let us say, flourished."

"I believe I shall make a call again to your hearth tonight, shall I, Vartan?" Mariam intervened quickly. "There was a matter we were discussing, an important matter, and we were disturbed, weeks ago, by births, by deaths, and by sickness." Her throat swelled at this last and she wiped at her nose.

"Yes," Vartan agreed readily. "Let us put that right, Sister Mariam. We shall wait for you."

That evening, Raffi tried not to use the butt of his rifle for balance as he walked in the snow. Their rifles were different from the ones the Turks used and it would cause his trail to be followed.

He moved further and further away from his father's house, but a huge sense of relief went with him. He would keep Anno's shining face in his memory a long time. She had leaned her forehead against his arm and cried tears of relief and joy. They had wracked her body in such a frightful way. She had not asked what the reasons were for her father's change in decision. She did not care. They had always been important only to him.

She had promised him, promised sincerely that she would begin to eat and drink again. Or, he had told her, she must not be surprised if Daron looked at her and fled. She promised, knowing that truth about her appearance lay in his jokes.

Mariam would be busy again this night. She would take word of the Vartanian clan's consent to Nevart.

He had made two hurried visits after that morning's meeting with Mgro. He had gone to see Lucine. He had wanted to, of course, but he also went because Aram would ask of her when next they met.

Then he had gone in search of Daron, wondering at how so many people so close to him had suffered these last weeks based on a falsehood. He did not dwell on what would have happened to them all if he had not come.

Daron was in the stable planing wood. He shaved a two-foot length of walnut, but it was in the rough, early stages and Raffi could not make out what it might become. Daron had not seen Mgro yet, and Raffi's entrance into the dim stable startled him. He stood quickly and tool and wood fell to the ground. "Anno?"

Raffi thought how tired he was of seeing spare faces and anxious eyes looking back at him. Daron was Vrej's height and age, and just an inch or two shorter than Raffi, but he seemed older than them both. Raffi sighed with regret.

He clasped Daron's shoulders at once and spoke sincerely. "I have come to thank you for saving my sister's life. It is a debt my family and I will carry always." He hugged the surprised boy to him warmly.

"You will forgive my family's mistakes. They were not at fault. They will, after all, soon be your family too, and why start a life with your beloved and keep blame for them in your heart?"

Raffi had not thought it possible for Daron to pale even more.

"All will be sorted out by tomorrow," he had promised. "Let us have a spring wedding."

Now Raffi listened to the crunch of his footsteps as they took him further and further away from Salor.

CHAPTER 30

"*My* girl, your face and that wall you see there are the same color!" Aunt Marie, relieved and liberated as they all were with Anno's promise to Daron in marriage and the festivities to come, had loosened her tongue once again.

"My daughter," Yeraz pulled her aside in her own diplomatic fashion. "You will eat small portions, all day. It will be gentler on your stomach and easier for you, in general. You will be yourself again quite soon."

Anno cooperated fully with all their instructions and demands. She wanted, more than anything, to see Daron and not have him disappointed in her appearance. But she also longed to be able to go outdoors again. There were short, unexpected periods of sunshine, and she ached to turn her face toward it.

The New Year's approach coincided with Nevart's first formal visit to her future khnami. The older woman contemplated the snow-covered, icy road. A coarse wool scarf covered her more decorative head covering underneath. Naomi walked two paces behind and pushed her mother-in-law forward when necessary. Both were unrecognizably bundled against the bitter wind and snow, but not even a blizzard could have deterred them that afternoon. They carried one large tray of wrapped almonds and candy and picked their way past the icy portions of the lane.

It was that visit which demanded the Vartanians' return visit to-day. It was early January and the eve of Christmas. Anno would at last see Daron again. It had been just over two months since she and Turgay had tried to pass over the stream. She was more herself again in appearance. She smoothed her hair. The mirror had reappeared somehow and she used it often. She wore Lucine's old coat, but underneath was a new, dark-green dress that she and Yeraz had sewn together. The sleeves and skirt were the perfect length and her wrists and socks were no longer mockingly exposed.

Their entrance into Mgro's vegetable garden bore no similarities to the last time Anno had been there. She wondered if she dreamed the sight of Daron's father now leading Vartan past the snow-patched garden. She looked at the muddy rows to her left where once the purple eggplants had grown fat in the summer sun, and then she stole a sidelong look at Yeraz. Her mother winked back at her. She, too, would not forget that pivotal day.

Once inside, Anno was dizzied by the number of hands she kissed. She paused when she came upon Mgro's father. She had never been this close to the old man. The fingers of one rugged hand spread wide and he patted her head reassuringly. It was good that she was not required to speak, because she glimpsed flickers of Daron on his worn face and this peek into the future brought tears to the surface again. She kissed his free hand and squeezed his fingertips with spontaneous affection, breaking the rules of custom, but lifting his heart.

At the end of the circle of family members, she knew Daron was near. Patience thinning, she hurried, reaching for Old Mariam's hand without looking to see to whom it belonged. The old woman's belly laugh caused her to look up, and good friends once more, Anno laughed as well. She broke the second rule of custom and threw herself into the old woman's arms.

At last, she stood before Daron, and they were mirror images of one another. Their hands hung limply at their sides and their weary, drawn faces gazed back at each other. They had trudged and stumbled but made the long journey home. Daron's face haltingly lifted into a smile as Anno drew near, and there she saw a new maturity and depth of ardor. Flecks of gold lit Anno's eyes at the sight of him.

CHAPTER 31

*T*he long winter had finally ended and the sowing had begun. The rivers and streams were dangerously flooded now from the rains and the melting snow. Anno had walked to the stream's edge with Vrej once she was able. They did not speak at all when they reached the crossing where she and Turgay had been found. The currents crackled and bounded mischievously over the banks. It seemed they would wash away the memory of that night long, long ago. Anno wished they could.

Anno was almost completely recovered and was well encouraged to spend time outdoors to restore the color to her skin. Yeraz watched her stroll away instead of helping with the midday meal and its delivery to the fields and did not say a word to stop her.

She and Daron were to be married after Easter, well before the harvest, when it would be possible to spare time for a wedding. Aunt Marie and Yeraz had already put their heads together and scrutinized Anno's figure to plan a becoming wedding gown.

She decided to walk to the end of the village and then to the orchards. The fruit trees bloomed now like endless rows of enormous bouquets. She walked between the plum, cherry, and apricot trees with their shades of white, pink, and purple blossoms and tipped her head back as a breeze shed their lacy petals on her hair.

By the time she reached the cornfields, she had tired, and she seated herself on a tree stump to rest. She watched the oxen pull the steel-tipped plowshares and turn the hearty red soil. Anno searched each figure. She was not at all certain if Daron would be here. He could be in any of the fields, but her legs had carried her as far as this one.

Someone in the distance straightened and broke away from the others. Her face broke into a proud smile as he walked toward her, unhurried and almost thoughtful. His shirtsleeves were pushed to his elbows and his head was again bare.

Anno knew she should not be here. There were designated times and places for betrothed couples to meet, but it was she who would receive a scolding later that day and she was past caring.

"Anno! What are you doing there?" Daron called out to her laughingly.

She watched him, straight and spare. His eyebrows were not great and coarse like so many of the village men's and his black eyes were not overshadowed by them. His nose, she had teased enviously, was as if it had been drawn and shaped with the use of a straight edge. His mouth, she now knew, was silken.

Anno shrugged and spread her hands. "My mother still feels I am not truly well enough to work, so I am free to roam on a morning like this."

"I am glad." Daron smiled still. "I am glad that this is where you wanted to roam to."

"Well, if I had not found you here, I was going to begin climbing the hills next, one by one."

"I believe that," he answered.

They watched each other's faces intently. Private moments together were still so rare.

"Anno, I shall never let anyone else decide what is right or wrong for us again. No one."

Anno was taken aback at his sudden seriousness.

"I nearly failed you."

"No! You did not..." Anno began, but his raised palm silenced her.

"No one," he finished.

CHAPTER 32

$\mathscr{L}$ucine snatched the needle and cloth from Anno in annoyance.

"Oh, Anno! What do you think of walking to the church on your wedding day with a crooked dress? At least pity Daron. Do you wish to embarrass him?"

Lucine's belly was in her way regardless of what task she tried to perform. Things simply slid to one side or the other. There was less than a month left until her delivery, and she had come to spend that time in her father's home as well as to help prepare for Anno and Daron's wedding within the week.

Anno knew it was Lucine's discomfort causing her to speak so sharply, and she did not care. She did not care what anyone said or did or whether her dress collar sat straight against her neck or not. She was to be wed in five days.

EASTER HAD COME and she and Daron had sat in Vartan's courtyard beneath the silky grape leaves and tendrils newly unraveling along the length and curves of the vine. She had held a good-sized, braided chorek topped with a red-dyed egg in her hands and gazed at it, unable to take a bite out of its crisp, toasty end.

"It seems I cannot enjoy this, Daron. I feel as if Turgay Dade should come hobbling up to claim it."

"Anno, that old woman died that night because her mind was not right and her old body did not handle her wanderings. You know that, do you not?"

Daron worried about the guilt she still carried and wished to be done with it.

"If I could just lay this on her grave, I would be, at last, content," she tried.

"You cannot," Daron answered simply and sharply. They could not place a Christian offering on a Muslim grave. It was unthinkable. His eyebrows had arched with aggravation and his eyes had narrowed. It was an aspect of him she had never seen and she knew her words had been the reason for it.

Anno turned her favorite part of the chorek to Daron instead and he took the first generous bite. His dark eyes locked with her honey-colored ones and thoughts of Turgay faded.

CHAPTER 33

On the morning of her wedding day, Anno lay awake long before the sun rose. She listened to the deep breaths and snores of her family. Their bodies were heavy with the marrow-deep fatigue of the urgent work and care of spring coupled with the preparations of the wedding and its feast. And the sad knowledge that yet another family member would leave them.

Anno had grown a bit ashamed at how eager she had been for this day to come. She still steeled herself at the start of a conversation in fear that the topic might be Daron, might be a new bit of information heard, and Vartan's consent might be a grave misunderstanding after all.

She blinked into the darkness and knew she did not imagine that the first rays of the day had fingered their way through the windows so that, at last, its arrival could not be denied.

Yeraz had lain watching her youngest child wring her hands as they rested on top of her blankets. She had been staring at the window for quite some time now and Yeraz knew what she waited for. She prayed her daughter's married life would bring her the joy she so fiercely anticipated. To witness Anno's happiness was all she wanted. It would help diminish the slicing pain she would feel when she stowed her pile of bedding on the bottom along with Lucine's.

Later that morning, Uncle Hagop sounded a good sigh of content as he shuffled to the front door for the second time since he had risen. He had already given the most favorable prediction there could be, and that was that their mountain shone down on them with clear distinction and that their girl's wedding day would proceed as it should, without a single hindrance. He studied Maratuk once more now and nodded with as much pleasure as if the mountain and he had planned the details of its splendid display. He was about to close the door again and turn back inside to oversee the bustle he so enjoyed, when Haig's wife called to him to hold the door. She had expertly maneuvered her wide hips through the courtyard entrance carrying a tray that matched her width. She was pulled into the circle of women who had finished dressing the bride.

There was an Armenian village a good distance south of Van, near the border of Syria, which was completely immersed in the making of silk, from the cultivation of the worms to the production of yards and yards of silk fabric sold and coveted in the nearby districts. The tailors of Van also valued this silk, and after much inquiry and trading, Mgro was able to obtain two square yards of it in alternating shades of red. Nevart had presented this fabric to Yeraz on Easter Day. It was sewn into a sash and twisted and tied snugly at Anno's waist over her wedding dress. Anno dug her fingers into it now, unconsciously, as she watched the commotion before her, so uncharacteristic of her father's house.

Anno's dress was not as ornate as Lucine's had been, nor had Anno participated in the cutting of it. The work had fallen largely on Aunt Marie and Yeraz and, at the last, Lucine. Anno had only fingered the material in passing. Its sole ornament was the sash at her waist and the coins on her cap and strung across her chest.

Their front room was filled with people, so many that Anno could no longer see the walls. No one cared to sit either. They clasped Anno and Yeraz and each other, and her father, even, seemed to have smiled more than a few times today already.

Eventually, she was aware that the room hushed. The door was locked and there was silence. Anno felt dizzy. Let this end, she prayed. Let her see Daron's face. Her eyes roamed the room until she found Old Mariam. She was seated comfortably on the divan, close to where Vartan and the other men stood. Her eyes had been on Anno for some time now.

Teasing and laughter carried through the closed door. Manuel's voice could be heard and the door was pulled open. Coins clinked into Vrej's hand. A fine lace scarf, long and voluminous, was presented to Yeraz. And at last, Anno saw Daron. He wore a simple tunic and shalvar of a matching deep blue. A fringed scarf wrapped across his forehead, and at his waist was a dagger, sheathed and housed in a red sash. Anno went to his side before it was time, causing bursts of laughter at her eagerness. Uncaring, Daron pulled her with him to kiss Yeraz's hands.

Later, of her wedding, Anno was only to remember standing at the altar forehead to forehead with Daron. She wore his mother's wedding ring and squeezed her fingers tightly to feel its presence. Cords were tied around their foreheads and Anno breathed in the familiar dampness of the ancient walls.

In the church square, the skewers of lamb sizzled and drippings fell into the fire until the meat was wrapped in lavash and distributed to the guests. There was oghee and dancing and the meat was pulled again and again and served with potatoes and mushrooms and greens. There was cheese and pastries and the men clenched fists with one another and, shoulder to shoulder, danced in circles around the bride and groom until the ground beneath them shook.

Their bed was in a small room just above the stable, made ready for Daron and Anno. It had one small window and it lent a clear, although narrow, view of the orchards beyond. Anno was enchanted by it, having spent her life in a space that offered no free view of the outdoors.

Grape hyacinths, tulips, and iris could be seen blooming from the window. Their colors dotted the flatlands between and around the spaces least trodden. But most of all, Anno was glad to see the poppies. Blood-red with their black faces pointed in every direction, they seemed to watch over the land. As a child, she had plucked them from the ground only to watch them wilt and fold over before she could walk the road home with her short legs. She had learned soon enough that they would stand sentinel for long days in the early spring, but would not survive if ever separated from their roots. She had learned to only finger their silky petals, only peek into them as the bees bore themselves into their powdery pistils, and only watch over them as they watched over her.

The red petals were closed now with the night and Daron stood soundlessly behind her. His head was bare and he had undone the top buttons of his tunic. His coarse brown hair had fallen onto his forehead and his eyes and body were heated from the long hours of revelry and songs and teasing and waiting.

Two candles lit their tiny room and the covers of their wide mattress had been folded back to reveal an uninterrupted expanse of white sheets and cases etched with delicate embroidery.

Daron lifted his shoulders. "Do you like it, Anno? Our room?"

They both knew the room itself did not matter to them. But his family had taken great care in its preparation and Anno was touched by what she saw.

"Daron, we could be happy together in the stable itself. But *this*," her arms swept around her, "this is a heaven."

"Our heaven," he smiled.

His voice had turned gravelly, as it had been once short days ago when they had been too long under the cover of the willow tree.

She fell against him and they had their first deep kiss, free of watchful eyes, ending only when they chose, to tug open buttons, to unravel sashes, to explore planes and silky skin, and spill, finally, tightly entwined into an ocean of release.

Later, in complete darkness, the candles snuffed, they listened to each other's breaths. Anno marveled at the force of Daron's heartbeat, her cheek on his chest. She had risen on one elbow to look into his face. He pulled her back tightly to him.

"You will never leave me alone, then, Anno? Do you promise?"

A strange memory came to Anno, clouded and distant. Her father's home had been so silent. She had thought herself alone in the front room. Anno had lifted her head from a cushion that she had been hugging to her cheek. She sat up on the scratchy carpet she lay on, disoriented from her deep daytime slumber, and rubbed her plump fists into her eyes to clear them. There was perspiration in the folds of her neck from her heavy hair and the heat of the summer afternoon. There was movement by the kitchen space. Her parents stood alone as if the only two people in the house, her own presence well forgotten. Vartan slapped Yeraz on her rear. Anno was instantly alarmed. She had never seen such a thing. Was her father angry with her mother? Had he hurt her? To add to her confusion, Yeraz turned to Vartan, and smilingly she caressed his face, his chest. Vartan's hand lingered, he gathered the material of her skirt, and more, into his palm. They pressed against each other and then parted abruptly. She remembered their heads swiveling in her direction. The memory, suppressed, came so clearly to her now, so poignantly understood.

"I promise, Daron," she answered him. "We shall have a lifetime of love."

CHAPTER 34

*O*ne week later, the Markarian men escaped as soon as they saw Yeraz and an array of women lower a carved wooden chest from the back of a wagon. Before the men's cigarettes were even lit in the church square, the chest was opened and Anno's trousseau displayed.

Once Yeraz had been certain that Anno's recovery from pneumonia would be complete, she had begun lecturing her anxiously as to the attention she should pay her new duties among her husband's family. Anno had been spoiled for so long, Yeraz worried she would not perform her chores well, as daily and repetitive as they would be. Anno had nodded distractedly and vaguely at her mother's words and the older woman had begun wringing her hands with dread.

As it was, Anno embraced her duties, every aspect of them. Hers was a marriage of love and she could not do enough for Daron, for his sister Nairi, or for his family, who had, as it turned out, always wanted her.

The rhythm and schedule of all the households in the village was the same, but Anno found that living on the edge of the long lane of houses allowed her to see many more people during the course of a day than in her father's home. Everyone passed this way when heading to the orchards and fields. Also, the wide display of wooden and bone combs, scissors, precious mirrors, copper and tin bowls, earthenware jugs and baskets brought browsers often. Often, too, they would look at Mgro's supply and order something similar, something larger or more affordable for him to bring back on his next trip north or south. Anno was surprised to see that he never grumbled or complained about the people who came to look and touch but never buy. People like those, it seemed, were more a part of a merchant's life than the ones who actually produced coin or traded.

During the day, Anno was everyone's sister and daughter. But not long after the sun set, when eyes and arms fell in weariness, she had Daron to herself. In their tiny room with their tiny window, they watched the night sky deepen and spoke of every detail of their days. Daron spoke of the work he preferred with the crops and that which he detested, shepherding the animals for hours on end. He spoke of his brother-like bond with Kevork and how he wished his sister had not been deprived of her mother. He spoke of his wish to take Anno with him to other villages and other cities some day in the other provinces so that they could see how life was outside Sassoun, when he himself would do the buying and trading without his father.

Anno had never left Sassoun. She had, twice, left Salor to go on a short pilgrimage to a larger church in the neighboring village to the north. She remembered playing in the spring there by the huge church ground and eating by the water's edge before they all made their way back home with the setting sun.

There was so much to look forward to, Anno thought. She even did not mind rising with the early morning sun any longer because it was Daron who woke her.

CHAPTER 35

*A*nno was pouring cold water into a smaller pitcher for Naomi to mix with yogurt when they heard a call from the door downstairs. She started at the sound of the familiar voice and dried what water she had spilled while Kevork called down the stairs for Vrej to enter. It was so early still that the men had not finished their breakfast. Anno looked at Daron uneasily, but then they heard a laugh on the stairs. Vrej entered, apologizing for his early-morning disturbance. Watching him move around the room, Anno already guessed the reason for his presence, his eager greeting of each family member, his disheveled hair and his twinkling eyes.

"Well, I have come to say that our Lucine has had her baby." Vrej's eyes met Anno's for the first time since his entrance.

Murmurs of pleasure circulated.

"The baby was born hours ago, really. Perhaps it has been four or five hours now. It is a boy. A large boy." Vrej showed by the spread of his hands that the child was as large as a watermelon. "Sister Nevart, if you will pardon my asking, Sister Mariam has sent me for almond oil. It is for the baby. Perhaps it is downstairs?"

He turned to Mgro again to see if it had been better to ask it of him.

"I, myself, shall bring that oil!" Nevart was already untying her apron decisively. "Vrej, my boy, no need for you to wait. You return home and tell your mother I am on my way."

She immensely enjoyed her new relations with the village leader's family and here was another opportunity to go calling, filling a role of no small importance. Her apron flew off her head.

Anno's eyes went from Vrej to Nevart. She was certain Daron's grandmother had forgotten her existence completely. Nevart disappeared into a room and then returned immediately with a small bottle of the precious oil from the almond trees of Van.

Naomi's mind had already raced ahead of Nevart's, and as soon as the men rose, she winked in Daron's direction.

"Akh, Mother, I am feeling uneasy at this," Naomi began. "Do you not think it wisest that you yourself take our new hars to her mother's home first, before every other neighbor trails by?"

Minutes later Anno and Vrej found themselves trotting up the road beside Nevart, who, in her desire to reach her khnami's side, thrust her body forward from the hips and assumed a heel-smacking gait that gave the impression of generating a good deal more speed than it really did. They kept up comfortably, only glancing sideways now and again to be sure that the jarring to which Nevart was subjecting herself did no real harm.

Vartan's front door gave the familiar clack and creak as they entered. They were met with embraces of joy and welcome. Lucine's baby, swaddled tightly, was placed into Anno's arms immediately as *daross* so that she, too, would soon bear a child. His eyes were screwed shut, but she could see that his complexion was fair like that of his parents. He yawned and Anno's heart warmed at the sight of his pink, glistening mouth against cottony-smooth skin.

Anno looked around her, into every corner of the dear, familiar room. Avo dozed against a wall while his mother was conversing deeply with Old Mariam and now Nevart. Lucine and Yeraz, in their corner, smiled contentedly at each other and the baby.

The need for almond oil seemed to have been forgotten. Anno searched the baby's face for a rash or irregularity.

"Lucine, I see no rash," Anno whispered, Nevart only feet away.

"There is no rash, Anno."

"It was cured so quickly?"

Lucine giggled and Yeraz looked unashamedly smug.

Anno's eyes widened.

"We wished you here. With us," Lucine stated simply.

So much happiness, Anno thought, so much fullness—then why had this persistent, tiny fear bored itself into the base of her throat?

CHAPTER 36

*A*long the skirts of their mountains, knolls, plains, and ravines, in July of 1914, the Sassountzis were busy with their harvest.

Mgro went more often to Moush as soon as the weather allowed. He sought newspapers first. Through him, they learned of the shooting of the Archduke Ferdinand of Sarajevo and later that the Ottoman Empire was preparing for war alongside Germany against Russia and the European Allies. But the people themselves were most keenly aware of the golden stalks of wheat bending heavily with the dry breeze and sun. They were more watchful of the tobacco fields, green and lush with their rolls of leaves, the fields of barley and hemp, and orchards that presented them all at once with all they would need to harvest and store for the winter that would creep in on them in four short months.

Kevork and Takoush could be seen crossing paths more and more frequently these weeks. Takoush at first had begun presenting herself at many odd times of the week in search of Anno. But now, it was suspected, she came in search of Kevork as well.

One late afternoon, Anno and Nairi had laid carpets and cushions under the shade tree near the vegetable garden. Dusk was Anno's favorite time of day. Lazy and infectious, it had called her outdoors to await Daron's return home with the rest of the men.

Eggplants, deeply purple and glossy, grew in rows once again and the bees left their hives not far from the stables to claim what they could from the garden blossoms. Eggplants of the same seed now grew in Yeraz's garden, as well as Old Mariam's and Aunt Marie's.

Takoush, her cheeks overly pink from the heat, threw herself with relief under the shade of the tree beside Nairi. She leaned over for a handful of chickpea pods. The legume had enjoyed a long season this year, and while a great amount had been dried and stored already, Anno and Nairi had harvested this last trailing batch while still green to be used for a meal tomorrow.

Anno had entered her third month of pregnancy. Daron had watched her at sunrise, one day in May, blinking at the floor of their room, a shawl thrown over her bare shoulders. He was already nearly dressed and she still sat, lost in thought, her long hair loose and offering the same meager covering as the shawl beneath it.

"If you are waiting for me to brush your hair again, I will, but do not blush so when they tease us for being late."

"Daron?"

"Anno?" He tried to glimpse her face. Her tone was strange.

"We have been wed four weeks now?"

"Yes." His hands dropped, his shirt left open.

Anno turned to him. "Then I should have bled by now." Her smile was luminous with certainty.

They had fallen back onto their mattress, their laughter muffled, their joy a bursting secret and their own for only days more. Naomi had caught her out, yawning too often by midafternoon and eating great mouthfuls of pickled turnips with bread and yogurt and cheese between mealtimes.

"Now where does your mother think you are, Takoush?" Nairi giggled. Her eyes twinkled at Takoush's presence; the girl's daring and frankness was something new to her and exciting.

Anno knew Nairi should not hear of Takoush's small escapes

from work and her schemes and tales to make them possible, but she could hardly keep her head upright and her hands from dropping to her sides. She wished to close her eyes for just five minutes, to lean against the tree and surrender to the cool summer breeze.

"I shall tell you, Nairi. She thinks I have gone to gather the dog rose berries. And I shall. I just did not mention that I would gather them from the bushes near your house and not mine." Her head turned suddenly in mild apprehension as she searched the brush around her, wondering for the first time if the berries did at all grow near Mgro's house.

Nairi's mouth fell open at Takoush's cleverness and her eyes shone in admiration. Anno promised herself she would stop Takoush from teaching Nairi these deceptions, but not now. Now, her eyes could close a few minutes because Takoush was shelling her portion of chickpeas at a furious speed.

She awoke, what seemed only seconds later, to see Daron staring over her. The cloth twisted and wrapped around his forehead was darkened deeply with perspiration. He smiled down at her, but she sensed a reserve there. She pulled herself off the tree trunk and was surprised to find the chickpeas and bowls cleared and herself alone on the carpet. He did not approve of her laziness, she thought. She was an embarrassment to him.

She struggled to her feet. Closer now, she looked into his face and saw that he was not disappointed. There was something else.

"What is it?" her voice thick.

"Anno, Raffi has come."

She gasped. Again, that fear at the base of her throat.

"Is he all right?" She pinched the material of his sleeve.

"Yes. Yes, I think so. I did not hear that he was not."

Anno was dizzy. Daron returned with some cool water and a large spear of cold boiled potato. She consumed both swiftly as he watched her, no longer taken aback at the zealousness of her appetite.

"Go wash your face, Anno. We shall go see him now."

Anno and Daron reached the lane to Vartan's house and slowed. Daron was glad to finally see Raffi again, to thank him again for his intervention in making their marriage possible. That other time, he had been too weary, too distrustful still to speak to him as he had deserved. Anno, however, felt such trepidation, as if her legs were too heavy for her.

Raffi was seated on the divan not far from where Anno had lain ill for weeks. Her senses, heightened with pregnancy, took in the aroma of boiling whole wheat along with the metallic sharpness of cooking vegetables. The woody, buttered juices of the mushrooms released themselves next and brought a knowing smile to Anno's lips. Raffi's favorite foods would be happily prepared just for him. Several golden egg yolks would be broken on top of the mushrooms and sprinkled with salt and herbs until the wheat and vegetables were ready.

Raffi stood at their arrival. Anno's eyes filled and she felt Daron leave her as he went straight to Raffi. Yeraz turned away from her pots and skillets to watch their embrace.

Raffi was intensely relieved to see that Anno was almost plump now and, with the unfamiliar head covering she was now required to wear, looked a wiser version of the little sister left behind just months ago. He felt a tiny regret, but ignored it and hugged her to him.

No words were exchanged after all about the situation he had found them all in last winter. It was not necessary to look back. They desperately needed to look to the future.

Later, food eaten, Raffi spoke.

"I have left you months on end, with other fedayees, to spend days and nights in the homes of those who receive information from the capital as to what the Young Turks *really* plan and hope for their empire and for we Christians who live here.

"As you know, there is now forced conscription throughout the country, including Armenians."

"Hah!" Uncle Hagop's reaction was scornful. "*Now* they consider us their equals? We are finally fit to fight side by side with them?"

There were nods. They knew. Mgro's newspapers were in tatters after being passed from one house to another. Those who could not read crowded close to sons who could. Vrej, too, had been schooled in Moush and read the black inked lines repeatedly to Uncle Hagop and his friends until he had them nearly memorized.

"War will likely reach us here," Raffi continued. "With the Russians coming from the east and the Turks from the west, our lands are a natural barrier between the two enemies."

"The Europeans are caught up in their own troubles now and are too busy to draw up treaties and make hollow promises for a safer life for us. Many, many of our fedayees are searching for guns, but the leaders say wait. They too sense something different and more dangerous than ever before."

The base of Anno's throat squeezed in on itself.

"The Germans have sent a chief inspector to Constantinople to try to train the army." Raffi's voice was a tired monotone of dread. "The Ottoman government has promised us autonomy after the war if we help them liberate the Armenian provinces in Russia."

No one was impressed. They waited for more.

"The Russians have promised much the same, if we support them."

Empty-handed and used as a pawn at every turn, they did not know what to expect. Or where to place their trust.

Silence fell and soon darkness.

Not one month later, a similar gathering took place again in Vartan's home. This time, the world was at war.

CHAPTER *37*

$\mathscr{V}$artan felt Yeraz's eyes on him as he returned home, up the twisted road to their door. He had been part of a small delegation of Sassountzis called to Moush. Raffi and Uncle Hagop crowded near to hear his news.

"We met with Zengin Pasha."

Raffi nodded at the well-heard-of name.

"The entire meeting was quite short. And we had our own appointed spokesman. It was not I, Yeraz."

Yeraz nodded in relief. The less notice taken of Vartan, the better, she felt.

"Zengin Pasha was well agitated. The Ottoman Empire is at war and he said that he wants all the men of Sassoun, aged twenty to forty-five, to join the armed forces.

"We stood in a row. We offered no argument. When we left, the Pasha looked pleased with himself." Vartan chuckled ruefully. "I do not think he was impressed with the fierce, fighting mountain men he had been warned of. He fed us and sent us on our way." His face sobered. "It is as you say." Vartan looked at Raffi. "Something is different this time."

In deep autumn Zengin Pasha sent his authorities to Sassoun to collect the volunteers their village leaders had promised. They arrived in Semal, passing herds of sheep but no shepherds. The roads were curiously empty of people, yet they felt as if they were being watched. They saw an occasional donkey and heard only the distant clucks of the chickens. They decided to pound on the doors, to shake off this eeriness and have their needs met at once. They were a delegation of three but decided not to separate. It was better to have one another's support and nod of encouragement when dealing with Christians. Sometimes they provoked.

The doors did not open, but a boy appeared. He was disturbingly fair-skinned and the short, coarse hair on his head was the color of wheat. His large, brown eyes stared up at them anxiously. His toes would finally bore holes through the tips of his shoes within the week.

"Please," he bowed and beckoned.

The delegation would rather have kicked him aside, but followed him instead to a house built into the sides of a hill, the first in a row of four. They passed through the open door to find the dwelling deserted save for two men, the village leader and the priest.

The Armenians said they were not prepared. If they would be forgiving, would be patient, they might move on to Geligouzan, and by their return, their volunteers would be ready.

The room was bare. There was nowhere to sit save the floor. There were no smells of bread or boiling, bursting grains and spices and onions. They saw only a lone jug of water and a cold toneer. They did not wish for water and, their annoyance in their task rising, left.

Outside, the boy had vanished. Two of the delegation stopped to urinate into the mud wall of a house before climbing onto their horses. Geligouzan was a larger district with almost fifteen hamlets. They would see that their needs were met there. They headed south, not knowing that word of their coming was traveling faster than they.

In Geligouzan, they dismounted almost immediately to ease their muscles. They had missed enjoying their long midday meal on their embroidered cushions, their pastries served with their coffee, their slow afternoon's nod and slumber.

Here they at least saw movement on the roads. On the right, an old woman sat cross-legged against a wall of rocks stacked in varying shapes and sizes. Her head was tightly wrapped, revealing only a face slackened and deeply folded. Her hands, the same shade as a dried tobacco leaf, gripped the end of an earthenware churn and rocked it. Her eyes dully followed the Turks' movement, but she did not care enough to turn her head to follow their progress down the road. If she was to expend energy, better to swat the flies that gathered at her eyelids.

The delegation headed for the church square. It was not long before they were directed to the entrance of another house. The room was a bit larger here. There were rugs on the floor, and they were seated. Two old men sat sentry at the door. The delegation was dryly welcomed by the village leader who resided there. A low wooden table held bread and yogurt, tomatoes and oghee. They stretched their legs and ate a few mouthfuls quickly, directing the old men to send word that the volunteers must meet at this location at once.

"What volunteers would that be?" asked one of the four Sassountzis seated before them. "You want young, able-bodied men for your army. We have had none for the past twenty years."

The tassels atop their fezzes swung like pendulums with the swift swivel of three heads.

The Sassountzis shrugged back at the challenge in their eyes. "Twenty years ago the government demanded back taxes from us, many years' worth. If we had the coin to pay for even one year we would have. We eat what we grow. Look around you. Do you see anything we have that you would even care to carry back? Our cattle and our sheep, which put the very food in our mouths, were stolen and slaughtered by the Kurds. The Kurds the government armed specifically for that reason. The great Sultan sent in his army, and together with the Kurds, they killed our boys and young men, the ones you have come for now."

The village leader spoke without emotion, his voice even and conversational. The Turks half expected the conversation to turn in their favor at any moment.

"Ten years after that, you returned and did more killing. Your soldiers lived at our expense. You filled your prison with innocent villagers and then, because that was not enough to assuage your fear of us, you killed again the men and boys you have come here today searching for."

The delegation returned to Moush and the few men of Geligouzan descended from their hiding places.

When the same thing occurred in two more villages, the delegation was fired.

The Sassoun village leaders and elders conferred and decided that their men would be hidden each time they were asked for volunteers. At the same time, they would begin training for their own self-defense.

Before the ground froze, the "ovens" of Talvorig village were filled. They worked furiously. The iron ore in their mountains was close to the surface. Very close. They dug large wells and filled them with oak and hazel wood. They refilled the wells with the same iron-rich soil they had dug out. The wood burned, and in the extreme temperatures the melted iron flowed within the well. Once the well cooled, the iron was collected and moved to the forges.

Sassoun's isolation was such that they knew they could not expect help from others and were cut off from most communication. The Kurds who lived around them in effect surrounded them and were already well armed with guns and ammunition. The Sassountzis would have to make their own.

CHAPTER 38

Winter came and they had news that those Armenians who had joined the Ottoman army were being removed from the ranks. They were disarmed and forced into labor battalions. Underfed and scantily clothed, they built roads and dug trenches. The trenches were often their own graves.

Again there was a gathering in Vartan's home.

Aram, too, had returned to Salor and now sat across from Avo. Aram's fists lay clenched on his thighs and he did his best not to look at Lucine's husband. Blessedly, the younger man seemed not to notice. Aram concentrated on the reason for their meeting.

"Gendarmes and soldiers gather peasants from their fields and march them away instantly," he said. "Their wives run after them with quickly wrapped loaves of bread and clothes."

Eyes did not move from his face.

"Many times, these men are simply shot dead as soon as the first hill is rounded."

"You have seen this?" Mgro demanded.

"Yes. You will not read of this in the newspapers from Moush," he continued. "They have lists now of the number of people in each village and their gender. Burning houses simply means that the gendarmes did not find all the men on their list. They do not wait."

It was as they had heard.

"No Armenian is allowed to own so much as a razor. If *I* were found with one, all of Salor would be burned to the ground."

The men looked at each other as the same thought passed through their minds. When would the Turks turn their attention to the remote highlands of Sassoun, where their scanty collection of ammunition was being painstakingly manufactured and hidden?

Their mountaintops were blanketed with several feet of snow. The wind blew through the passes and the trees, and the roads in and out of Sassoun became impassable. Raffi and Aram did not leave Salor.

Eagles and hawks soared above and the people sheltered in what appeared to be an idyllic winter retreat, cocooned in their homes, perched on their mountains. In truth, they passed their days meeting and discussing and preparing, though they did not know for what.

The New Year came and 1915 began. On Christmas Day a great pot of hereesa bubbled over a slow fire in Yeraz's kitchen. The contents were simple. Wheat, lamb, water, and salt boiled from sunrise to mid-afternoon. Long wooden spoons were kept close to beat the mixture with strong hands, several times each hour, until all the ingredients melded into one another. The fibers of the wheat softened and finally melted and the meat became tender threads of flavor. Drizzled on top was golden butter, the color of a sun they had not seen for months.

In her last month of pregnancy, Anno was given the seat of honor on the divan. Daron sat with his bowl of hereesa on the floor next to her brothers, the table before them holding only the customary lavash and oghee.

Vartan, Mgro, and the other men were smoking in an adjoining room and the women intermingled and went where they were needed.

Lucine and Avo's Daniel was the center of attention. At nine months he was a fat, happy baby with sparse wisps of brown curls upturned all over his round head. Anno watched Lucine's thin arms carrying and shifting him all day. She longed to play with him now but was not permitted to lift him. The older women feared his weight would be too much for her.

Anno's pregnancy had passed quickly. Except for her early yearnings for food and sleep, her body was not especially weighted. She would have enjoyed a long walk and a chance to take deep gulps of air away from their cramped rooms filled with restless minds and wringing hands, but the weather had transformed the lanes into icy courses of treachery. Through the walls, the wind's squall still came to them and the snow flew in every direction. No one would ever allow her to walk three feet from the door without being lifted bodily off the ground with cries of warnings and caution. Nothing less than the arrival of Christmas would have softened Nevart enough to allow her to come even this far.

The small of her back was aching again. She had not removed her eyes from Daron and her brothers. Their bowls of hereesa were nearly untouched. The lavash had dried and curled at its corners. Cups of oghee were held but never lifted to their lips. They spoke of flintlock pistols left and forgotten since the 1904 massacre in Sassoun. Even those single-shot weapons were being unearthed and restored.

She needed to move a bit. Her back felt twisted. "Mama, do you need anything from the stable?" she asked. In the cool ground there, containers of preserves, cheese, potatoes, and vegetables were stored.

"No, my daughter."

"I shall go, then, and stroke sweet Meghr's nose a bit." *And let the chickens peck at my skirts,* she thought. How many were there now? What had the Kurds left them with this last autumn?

Yeraz wrapped Anno in a scratchy shawl, the weight of which caused her to spread her legs for balance. Daron watched Anno allow Yeraz to wrap her as high as her neck and then pass them to disappear into the grain room that led to the stable. The only heat there would be what came from the bodies of the animals.

The cows, all four, greeted her with their rumps first. They were gathered at one end of the stable, much like gossipy women. Their heads turned at her entrance and bobbed in greeting. The hens and their chicks were roosting everywhere, high and low, and Meghr, standing in the middle of the stable floor, unused to days of inaction, days of only eating and waiting, pricked his ears and turned to face her in hopeful readiness.

Anno laughed aloud at him. He did not need to speak. She understood that he missed his mountain trails, his leaps and swims, and his nights outdoors. Standing in a stable with these placid beasts was hurtful to his dignity.

Anno hugged his neck and stroked his nose, all the while apologizing for their mistreatment of him. The light in his eyes told her he understood and he dropped his head to accommodate her height. They stayed that way a while, and then Anno thought to collect some eggs. She was not cold and did not wish to return to the smoke-filled room to sit again.

She found two eggs right away and was snatching her hand away from the hen's beak when her fist closed in agony. The warm yolks oozed between her fingers and down her wrist as she threw her head back in shock. Her arms reached out and grasped at nothing.

The tearing pain in Anno's groin dropped her to her knees and her mouth opened as if to call out, but only trapped air escaped. Clutching her belly with her left arm and balancing on her right, she looked back toward the grain room. It was so far, she thought. When had she gone so far?

Her chest heaved repeatedly as she sucked wide-mouthed at the frosty air. Her mind worked through the shock of the pain, but her limbs would not cooperate.

The next contraction turned Anno's arms to rubber and she rolled to her side and ground her head into the straw and dirt beneath her. The urge to push the baby out was all she knew and she growled as she ripped and tugged at her clothing.

The wind's squalls had turned to screeches that rattled the heavy walnut door, and Daron began to regret their having made even this short walk out today. How could he ensure that Anno did not slip on their way back down the road? He would walk just ahead of her and clear her path, or perhaps, he considered, she should stay the remaining nights in her father's house, after all, until the baby's delivery. No, he knew she would never agree to their being parted. They would not stay much longer then, he decided.

Anno screamed now with the tearing. She knew she screamed and that someone should certainly hear. Meghr stood close, his nostrils quivering at the smell of blood.

"Now Anno has stayed too long in that stable," Yeraz commented disapprovingly. "She will catch cold."

"Lucine, call your sister," Avo instructed. "Then we must leave. It seems this wind and snow is not thinking of resting."

Lucine stood in the relative warmth of the narrow grain room. Her calls to her sister went unanswered, and, annoyed that she would have to enter the still colder space of the stable, she opened her mouth to speak sharply. But Meghr's anxious snorts stopped her. His nudging at something lying on the ground brought her to a full understanding, and Lucine's screams penetrated the walls of the house to mix and swirl with the howls beyond.

Only seconds later, Anno knew she stared into her mother's face. She was aware of her shoes, her pantaloons being pulled off. She heard Daron's voice, so close, and the thump of Meghr's hooves as he nervously beat the hay-covered ground she lay on. Strength came over her and she responded with instinct.

Yeraz and Lucine grappled with her straining body.

"Anno, my daughter, you must turn. Turn before you try to push."

Yeraz abandoned any thought of carrying her into the warmth of the house. It was too late for that. But she at least was determined to position Anno on her hands and knees, so that the delivery would be easier. As it was now, Anno fought her mother as fiercely as she fought the pain searing through her.

Daron was pulled away from Anno's side by her brothers. They averted their eyes, sick with guilt that they had not come searching for her earlier.

Anno's contraction eased and Yeraz and Lucine quickly turned her onto her knees.

"Now, Anno, calm yourself. This cannot be rushed." Yeraz pulled the thick, damp curtain of hair away from her face. "All is as it should be. Only push again when you feel ready."

"Where is Daron?" Anno panted.

"With our brothers," Lucine answered.

"He must not worry..." Anno bore down until exhaustion again overcame her and she dropped to her elbows, forehead grazing the ground. "Daron must not worry. Tell him that I will be all right." Her voice was just above a whisper.

Yeraz and Lucine exchanged glances, but neither moved, believing it was Anno who needed their attention, not Daron.

Anno felt their doubt, their stillness. "*Tell* him," she growled as the pain returned. "I am not like his mother."

Yeraz gasped as her insensitivity toward her pesa dawned on her. She had completely removed the reason for Daron's mother's death from her mind.

Guilty as well, Lucine had already scrambled to her feet.

"Hurry, my daughter. Tell him all is well. It should not be long now." Yeraz bent over Anno again as she strained and pushed with new determination.

Clean white sheets had been brought from the house and Yeraz spread and readied them. Now Daron and Lucine both knelt close to Anno. Daron spoke in a low voice to Anno and smoothed her hair time and again.

It was not long before a baby girl emerged. Their daughter, tiny and pale, with traces of feathery black brows framed over tightly screwed eyes, squealed in protest in Yeraz's hands.

Lucine held the baby while Yeraz worked quickly with the cord and afterbirth. She was not overly concerned with the place the babe had chosen to be born. Raffi's square of ground had not been much different. But the cold was a dangerous factor. She stole glances at Daron. He would not move away.

"Hold the baby, Pesa. Cover her and take her inside near the fire."

Daron reached for the baby as he was told, only to hand her to Vrej, who stood expectantly at the opening of the grain room. He then returned to stand close to Anno.

Yeraz and Lucine glanced at him with discomfort. They realized that he stood ready to deal with the cord himself.

Soon, Anno was covered. Her teeth had begun to chatter, whether from shock from the quick delivery or from the cold they did not know, but a small army of men hovered nearby to carry her in when ready. Yeraz called out now. Daron gathered her into his arms.

Uncle Hagop himself had prepared Anno's mattress. He had even pulled her own bedding out from the bottom of the pile. But how different everything was from the last time she had lain on her mattress in the front room. How grateful they all were to divert their thoughts from the Turks and the war. Instead, they grasped the tiny fingers and exclaimed, too loudly, when her dark gray eyes grudgingly opened. They laughed at her perpetual scowl and exclaimed at how she ever so slightly resembled her uncle, Raffi.

"What is her name to be, Anno?" Vrej asked.

Anno looked to Daron and he announced, "Sossè."

"Sossè." The name echoed around the room and then was tested again. All were amazed at how good it was that she be named after the graceful plane trees that dotted their land.

CHAPTER 39

In late February, Raffi and Aram left Sassoun. They could bear their seclusion no longer. They would see for themselves what was happening in the other villages, and they would get news from the capital.

Weeks later, minds and bodies numbed, they returned to Salor.

Families clustered at Vartan's and Mihran's doors to hear their news, too many to be ushered inside. With all his strength, Father Sarkis beat the clubs against the walnut slab, and the people of Salor filled the church.

Raffi stood before them all, his back to the darkened altar. "They are emptying the villages of all our men. They leave just the women, the old ones, and the…" Raffi's voice faltered. "The smallest of children."

All strained to hear.

"They lie to them about where they are going, when they will return, or do not say anything at all. But they kill them. Right away. Mass graves are everywhere." Raffi bowed his head and Aram stood and continued.

"Once they finish emptying the villages of the men, the rest is made simple. All Christians are driven to the deserts or the rivers to die. The Kurds are thoroughly armed and they perform much of this work themselves because they know that the remains of the villages will be theirs. The livestock, the crops, the goods in the stores, the stores themselves, the houses..." His head shook with the memory of so much plunder. "They even have schedules made for the deportations of the Armenians in each *vilayet*, each city, each village."

Raffi's head lifted. "It seems they concentrate on moving the people to the south. But they are always moved to places where the foreign diplomats cannot see.

"Our people," Raffi took a breath and spoke more loudly. "Our people walk unarmed, with scarcely more than the bread they have been able to bundle for themselves, and are not even allowed to drink water along the way. They stop the caravans of people right near the fountains our own masons have built, and yet they are not allowed to drink." He paused to ensure that his voice would remain strong, then added, "Not even the babies. There is no one to help us. Their plan is to make Turkey for the Turks, and any Muslim who aids us is killed."

"We have seen Turkish women carry away the rugs, the lanterns, the furniture of the emptied homes..." Aram interjected here but could not continue. Raffi knew what his friend had meant to say, and he continued for him, his voice hushed once more.

"And the children. They snatch the youngest children from their mothers and take them as well."

The people had heard enough. They spoke to each other at first in hushed voices that began to rise in panic, and amid the din, one person called out after another.

"Do you think they will do the same to us here?"

"How long before they get to us here, on our mountains?"

"Are you sure they will not stop soon? We have seen this before. They raze a number of villages to scare us, but then they stop."

Raffi held his hand up for silence. "Our treacherous mountain trails and harsh weather should shield us for a while. But I do not know if we will be spared."

It is true. It is different this time. He did not speak this last out loud.

One week later, the sky above Salor cleared and the sun began to make a daily appearance. Uncle Hagop, encouraged by his clear view of Maratuk, dragged himself from the house to the village square.

He did not expect the uproar he saw there. News had come from Moush. It was repeated over and over again. He swung back on his heel to make his way home again.

The melting snow dripped incessantly from the tree branches above. Uncle Hagop swore as an icy trickle caught the back of his head but did not slow his pace. Six hundred Armenian writers, poets, lawyers, and educators living in Constantinople had been put to death.

RAFFI AND ARAM set off for Van. Van did not have the mountainous advantage Sassoun had. The city had been attacked and the people there had organized their own defense.

Anno and Daron stood alongside a hundred other villagers of Salor and waved their young brothers away with blessings and tears and dread. The pain in the base of Anno's throat choked her. She went to be near Lucine, who stood apart from the rest.

Her sister stared after them, still and tearless. Her eyes were rounded and glassy and her pale, tender lids were swollen and dry. Her lips moved but Anno could not hear what she said. She leaned closer.

"I gave him a lock of my hair," she rasped.

"Who?" Anno asked.

Lucine's lips moved again. Anno had to move closer still.

"Aram."

Anno stepped away, confused.

"But why?" she frowned.

"Because he asked it of me." Tears began to flow. "And it was all I *could* give. Now."

"Now? Lucine? What do you mean, *now?*" Anno could not form the words. Could not continue.

Lucine turned to her sister, slowly, as if her skull was weighted and not her own. She squarely met Anno's eyes.

Understanding dawned and Anno pulled Lucine further away from the crowd of villagers. "Lucine, do you *care* for... for *Aram?*"

The glass-green eyes never left Anno's face until finally words, words learned and recited, came from her throat.

"No, Anno. Nooo. I am married. I have my husband."

Her words, weak and false, thrust at Anno's heart. She knew, at that moment, as no other could, how much life and love her sister had missed.

"Oh, Lucine. I am so sorry. I never knew. Never."

She thought of Takoush. Her friend could have never kept such a thing to herself had she known her brother's feelings. Anno was certain that they were something Aram had kept to himself, as a desperate secret.

"It does not matter now, Anno." Lucine's voice reached her ears, lilting almost, as if to try and cheer her younger sister. "I am married to someone else. And Aram will not return."

CHAPTER 40

Raffi and Aram stole into the Walled City at night, covered in dirt and gunpowder. They had watched the cannon fire coming from the Turks all that day. They had watched the Armenians' calculated and less explosive responses.

They were familiar with the vastness of Van. Of its two thousand villages, two hundred and seventy-five were inhabited by a majority of Armenians. They watched aghast as survivors, thousands of them, dragged themselves into the city alongside them. They, too, had heard that the people of Van were trying to hold out in their own defense until the Russian army reached them.

"Let us head to the citadel, Aram. That is where we should receive our instructions."

People skirted to the right and left of them, anxiously seeing to their needs in the relative safety of the night. Livestock, hastily herded in, stood in makeshift pens. Raffi and Aram found their way to where the leaders of the defense gathered.

One fedayee, well known to them, rose excitedly as they approached. He pulled them in closer to the table where the military counsel sat studying drawings of Van. Raffi noted that the Garden Town, heavily populated with their own people, was boldly etched.

The defenders were desperate for men familiar with guerrilla fighting. They were told that the fedayees had trained bands of young men to protect the street corners and boundaries of the Armenian quarters.

The discussion continued, and they listened closely. Raffi's eyes rested on the markings of cannons and artillery surrounding all of Van and pointed into every corner of it.

Once the meeting ended, Raffi reached across the table to lift a copy of a manifesto the defenders had long distributed to the Turkish people of Van. It stated simply that their fight was not with them who had been their neighbors, and they hoped that in future, they would live as neighbors again.

Raffi heard his name called and let the paper float back to its pile.

A man not ten years older than Raffi himself stood waiting. Legs bowed beneath him, he took in Raffi's cartridge belt crossed over his chest and his sword sheathed at his hip. His wary eyes rested on the Mosin.

"What is its range?" he asked, voice hoarse.

"Two thousand feet."

The man grunted. "Smokeless?"

"Nearly," Raffi answered, and realized he had just met his commander.

He and Aram were to be separated. They cupped each other's faces briefly and clapped shoulders.

"God be with you, brother." Their voices were filled with emotion. "We shall meet now and then, I feel certain." They smiled wanly at one another, a lifetime of knowing in their eyes. Aram lifted his own rifle and hastened away.

CHAPTER 41

*B*arrages of cannon and rifle fire burst around them from sunlight until dusk. Shrapnel flew as the Armenians attempted to tunnel past the Turkish lines while the Turks attempted to tunnel into the Walled City.

At night, the well diggers dug trenches furiously and bored openings between the walls of houses. Merchants, tradesmen, and shopkeepers reconstructed defense lines. Cartridges and bullets were manufactured daily, and the women took over the supervision of the food and clothing supplies.

Raffi learned at once that the American and German missionaries were sympathetic to the Armenians and aided and housed the wounded in their buildings, beyond their capacity. He learned, too, that the British Consular building was occupied by Turkish police and that gendarmes used their position to halt communication between the Christians in the orchards and streets.

The violent shelling continued for days. Raffi lay in an isolated house, surrounded by mostly inexperienced young men, all holding their positions through sheer stubbornness. It had once been a large home, but its walls crumbled now around them and their ammunition was almost gone. Raffi, no longer believing that the promised reinforcements would come, watched in amazement as men dragged their way toward them through a deep trench. He did not move even as they spoke to him.

Fatigue did not allow him to react. He was lifted bodily from his place by a window and ordered back to the Walled City for two days' rest.

The shelling never stopped. Raffi struggled to sleep, but could not. He rolled over once again on the stone floor of the shop that served as shelter and sat up. In the next room, where the shopkeeper had probably napped cozily in the late afternoons, position commanders planned strategies that would use as little ammunition as possible.

Raffi slipped his cartridge belt back on and reached for his boots. He frowned at the condition of his feet and decided to see what he could do about them, rather than lie flipping from one side to the other.

He walked onto the street and looked around him. A city the size of Van, with all its food stores and tradesmen and hospitals and buildings, was straining under this siege. How would Sassoun manage to survive, he wondered? They had only had barely enough under the best of circumstances.

The streets were not safe. Stray bullets caught people regularly. Still, he needed to move. His throat was perpetually coated with smoke and each breath burned.

He wanted to see the refugees. He wished to hear where they came from and exactly what method of operation the Turks were using now. But what use was that? He reminded himself of why he had risen just moments before. Better to concentrate on what could be done now, for himself.

Raffi turned to a woman hurrying by, hunched over to protect a basket containing something presumably very precious.

"Sister!" Raffi called out.

She spun around, her brows, her face, anxious and wide-eyed. Her body was steeled as if to accept another blow.

"Where are the women who are sewing shirts and socks?" he asked.

She took a step forward, certain that she had not heard him correctly.

"For the defenders." Raffi felt foolish, but the fact was that his right foot had ripped through the toes of his socks entirely and his foot was bared and rubbed raw against the sole of his boot. He needed socks, or one sock at least, or he would be bleeding when next he needed to run.

The woman looked back toward an open door and pointed.

Raffi sheepishly entered the schoolroom appropriated for the sewing committee. The sound of the shelling outside mixed in with the whir of the sewing machines lined against the walls. Women bent over long tables piled high with, it seemed, every article of clothing one could need. They conversed rapidly with one another, noting shortages and surpluses. They sorted and folded.

He was relieved to see a few other men there as well. He saw the women sewing underpants as well as shirts and socks and was glad he did not have to ask for those. He would approach the first person he saw with socks and then leave. His eyes soon landed on what he had come for.

He hesitated, not accustomed to asking for things. But in the snow, in this condition, it was better to ask than to lose his toes.

"Your pardon, I have come for a pair of socks." He spoke with head bent, already examining the sizes before him.

The woman counting and stacking an unruly pile slowly looked up. She saw a lean torso belted with a pistol and sword appear before her tired eyes and her counting faltered, *sixteen, seventeen...* Her eyes traveled up the cartridge-laden chest to the gray coat collar and stopped. Her body was straight, but she was quite petite, making it necessary for her to lift her chin further to see the man's face. Her hands stilled and the socks toppled over.

Raffi gave a short sigh of annoyance and looked up, for the first time, to see who this person was who was delaying his escape.

He saw brows dramatically upswept and arched, framing deeply brown eyes.

His mouth fell open and she laughed at him outright.

Raffi pulled himself away from the table in confusion. Now he could not take his eyes off her mouth. The old women called teeth like that pearls, did they not? What a foolish thing to remember!

He inhaled to collect himself. He felt he was behaving like Vrej. She was still smiling at him and he found himself smiling back. It had been a long time since he had laughed the way she had, but he began to feel as if, possibly, he could.

RAFFI WAS SENT ten miles north with eighty other armed men. Turkish soldiers and Kurds together were massacring the villagers there.

"You will find the people of three other villages there as well! Reach them!" his commander had barked.

It took a day's walk. Raffi studied the men around him, the urgency in their step, the resignation in their eyes.

Then he would see another pair of eyes, deep brown against black, upswept brows.

Almost as soon as they reached the village, Raffi was positioned strategically near the front. His accuracy with a pistol had been noticed from the start. For five days they held their position until their ammunition ran out. Reinforcements marched in just in time to drive the Turks away. All the surviving defenders were ordered back to the Garden City.

They trudged back, eyes hollow and bloodshot, hands and faces blackened.

The ringing in his ears from the gunshots and explosives came to him even more loudly in the relative silence of their journey. His body craved sleep, but he brought one boot forward, then the other. Then his ears would suddenly fill with the sound of her laughter.

He felt a new, daily yearning to be with her.

AS HE ENTERED the Walled City, Raffi looked around him in disbelief. Fifteen thousand more refugees had dragged in.

The food stores were nearly depleted. Even the fighters' rations were cut back. He sat to eat and the plate handed him was nearly empty.

Raffi was given one day's leave and he headed straight to the sewing compound.

All he knew was that her name was Noushig and he owned two pairs of socks that she had knit herself.

He entered the schoolroom and searched the table where he had seen her last. There was no one there. He searched the room, walking its entire length, even leaning over tables in case she had bent to retrieve something from the floor. He did not see her. He asked a passing woman where she might be.

"Noushig has gone to make a delivery to the American hospital," was her reply. "She left not long ago."

Raffi made his way to the southern edge of the Garden City, where the American compound was, and its hospital. He wondered how often she made this trip, because it was far and could be risky. The Turks' ammunition was limitless and they fired all day, often at nothing.

Once he was inside the compound, the church stood before him. It was his first glimpse of Western architecture. The church had glass windows that reached from floor to ceiling under a slanted roof, but it was modest, not at all like the structures he had seen in Constantinople. He hurried past its closed doors to the adjoining hospital.

He left all his weapons at the door before entering, as was the requirement there. Inside, his eyes ran up and down rows and rows of beds, rank with people. They had even tucked some of the sick under the beds for lack of space.

Raffi saw that the men were separated from the women and children and he found himself peering into the women's ward.

There was very little noise, save for the sound of the bombardments coming from outside. People were bandaged heavily and most stared blankly into space. These were the refugees, his people, who had survived at least in body. Limbs missing, emaciated, children clutching at mothers who could not respond, left with no strength to cry in protest.

Nurses in white were everywhere, American and trained Armenians both. Bottles of something were being distributed to the babies. Apart from all the rest was a woman with two smaller figures lying at her side. Their faces and necks were entirely concealed and bandaged. Raffi could not tell if they were girls or boys because their bodies as well were covered with sheets. Their mother, presumably, lay with her eyes wide open. He started, thinking her dead. He almost rushed toward her, but just then, she blinked once.

He felt a hand on his arm and turned, agitated, to see Noushig. She pulled him away.

"They are her sons. Twins. The Turks tied them to a tree and sliced their faces with razors. Then..." she stopped.

His eyes told her to continue.

"Then, they pulled the skin away with pliers. They were so intent on what they were doing they did not see the village women come at them. The children were carried here just two days ago."

Raffi followed her out of the ward. He asked himself again and again the same question. Was this what an Englishman did when ridding himself of a people and taking their land? Was this how an American fought? A Chinaman? Did they not fight like men, with guns or hand to hand with daggers? Or did they dehumanize their victims like the Turk? Did they kill the men simply to rape and torture their families like the Turk? Did the Turk really fight to rid himself of the Christians, or just to get the spoils?

Noushig had led them to a supply room. There, she lifted a basket filled with garments. She would take them with her to be mended.

Her hair seemed lighter in color than he remembered. Perhaps it was the light from these enormous windows. It hung in one single braid down her back and her head was uncovered. Her dress was also of the Western style. It was of a thickly woven material, high-collared and long-sleeved, and showed her curves quite plainly.

She seemed very familiar and at ease here within the rooms of the hospital.

"Do you work here at the American compound?" he asked.

"I did before. They raised me. I am an orphan. Now they need my help with the sewing as well, so I spend my time in both places."

Raffi asked her to wait while he retrieved his weapons. She watched him walk toward the orderly who had stowed them, his stride slow, still taking in the unfamiliar surroundings as he went.

He slipped everything into place and reached for her basket. As they walked out of the hospital and away from the compound, she asked him, "So, you did not come here looking for me?"

Gunfire sounded from a distance and the metals of his gun and sword clinked as he moved.

"Well, yes," he answered honestly, "it seems I need more socks."

He watched her fleeting indignation and her preparation to defend her handiwork and then seeing the smile on his face, she laughed outright at him again. His heart hurt at the sound of it.

"You make this trip back and forth every day?" Raffi asked.

"Yes."

"Is it necessary?"

"It is my job," she stated, surprised. "And I sleep here."

"You are careful." His voice was urgent.

Noushig stopped.

"I know what can happen, Raffi." She motioned back toward the hospital. "I know because I see it every day. I lived it once before." She slipped her hand into her pocket and pulled out a small dagger. It was smaller than any he had ever seen. "It belonged to my mother." It did not offer her protection as much as comfort, they both knew.

He had walked Noushig back to the American compound that

night as well. The tune of "Our Fatherland" was being played by the boys in the Armenian school band and the music drifted to them through the streets. He asked why she was not married, being in her eighteenth year.

"Who would want a penniless orphan, Raffi?"

He had stared incredulously.

"Is that truly why?"

She shrugged and nodded.

He had wanted to hug her to him and ask her to marry him, this minute, but reality was everywhere. It was in the thickening layer of gunpowder on their skin and in their hair and the unnatural lights in the sky from blazes and guns and a world that was no longer ever silent.

He lifted and kissed her hand as they parted.

THE TURKS HAD learned the terrain and their tactics had improved. Cannon fired and rifles shot as they screamed "Holy war!" and plunged forward.

Dusk finally fell and Raffi remained seated in a trench. He had been tossing brickbats all day. Men filed by and he shook his head at hands outstretched to help. He should join them and find something to eat, but he stayed, instead, and watched the young girls and boys run into the darkness to collect empty shells. They would be refilled again and again.

He had not seen Noushig for two days. He closed his eyes and imagined them walking side by side, up the twisted lane to his father's home.

THE SUN BEAT down on Raffi's dark head and it seemed as if that day darkness would never come. He heard the pounding of boots and mechanically moved aside for a labor battalion to rebuild the rampart he stood behind.

He leaned against a pile of brickbats and watched them as they worked. A defender offered him a sloppily rolled cigarette.

"Did you hear?" the man drew on his cigarette deeply. "The German *and* American missions were fired upon."

Raffi's hands froze. She would have no reason to be there now, would she? he wondered frantically. Fruitlessly he looked in the direction of the missions. The entire sky was filled with smoke.

He closed his eyes and prayed.

The day finally merged into night and the men crawled into a sheltered corner to rest. Raffi had been unable to gather any more information about the condition of the American mission. He drifted into an uneasy sleep.

"Take your positions! Take your positions!" Raffi jolted awake at the sound of his commander's bellowing voice. He and the defenders raced ahead.

Two hundred mounted Turkish soldiers followed by a number of Kurds on foot were attempting a mass attack.

Raffi fired and refired his pistol. He nodded as he was given his allotment of grenades and turned back to fire again. Darkness fell and the Turkish shelling still continued.

The first wave of the attack failed, but the second brought the attackers not twenty feet away from their line of defense.

NOUSHIG WATCHED THE door to the sewing hall. She looked over her shoulder in the streets. He had not come for days. She searched the Armenian surgery. He was not there.

The Turks were preventing thousands of Armenians from entering Van. They were allowed to starve a bit more each day before they were finally ushered toward the Garden City. They dotted and then filled the inner streets and orchards like walking skeletons. The strategy was that this would once and for all deplete the food supply in Van.

Raffi's right arm had been grazed deeply by a bullet. The bleeding had not affected his shooting, but he was nevertheless finally sent to have it checked for infection. Raffi looked at his area commander and did what he had never done before. He asked for a few hours' leave. Alarmed, the commander examined his face.

"Why? Is there something else you are not telling me?" It was dark and hard to see, but his words were harsh. Their situation was desperate and he could not afford the loss of a trained man.

"Nothing. It is the truth. I shall return in three hours if you will permit it."

"Go! But see that your arm is taken care of."

Raffi would have run, but it caused the blood to flow once more, and he was lightheaded. That was more from lack of food than the gash in his arm.

At the American mission, he again handed his weapons to an orderly, and when his wound was noticed, he was directed to a nurse. She seated him away from their more serious patients and began to examine his arm, assuming that there could be no other reason for his presence. He did not object but turned his head right and left, searching.

"Did you want something?" the American asked.

Raffi did not understand her words, but he understood the query in her eyes. Time was running out.

"Noushig," he attempted.

The woman paused. She again took in his smoke-blackened face and hands, at his grizzly face and lastly, his anxious, falling eyes.

"I shall call her. She is here, I think." Her palms opened at him and she motioned he should stay where he was.

His smile was rewarding, indeed, the nurse thought as she walked away.

A word or two to a passing woman and she came to complete the work the first nurse had started. His wound was cleaned and bound tightly.

"Wait here. She will come. She is not far."

Raffi closed his eyes to the sound of her reassuring voice. The ringing in his ears intensified.

He liked to think of Noushig here. The foreigners were neutral and they were somewhat protected, were they not? They already held themselves apart, in their confidence, in their tranquility. Or perhaps it was their faith ...

He turned as steps hurried closer.

"Are you hurt?" Her face was anxious.

"No. Just... It is nothing. I wanted to see you."

A white apron covered her dress. Her hair was hidden under a cap.

"You need water. You are so pale." She helped him stand.

They entered a room. There was a high table for eating on and chairs of wood arranged all around it. A pitcher of water and many cups glistened with cleanliness. As he drank deeply from one, she lifted a napkin and pulled out a boiled egg from beneath it. She peeled it and handed him this precious bit of food. Raffi's brows lifted in surprise. Her laugh was low and short, but her worried eyes lingered on his and filled with tears at once.

He had made his decision days ago. "If we live through this, Noushig, we shall be married. I shall take you home, to my family, in Sassoun."

She nodded and her tears trailed her cheeks.

"It is not like Van. It is small. We do not have schools and buildings and, and foreigners..." His voice was apologetic and she did not want that. She did not care about the size of his village and she shook her head to silence him and tell him what she did care about.

He kissed her and held her to him for long minutes. Eventually they moved apart, streaks and smudges of black and gray on her face and her apron. He tried to clean them and the stains darkened further from his coal-colored fists.

"Please. Please come back, Raffi," she pleaded.

THE TURKS OPENED fire and the American mission's cemetery was struck as well as the church and the boys' home.

Away from the business center of the city, Raffi was positioned inside an old home bombarded by cannons. As the house crumbled, they were all left without cover. It was nothing they had not experienced and they simply continued firing upon the Turks, using the rocks as cover. The Turks advanced alarmingly with their bayonets pointed. The defenders pulled forward to meet them, and some of the peasants threw rocks when there was nothing else.

Raffi had no grenades left. He would use his pistol and sword. Beside him, breathing heavily, blood in his eyes, a boy of nearly sixteen years clutched a rifle backwards. He would use the butt as his weapon.

Raffi began to sprint toward a heap of rubble. He could pick off numerous advancers there. The boy he left behind him screamed. Raffi skidded and whirled. A bayonet had pierced the boy's chest. Raffi shot the Turk who had thrust it and watched him collapse beside the boy.

He had left his back exposed too long. He swung around again in time to see the rifle pointed in his direction, held by a wild-haired man. Raffi's arm lifted, light and sure, and fired first. But to his right, Raffi never saw the face of the Turk holding the sword that split his side.

His death was instantaneous, but his body was not recovered until well after dusk, when his countrymen walked the bloodied fields and collected their dead.

A barrel-chested well digger bent over Raffi's body. He recognized the young man at once and groaned out loud at the sight of his body, bloodied and still. Once, he could have lifted a man of Raffi's size with no effort at all, but he was weakened with hunger and tears and needed help. He carried Raffi's body off the field, never once suspecting that there was someone beloved to the young man, in Van, who would search for him in vain.

CHAPTER 42

*A*nno plunged her hands into the already tepid water and scrubbed at the last of Sossè's garments with not nearly the detail they deserved. No task was performed well anymore. Eyes and ears were to the hills around and the slopes below them. When would their turn come? How would it end?

She wrung out a tiny dress, a blanket, sleeping clothes, and undergarments and left them twisted and rolled in a dripping pile. She carried the wash water downstairs and emptied it onto the middle of a lone mound of snow that refused to melt, just outside the door. Spidery rivulets of water sketched and ran over newly formed ridges.

Her wet hands stung with the cold and she pushed the door closed with her hip, having to execute two good thrusts to crush the wind's obstinacy. Spring had arrived and their protective blankets of snow were gone.

Sossè squirmed in her cradle, testing throaty sounds and focusing on her own thickly clad legs pointed at the ceiling and swinging before her own eyes.

Anno's fingers, bright red and wooden-like from the cold, reached for the silver bracelet she had placed on the edge of the bench. It was a bangle, shaped from one smooth strip of silver, an inch wide at its center, tapering off only slightly in the back where it clasped shut. The jeweler had crafted two openings to slip the hook into, accommodating the size of the wearer's wrist. Anno used the further opening.

The bracelet had been a gift from Daron, given to her after Sossè's birth. Trailing flowers and leaves were engraved over its surface, with twin roses in a circle at its center.

She removed it from her arm grudgingly and would not wait for her fingers to regain their limberness to refasten it.

They had been forced to leave their tiny bedroom in late November. The heat of the toneer had not reached them there. They had clung to their haven, to each other, until one moonless night, when icy sheets of air came at them through their window. The coldest part of the night was still hours away and the heated stones warmed only inches of their body for brief minutes. Anno turned to Daron in defeat. They could not face the rest of the night with wool blankets that seemed to have opened holes to receive and absorb all of winter in their fibers.

Daron had dragged their bedding to the front room and seen rolls of bodies covered to their heads near the fire. Aunt Naomi's frizzled head had poked out at them in relief. Nightly, she and Nevart had worried at how long they would cling to their privacy and risk illness, with Anno greatly pregnant as well.

Naomi called out sharply and a generous space near the toneer was created for Anno near Nairi. Daron settled a way off, near Kevork.

"Daron," she had told him after Sossè's birth, "I want only to see spring again so that we may return to our own room. The three of us."

"Anno," he had started slowly, almost reluctantly. "Do not be surprised if you find Kevork and Takoush there in that room instead of us, sometime soon."

He had shrugged and left her gaping. She did not know how to react, torn between the joy of her and Takoush living in the same household and the sting of having to surrender her haven to the next newlyweds so soon.

"Do not worry," Daron had encouraged her. "There are other rooms."

"Yes," Anno brightened, "and we shall give one of those to Kevork and Takoush, then." She had decided instantly and Daron laughed at her possessiveness.

Sossè's garments were strung across the room and Anno rubbed her hands to warm them. New, hungry cries came from the cradle and Anno's breasts stung and flowed in response.

Her nearly flat chest of a year ago had rounded impressively with her pregnancy and remained that way, consistently engorged with milk. Nevart had bitten back boastful words many times to neighbors, wanting to let them know that their hars, so diminutive when full-bodied, plump girls were coveted, had not only produced a baby nine months after marriage, but had enough milk for two! But she feared the evil eye, and she had bitten back the words, though it was regretfully hard.

Talk of Takoush's marriage had ceased since then. There was only preparation. And a furtive scanning of horizons.

Sossè's head was cradled in the crook of Anno's left arm. Her brows lifted and closed in satisfaction as she drew in long swallows of milk. Anno pushed against her other breast with her arm to try to staunch the even flow. As her milk soaked through her blouse to her sleeve, Naomi brought a cloth folded many times over and wordlessly pushed it inside Anno's open blouse to prevent the milk from dripping further. Anno smiled her thanks.

Her daughter's eyes, darkened to slate now, had opened at the disturbance, but dropped closed again as her belly quickly filled and the possibility of sleep overcame her. Her dark hair, fine and straight at the top of her head, rolled outward in the beginning of a voluminous curl above the tips of her ears. Her eyebrows already were well defined and would be thick and lovely one day.

One day.

Mgro had procured three rifles. One was a single-shot Mosin. The other two were refurbished Russian Mausers. One had a bayonet attached. The farm tools were kept close to the door now when not in use. They were never left as far away as the stable. Most of the villagers had no guns at all. Anno was certain her father would have something; Raffi would have ensured that. But what about cartridges?

Easter had come and been all but ignored. The day after, however, the cemeteries had been full as always. Prayers were made, but it was hard to say whether they were made for the dead or the living.

Vartan learned that the government had left it to the Kurds' discretion to attack when they believed the time to be right. He accompanied a handful of other village leaders to meet with Kurdish clans known to be friendly with the Armenians in the past. The Kurds told them they could offer the Christians no help, and they were turned away.

Anno shifted Sossè to her right breast now. Her daughter's eyes, large and unblinking, locked with her own and Anno marveled at their silvery, shifting depths. Yeraz had said that eyes this shade would not hold. So unique a shade was only a gift of birth and would surely deepen with the days. To Anno they resembled the reflection of a cloudy sky on a water's surface.

A clatter of metal and wood sounded downstairs. Feet pounded the earthen stairs and Anno knew already, from the gait and the weight of the ascent, that it was Kevork. His head appeared and Nevart turned to him.

"We have finished for the day," he confirmed and disappeared again. The evening meal was laid out.

He and Daron would be standing guard tonight along the eastern length of the village. There would be another hasty evening meal and a long evening of short conversations. There would be nothing to keep them from hearing, from being forewarned.

CHAPTER 43

May came and brought a spring so brilliant, so forceful in its arrival, that its detail could not be ignored, and Daron and Anno, together with Sossè, returned to their tiny room.

There were the blossoms in the orchard, some still folded and tightly anchored in promise to leafy green branches, soil that now yielded to the plow and hoe and turned richly red. It brought the return of the starling, the dove, the crane, and the stork, all greedily padding and tufting their nests, from the very roofs of houses to the widened banks of the rivers.

A male nightingale sang below Anno and Daron's window now, nestled in the brush. Anno lay with her back tightly pressed into Daron's chest. His arm gathered her to him as he slept, and she lay wide-eyed, her gaze on the airy patches of dust illuminated in the dazzling morning rays. No sound came from Sossè's cradle and Anno scarcely breathed.

We are those particles of dust, she thought. *We inch our way forward, as if permitted, or unseen, and then we are blown away, unexpectedly, and left floating again.*

Daron began to move. He had stood guard again until past midnight and was now allowed these extra hours of sleep past daybreak. His body, unaccustomed to sleeping with the sun, would rise soon, she knew.

"Anno?" His breath was on her skin.

She hugged his arm tightly to her in response.

"Anno, your poppies have bloomed again. Did you see?"

He spoke into her hair and she smiled, his words muffled and low. He would not speak of what else he knew, what was discussed during those cold night hours seated on the hard ground, the men clutching their outdated, outnumbered shotguns and farm tools. Her finger ran over the etchings of her bracelet.

"Yes, I saw them," she whispered back, "but there were a very few."

"No. No. I meant on the far side of the orchard, they have bloomed well." His lips moved over her shoulder. "Today, let us take Sossè there. Wrap some bread and cheese for us. We can sit in the grass and let the sun warm our backs a bit."

He had grown almost gaunt this winter. While food was plied on Anno at every turn, Daron's very jaw and cheekbones had gained new prominence. His heavy-lidded gaze was framed in shadows now, and amid all this, he could speak of poppies and outings and dare to plan even a single hour. Then, she decided, so must she.

"Anno, wake that child."

Her milk had soaked through her bindings and onto his bare arm. He rose on one elbow to peer into Sossè's cradle, hoping for movement.

"No." She pulled him back to her. "Not yet."

The day being Sunday, Anno trailed back from the church square with the other women, wishing to hurry but not daring. Her late rising this morning had been her allotment for shirking her duties and she now maintained a dutiful proximity to her husband's family.

They had emerged from their room that morning making a great fuss about the extra washing Anno must tend to, with Daron carrying her wet bindings and sleeping clothes. Anno held a satiated, bubbly Sossè, whose eyes shone and feet kicked at the sight of her grandmother.

All surely knew the true cause of their delay, and none begrudged them their love. On the contrary, Naomi turned anxious eyes on Kevork at that moment. He sat with his eyes downturned and she wished, again, that her son might soon, God willing, know the joys and holiness of marriage.

Once home, Anno helped with the setting of the noon meal. Kevork and Daron had gone to check the sheep, which, although well tended, were grazed in fields much closer to the village than was normal for the far-flung bounties of early spring. They did not want their flocks, their greatest source of livelihood, so far from sight and protection.

A dense broth of well-seasoned bony lamb meat was served. Piles of newly gathered herbs were laid ready to be wrapped in doughy, disc-shaped bread. This particular meal was a favorite of Daron's, and when he returned to seat himself at the table, Anno watched to see how well he would eat. She watched all the men reach for only meager servings, their pleasure in a warm, filling plate of food having waned long ago. The broth found its way past the crevices of steaming bone and meat to chase itself around half-empty bowls. The rich juices settled and were never soaked with the men's usual appetite into tearings of crusty bread.

The women's portions were no different, but still, the food was not wasted. Their villages had been laid to waste times enough that hunger was real to them. Whatever was not eaten would be gathered together and served again as their evening meal.

It was not long for the cleaning to be done and for Anno to mix the yogurt and water and pour it into a bottle. She wrapped the cheese and lavash and dropped them all into a sack, ready for their outing.

Nevart watched Anno closely. Disapproving of the sack's simple contents, she reopened it to add pickled turnips and a round of gata. She pulled Sossè's cap down lower about her ears. She was glad of their decision but bit back words of warning. They were no less aware of the dangers than she. They must claim whatever happiness they could.

The bright green hills were dotted with livestock and the sky was speckled with birds. The breathtaking field of wildflowers they came upon made Anno stop for a moment just to breathe. The extraordinarily long winter was truly over, and their very earth did not care to alter its cycle of millennia by mirroring its people's worries and fears. It would burst forth and bloom when it was its time.

Not wishing to crush even a single flower, they spread their old carpet on the very edge of the grassland and marveled at the contrasts of red poppy dotted with grape hyacinth. They did not speak at first, but only breathed in the silence, the sweet scent of grass and soil. The breeze that came their way, they vowed, was created solely by the wings of thousands of fluttering bees to which the field seemed to belong. Even Sossè stilled in Anno's lap at the enormity of the space before her and the colors of a world she had never before seen.

Anno turned her head so that Daron would not see her tears. They flowed painfully for the beauty of their land and for the nomads the devil had sent to drive them out.

"Anno," Daron said, squeezing her hand, "do not cry for something that might never happen."

She did not answer, but instead laid out a clean cloth over the carpet and laid Sossè on her back so that she might enjoy the vastness of the sky. She shook the bottle of tahn so that the yogurt and water formed a frothy surface and passed it to Daron to drink.

They had chosen their spot well so that as the sun moved further west, its rays would filter over them through the leaves of a solitary hazel tree.

Sossè's eyes tired and closed and Anno moved closer to Daron. She wished he would sleep a bit as well, but he did not remove his gaze from the hills. Their fate was left to the discretion of untrained, unattached Kurdish Beys and clans, and attack on them could come at a whim.

She would use this opportunity instead to feed him if he would not rest. She reached inside the sack.

"Anno," Daron began, "do you ever think of places like America?"
She halted, incredulous.

"I mean, to go there and live," he continued.

She could only stare.

"Others do go, you know. From other villages, they do leave and go."

"I…" she faltered, "We do not know anyone who has done *that*."

"No, not from here. But I believe my mother has a relative who lives in a place called Nev York. That is in America."

Anno wanted to speak, to ask, did the women go too, or just the men? Was it for always or just to work and send money back? But she found all she could add was, "I would like, someday, to see Van."

Daron smiled. "The watermelons?"

"Yes." They were said to grow as long as your arm, and a donkey could carry no more than two at a time, one hanging off each side of its back.

Daron had never been to Van either, but for him it was still not far enough.

"Anno, I am thinking of Sossè and of other daughters we might have. When they grow, they too will have to cover their heads and faces and arms and live in deference to someone else's fears and beliefs. I do not think Van is far enough."

She said, stricken, "This is my land, Daron. Yours, mine, and our daughter's. They will not drive me out."

Daron nodded tiredly. "I want you to know my thoughts, Anno. That is all. You do want to hear them, do you not?"

"Yes." Her voice was shaken. "Of course."

"And I want to know your thoughts and so you have said. This is our land and they will not drive us out. Nor Sossè."

"Nor Sossè," Anno repeated, her eyes dark.

Sossè slumbered beneath the rustle of the heavy leaves. Anno tried to imagine a large body of water and a ship. A ship that would carry them all to some different type of place... She stopped. She could not even conjure an image of the ship itself.

"How long have you thought things like this?" she asked.

"Only lately. When we married and you put on this," he tugged at her veil. The band across her forehead had shapes of leaves using threads of gold and brown and green, and the long plain veil covered her hair entirely. "More often after Sossè was born."

Daron turned, away from Anno, and then jumped to his feet. Surprised, she followed his gaze and saw Kevork running toward them. They had not been gone even one hour. Daron ran to meet him and Anno's body braced for the news he would bring.

Kevork's face was colorless in spite of his fast sprint in search of them. He halted feet away from Daron, his arms heavy at his sides, barely breathing hard from his exertion. His eyes, leaden with regret, held firm with Daron's. "It has started," Kevork told them, "in Aghpig." That was a village not forty miles north of Salor. "Fifty Kurds and two Turkish gendarmes have captured an entire herd of sheep and four shepherds. Two messengers brought the news. Two of our people went to notify the villages to the south of us. There were two boys there, with the herd, that the Kurds did not see."

They hastened back to Anno, still talking. "Those boys went back and told the villagers. Whoever was armed went after the Kurds."

Daron's eyes lit with hope.

Kevork shook his head. "All was lost."

Anno had risen to her knees. Her legs quivered beneath her as she refilled the sack with their few items. She saw Daron's and Kevork's strained gestures. When they reached her, all that was left to gather was Sossè and the carpet she lay on.

They hurried home as quickly as they dared without jarring their baby, who, still asleep, was clasped firmly against Kevork's chest. Daron had tossed all else on his back and gripped Anno's hand, harder than he knew, as they hurried over the irregular course home.

CHAPTER 44

*M*gro spoke of the joining of villagers in Kermav and Vartan listened.

"They were able to steal the entire herd in Aghpig and were greatly encouraged by it, of course."

It was dusk and another day had passed uneventfully in Salor. But their knowledge of the massacres taking place in all the Armenian vilayets, and now in Sassoun, closed in on their minds and their movements.

Vartan and Mgro's friendship, a near lifetime late in forging, pleased and consoled them both. Vartan understood now why he had never been approached by Mgro, in all these years, for neither advice nor mediation. His stomach still twisted uncomfortably at how he had so completely misjudged the man.

Vartan's voice, a deep baritone, came to him clearly. He spoke, as always, not one more word than necessary, restrained and weighed. "Kop and Iritsank were not able to fight off their attacks. They joined forces in Kermav, but it was not until Semal sent fifty armed men as well that the Kurds retreated." He shook his head. It took the joint forces of five to six Armenian villages and hamlets, with their rusted remnants of weapons, toted by farmers and their sons, to beat back one Kurdish attack. "The villagers have not returned to their homes in spite of the Kurds' defeat. They have all remained in Semal," he added.

"The livestock? The crops?" Mgro's thick brows were perpetually furrowed these days.

They walked home now from their own fields. How could they be left neglected at this crucial time of year, for even a day? Did those villagers not expect to ever return?

"The men go back and forth and tend to everything alone. The livestock have been moved to other villages for safekeeping."

Their strides matched, stalwart and deliberate, marking the ground beneath them. The attacks were to the north of them, but only two days' walk.

Mgro waited for Vartan to speak of something else, and then did so himself, uneasily. "We should hear from Raffi soon, and Aram, whatever their news."

Vartan did not answer. All knew their absence had stretched too long.

As they approached Mgro's house, Vartan kept to the lane and raised an arm to wave his friend away, but Mgro did not continue home. "Our granddaughter has decided it is time to sit without aid. Come and see," he invited.

Vartan hesitated. The only place he went after a day in the fields was to his own hearth. But he reflected at how long it had been since he had seen Sossè or Anno. He would like nothing more now.

Mgro clapped an arm across Vartan's back and they walked through the garden. The doors were closed to his little store of goods for sale. No one had come to browse or purchase anything for almost a year now. They looked up to see Old Mariam clambering down the narrow staircase from the living quarters.

The men almost smiled in pleasure at the sight of her, but she did not lift her eyes to them. She only paused long enough on the bottom step to pat Mgro's arm and cup Vartan's face in a confused greeting.

Disappointed, they watched her back, more deeply bent than ever, as she teetered toward the lane.

Unable to listen to her sons' murmured whisperings and worries any longer, Mariam had thought how long it had been since Naomi had fussed at her to interpret her latest dream. Mariam had never let it be known how impressed she always was at their accuracy. She had decided that moment to visit Nevart and see what would pop out of Naomi's mouth.

There had only been one dream, Naomi told her, recurring in angles and pieces. "I see nothing but cutting and slashing and blood, Sister Mariam." She related it with ice in her voice and Mariam stopped now to lean against the base of a tree. Her legs would not hold her.

The next morning, Anno splashed her face with the cold basin water to wake herself. Behind her, she heard Daron's deep inhale as he accepted the morning's arrival and his soft rustlings as he parted the covers.

She gave him a moment to rub his eyes. Still facing the wall, but before a sound came from her mouth, he spoke. "Tell Takoush that today Kevork will be in the tobacco fields."

Her heart warmed at his thoughtfulness. A meeting could at least be arranged, if not a marriage, and together, the four of them arranged two or three a week.

CHAPTER 45

*U*ncle Hagop hurried from the church square. He no longer looked to Maratuk for his predictions. He felt powerless now to foretell even one day.

The news received in the square was never good, but today's talk was especially unnerving.

"It seems that the Kurds are aggravated that we have resisted them at all," Uncle Hagop nearly thundered at Vartan and Haig sitting in the courtyard. "Zengin Pasha in Moush had told them that their plunder of us would be simple and fruitful."

"What of it?" Vartan squinted at him.

"Well, now the Turkish gendarmes from Moush have been put on alert in case they are needed for the next attack. They mean to surround Sassoun and finish us."

"Shenig, its location...it does not look good for that village." Haig shook his head.

The Kurds did choose Shenig next.

"Your prediction was correct, Haig," Vartan told him days later. "The Kurds approached the outer ridges of Shenig's grazing land and the shepherds there. Two herds were easily rounded up and driven back toward the Kurds' camp."

Haig waited, sensing there was more.

"Not long after, nowhere near their own camp yet, the Shenig villagers stood ready to surround the Kurds and retrieve their livestock."

"And?" Haig's apprehension grew.

"And they did. And now the Kurdish clans are more roiled than they ever were."

YERAZ PUT A hand on Vartan's arm as he and Vrej prepared to perch on the northernmost elevation of Salor for the night. "How will this end?" she implored.

He covered her hand with his own. "It is only beginning."

In June the Kurds attacked the very village center of Aghpig. They were met with a furious retaliation from the men there, and with them came aid from neighboring Geligouzan. Sassountzis living in villages in the lowlands began moving to higher ground.

In Salor, the men agreed they would remain here, in their homes. The villages to the east of them had decided the same. If attack should come, those armed would rush to each other's aid.

ANNO DID NOT want to hear. She kept her eyes shut. If she did not wake, then these voices would be just another dream. But the voices came to her, not shrill and unhinged as in her dreams, but weighted and drawn out.

She gasped and sat up straight. Daron was not here with her. He was standing sentinel again tonight. Something had happened to Daron.

She burst from the tiny room in her bedclothes, with only her hair blanketing her shoulders. Her sight blurred in her body's race from sleep to agony, but once in the candlelit room, she spotted Daron and rushed to him at once.

He did not look at her. His attention, and everyone's, was turned to Mgro.

Heghin, to the west, was under attack. Salor's sentinels had brought the news. Help must be sent at once.

"*I* will go," Mgro ground out, his gun leaning close behind him against the wall. He was packing cartridges tightly into his pockets and into a sack.

Anno's eyes whipped wildly around the room as she realized what decisions were being made.

Manuel, Kevork's father, wrapped already in coat and hat, Mosin in hand, was clearly to go as well. That left one weapon available, for one more man.

Anno's head moved and tilted in inches to her left to take in Daron, who had stepped forward, toward his father. She recoiled at the fury in his face, fury directed at Mgro.

He wants to go, Anno realized. *He has forgotten me.*

She stepped away. Her body gone cold and her teeth chattering, she listened as Mgro turned to them all and announced that only he and his brother would go. The one remaining weapon would stay here, with them, to use if necessary.

His voice dropped only slightly at this last. Then he went forward and kissed Nevart's hands and then his father's before turning his back on them all. Manuel did the same, with one light stroke of Naomi's cheek as she swallowed back her tears.

After that, their days were no longer lived but witnessed as through a veil.

Anno waited for daybreak, to lay the table for the remaining members of the household, and then collected the dishes again. She tied a large cloth across her chest and tucked Sossè inside. She did not ask for permission and did not say when she would return. She trudged up the deserted lanes to her father's home. She must see who was left to her there.

Anno pushed at the door and stood in its shadow. Inside, she saw no early-morning bustle, the race to complete all their chores and to prepare their stores of food and grain. The toneer stood empty and cold.

Yeraz turned, her empty arms slackened at the sight of Anno. They studied each other, eyes desperate, with no words to offer, no hope in their hearts.

ANNO RAILED AT Daron. It was the darkest night. He held her tightly in her fury and rasped, "Did you want me to wait to fight them at our own doorstep, Anno?"

She did not listen, but wrested and wrenched at him, accusing him of leaving and forgetting her, until she fell asleep, spent and broken, against his tear-soaked chest.

Vartan had not allowed Vrej to go either. Yeraz at least still had one son. It seemed the men had planned to do it this way from the first. They would spare the youth.

"I leave their care to you," Vartan told Uncle Hagop before he walked away. The old man's head dropped onto his hands.

Five more villages were attacked, again to the west. The wounded men of Salor returned.

A man limped in, a long stick bearing the weight of his right leg. His face was heavily bearded and he watched the ground, concentrating on each agonizing step. He progressed for several minutes and many watched from their doors as he passed. Then a squeal of shock burst from a doorway and Takoush rushed at him. "Baba! Baba!" She raced to his side and turned in surprise to see her mother running alongside her, arms outstretched.

Unkempt and half starved, they straggled in. Haig, head bandaged, dragged a makeshift litter upon which a twisted body lay. Old Mariam could not run, but wiped at her tears and bobbed her head as his wife caught him tightly around the waist. She then gently pried his hands off the litter and heartily pulled it in his stead. She glanced back once to see who lay on the litter, but did not know the man.

News of anyone's return raced from house to house. Soon everyone was plying the men with questions of their own family members.

Any bit of information was precious.

"Heghin village...all seventy-five households are left with just a handful of survivors." Mihran wept and tossed his head as he related what he knew.

Each day more villages were attacked. And at last, one night a great banging came at Mgro's door and a boy yelled up to Sister Nevart that her son had returned.

"Her son," the boy had said. Huddled around their unlit toneer, the women stared into their needlework, into their spindles. Kevork and Daron were standing sentinel, so Mgro's father led them down the staircase to the courtyard to wait for him to be brought in. All held their breath. Naomi grasped the boy by the shoulder. "Just one?" she implored. The boy's eyes grew wide and he nodded.

Figures drew closer and closer in the dark. Anno recognized Daron from a distance supporting a dropping figure, with Kevork on the other side. She did not rush forward with the others. She clung to Nairi beneath a tree and waited. Cries reached them. It was Nevart, Anno thought, doubled over. Kevork made an effort to go to her but could not. Her husband stopped her from collapsing to the ground. Someone, a neighbor, steadied her and turned her toward home.

Anno's eyes strained to see who it was who had survived. But she knew. Naomi clung to Manuel as closely as she could, as if she would lift him into her own arms.

Nairi and Anno pressed closer. The child knew too.

And now, Anno accepted, the next time help was needed, Daron would go in Mgro's place.

It did not take long for the front room to fill. No sooner had Manuel been laid on a mattress than people swept in. They aided with the lifting and the assessment of his leg, which, with one ball deeply embedded in his thigh, was swollen and infected.

A few families remained with men who had not returned or who had not been accounted for. Manuel shook his head at them all, unable to help, except for Yeraz.

She entered on the heels of Old Mariam and Anno's eyes followed her. She did not ask details, just as she did not ask yet of Mgro's death. They sought to make Manuel comfortable first. The details they would mill over for the rest of their lives.

The filth of gunpowder and dirt and blood were washed from him as well as possible and he gulped tea made from boiled herbs. Then he waved all to silence. There was a will in his eyes and he needed to speak.

"This is not as we have known it to be. The Kurds steal from us, we turn a blind eye. The Kurds steal from us, we call a clan member to mediate. They kidnap one of our girls, and she is lost, or we pay for her return." He shook his head once, "No. By the time we neared Heghin we could see the smoke coming from the rooftops. We hid and waited for nightfall. Then we entered, once we were certain no Kurds had stayed behind. There was no one left." He shook his head. "Entire families were slain and their blood was painted on the walls and soaked into the very soil. The houses were emptied of the best wares and bodies lay one on top of another, unburied."

He turned to Yeraz.

"Mgro, Vartan, and I did not return to Salor then. This, we knew, was what they intend to do everywhere. Their joy at our extinction is absolute. The Turks are waiting to offer them assistance, but for now, do not need to.

"The Kurds had moved on to other villages and we decided, with our guns in hand and pockets full of cartridges, we would not return home to wait for our turn. We traveled south and fought there, however we could, however anyone could. When the bullets finished, as did Vartan's and Mgro's, our own deaths came."

He allowed himself to weep, as did they all, and the last was more difficult to tell and more difficult to hear as his voice choked and he could no more control it.

"They carried off so, so many of the girls. We three hid in the mountain range and waited for them. We sat at three separate points"—he outlined their triangle in the air with one bent finger. "When the Kurds were inside that triangle, we shot at them. We were mostly successful. They could not see us. But then"—he held out empty palms—"we had no more bullets."

There was no sound in the room. Daron's grandfather sat nodding his old head when Manuel spoke and when he did not. "Mgro's and Vartan's deaths were good ones. They were not found and hatcheted. They were not tied together like animals to have their throats cut.

"Vartan still breathed when I dragged myself to him. He asked me, 'Did the girls escape?'"

Manuel wiped at his nose and eyes openly. He pushed away the cup of tea Naomi offered. "Yes, yes, I told him. But it was a lie. Those girls were not able to escape this time, and neither would we."

But Vartan had smiled at that, a victorious smile that Manuel would keep with him always.

He patted Yeraz's hands as she clenched them trembling before her. "They lay together. Do not worry. I saw to that."

Manuel's screams reached the streets below as Old Mariam and Yeraz labored to locate and remove the bit of iron that was killing him.

Sossè shuddered in fear at the sounds and Anno left the house with her daughter and Nairi. Sensing that the extraction would take longer than they hoped, they went to Takoush's house, not too far up the road.

Anno had expected the lukewarm welcome she had always received from Takoush's mother, but instead the woman's stout arms pulled the unsteady group near the fire. She pulled out blankets and bedding. Anno only remembered being awakened the next morning by Daron, who stood over them, gray-faced. He had come hours before, Anno learned, but Mihran had not allowed him to pull them away from the warmth of the room.

Daron and Anno followed each other's whereabouts at all times of the day and night now. Anno knew which field Daron would work each morning and then the afternoon as well. And all knew that Anno would be with Yeraz for a part of each day, as would Lucine. Yeraz had only Vrej now.

As for Raffi, Yeraz had accepted that she was one of the many broken mothers who would live a lifetime saying that her son went and was never heard from again. Vartan, at least, lay in peace somewhere in Sassoun.

CHAPTER 46

*A*nno beat the wool filling of their mattresses a very few times and straightened to take in the view of Salor from the rooftop. Even when she was a girl, this task had been one of her favorites.

Early summer, every year, the mattress stitching was undone and the wool fillings were laid out on sheets on the rooftop. After a long winter, the wool had curled and lumped together. It was washed and spread evenly under the sun to air and dry. Then it was beaten lightly to flatten and separate the fibers before refilling and stitching the mattresses closed, ready for another year.

Anno inhaled the smell of clean wool warmed by the sun and gazed at the church top, the misshapen roofs and gardens beyond. From her father's home she had been able to see the twist of the river and the tips of the orchard, and all was surrounded and bound together by the soft rolls of the gradually expanding hills around them. She had memorized the landmarks and dwellings as seen from her father's rooftop, and she was doing the same now, from her father-in-law's.

Remembering Vartan again, her body went limp as she wept. They were all left with such a constant emptiness, everywhere. Without their fathers, they seemed to push along aimlessly to the next task, and the next.

Daron spoke yesterday of how locusts had filled the air of Armenian vilayets farther away. In the same breath he continued that the Kurds, under intense Turkish commands, had organized and mobilized and were to surround the Sassountzi stronghold around the Antok Mountains.

Daron and Kevork now took direction from no one. Their work outdoors took longer, as did everyone's, with fewer men to help. When the wheat and grain ripened, she and Naomi had joined them in the fields.

"There are fewer men to work, fewer to lead, and fewer to defend when the time comes," Vrej grumbled. Anno had found herself bent at work next to her brother. All families worked collectively now, ever more so than before.

She felt the frustration, the fury in him. Their fathers all dead, the men woke and worked with the women and children and elderly.

"I say we join the defense line to the south of Antok," Vrej continued. "Let us fight them back there, because if they should ever reach here, we are finished." She looked some rows over to see that Daron was watching them and had heard. His expression was unreadable.

A movement on the lane below caught Anno's attention. She recognized Takoush's dark-blue apron. Anno called out to her, wiping her own face. Takoush shielded her eyes from the sun and followed Anno's voice, then scrambled to the rooftop from the narrow set of stairs outside.

Takoush's movements had slowed. To look at her, Anno was reminded of the hollow months she herself had passed when forbidden to see Daron.

Takoush surveyed Anno's work. Before, she would have chided her friend's half-heartedness and continued the task herself, all the while chattering and gesturing in the air. Now, she only seemed able to do one thing at a time.

"I will wait with you until they return," Takoush told her.

"All right," Anno agreed, "but why?"

"I heard something."

Anno watched her. If there was something that concerned Kevork, then it likely concerned Daron as well.

Takoush's hands, agitated, caught at her apron as the breeze lifted and ruffled it.

"What do you know?" Anno persisted.

"I think they will be leaving soon, to Antok."

Takoush hated watching Anno's eyes darken. She dropped the stick she was holding and Takoush moved to her side. Arms linked, they watched the paths below.

The beauty of their village was not lost to them, even then, as emptied as it was of their fathers and brothers. The sun was dropping well west and the contrasting blues and greens of the sky and hills matured and deepened. The birds swept and perched on rooftops and hollows they had claimed as their own. The oxen and donkey brayed and slapped their tales along the road home and children scampered as far as they dared, snatching minutes of games before their absence was discovered.

Anno recognized Daron's walk, straight-hipped and sure. He and Kevork carried farm tools on their shoulders and their shirts and shalvars hung dusty and dark with perspiration. Daron's cap was pushed back and Anno thought how long it had been since he had held a razor. It would be a full beard in just one more week, she reflected, as he neared. She would not mind.

Daron had seen Anno on the roof. She knew just when that moment had been. His chin had lifted and for a second, it had been a happy moment. Then he took in her stance.

The farm tools were dropped somewhere near the house. Takoush rushed down the stairs. She and Kevork would speak somewhere less visible. Anno was alone when Daron wearily dragged himself up the last steps to her.

She had thought to say so much, so much to remind him of Sossè and Nairi, of their extreme losses already, and of the Kurdish camp a riverbank away, but she did not. They folded into each other's arms and sank to the floor, staring into the bundles of wool.

"How will I rise each morning without you, Daron?" she whispered.

Her heart thumped in her throat.

"I will come back to you, Anno."

She moved in closer.

IT WAS TOO delicate a morsel for hands such as his, accustomed to gripping ploughs and oxen the day long, or his wife's wide, swinging hips. The pads of Haig's fingers bore into the creamy layers of halvah and sesame oil glistened on his cut and chipped fingers.

They marched over and around the stubborn, misshapen stones the earth yielded. They were all there, Daron, Kevork, Vrej, and nearly thirty others.

Mihran, his limp hardly noticeable, carried a strangely curved blade sheathed at his side. Its only use had been, until today, to harvest honeycomb.

"Keep that halvah for later, for while you fight," someone called out to Haig.

"It will keep best in my belly," he retorted and tipped his head back to pop the entire chunk into his mouth.

Their laugh mingled with the wind and lifted to the tips of the firs and cedars of their mountains.

CHAPTER 47

The days grew intensely hot once Daron left, once they all left. It seemed to Anno that they were all gone, but it was not so. Their own village would not be left completely unprotected. Avo had remained behind. He and his family would help harvest Vartan's crops and fields along with their own.

Yeraz had stared at her remaining son with stricken eyes when Vrej told her that he too, would go.

"I have carried this name...this name, *revenge,* all my life for a reason, have I not, my mother?" he asked. "I can at least fill my brother's place."

Yeraz's head fell. "My son. We had not named you so in hope that one day you would go to fight the Turk! We named you in hope that you would *live* and *love* and build a large family of your own, right here on your own land, in *spite* of them."

How wrong she had been thinking that God intended to spare her children.

The sun beat down on them like a single ball of fury. It forced everything to ripen at once and Anno and the women left their homes to harvest the grain and pluck fruit from the branches. But, most dangerously, it forced the shepherds to move their flocks to higher ground looking for land less parched.

At night, Nairi slept beside Anno, taking Daron's place. Anno pulled Sossè's cradle close to her other side, and feeling some reassurance at both their closeness, slept.

Uncle Manuel lay in the front room, no longer bargaining with death, but simply waiting his turn. He had buried two men and then dragged his wounded leg through two days of brush and mountainside. The infection was beyond any help Mariam or Yeraz could provide. He lay covered in a clean sheet, a fetidness seeping into every corner of the house.

Anno listened to Nairi breathe beside her and twisted her silver bangle on her forearm. Her neck and shoulders were strained and burned from bending and pulling crops all day and she lay flat on her back, waiting for the pain to ease.

Four days later, Uncle Manuel died.

Nevart and Naomi had no tears left, and in utter silence all watched as his body was lowered into its grave.

Calls came to them from the church square and Father Sarkis stopped his prayers. Women and children had been seen climbing their way toward Salor, fifty, sixty in all. The priest rushed through the last of the ceremony and Mgro's family followed him to gather more information.

They were from the village of Danz and, like so many Sassountzis, were seeking higher ground. Their men had sent them, and they would stay until called home.

There was no han in Salor as there was in the larger villages for travelers to pass a night. Instead, with the priest's guidance, the newcomers unloaded their blankets and food and clothing to settle in the church, and when that was filled, they looked to other homes for shelter.

Yeraz took control of this organization at once. She was no longer the wife of the village leader, and some murmured as much to one another, but no one stepped forward to dare say she was not capable.

She let all know that if they did not have room indoors, then the nights were lovely and more than warm and the rooftops would do very satisfactorily.

Yeraz herself took an elderly man, his two daughters-in-law, and three grandchildren. She hoped he and Uncle Hagop would have much to discuss and decipher. She worried at the old man's loneliness and guilt at still being alive.

A week passed and the people of Danz joined them in the fields and on the threshing floor, making it clear from the first that they would work as hard as the families who sheltered them.

At midday, Anno drew away from the others in the fields to nurse Sossè under a shade tree. She would wean her soon, she remembered telling Daron. That had been one month ago.

Anno watched Takoush beat the wheat and wished she would come to her. She felt Takoush was avoiding her. Anno did not remove her eyes from her friend until at last Takoush looked her way. Her hesitation was brief, and then, head bent, she walked to Anno. She knelt at her side, but did not speak.

Anno turned warm eyes on her and searched her face.

"Anno, my cycle is late," Takoush whispered.

"It happens." Anno smoothed Sossè's hair. "It will come when it comes." Then her hand froze.

She felt Takoush's stare, close beside her, and her breath. Anno's head, suddenly heavy, turned.

"Ah, noooo." Sossè's head dropped as Anno's arms slackened, and Takoush reached across Anno to steady the baby with both hands.

Sossè coughed and spluttered, but still Anno could not respond. Takoush lifted the startled child to her shoulder and gently patted her back, soothing her with soft words.

Anno's eyes followed her. Takoush was calm, so calm.

Uncle Haig's wife reassured Anno that the men should be returning soon. At any time the sentries would let them know they were spotted and oho! There would be such a rush to feed those hollowed bellies.

"You will be separated from him at times, again, Anno girl, especially if he follows his father's work. A merchant is often away from home."

Anno had always liked Uncle Haig's wife. As a child she had watched, fascinated, as the large, boisterous woman spoke and then laughed out loud at her own words, almost as if everything she did was for her own entertainment. But now, Anno heard the falseness in her words, as they came from a woman who was letting the unfamiliarity of fear enter her.

"Yes." Anno hugged her, her arms barely able to enfold the woman's shoulders. "We shall hear some good news soon."

CHAPTER 48

Yeraz lay staring up at the black ceiling. She had intended to wrap herself in Vrej's blanket from now on, but the nights were almost as hot as the days and she only fingered it.

She used Vartan's pillow and Vrej's blanket and lay, a widow, alone in a corner. The tears always flowed at night and still she made less noise than those around her, who slept. The people from Danz had moved to the roof, but Uncle Hagop had not, and it was his snores she listened to most of the night.

They were rhythmic for the most part, with tapping sounds from his tongue as he shifted position. Then she heard something else. Such a low knock, then it stopped. Then, there, she heard it again, three low knocks.

Her heart seemed to stop. Could it be Vrej? Could it be he had returned, or, Holy God, *Raffi?* But why would her sons knock and then wait? Why not burst into their own home as they had always done?

Yeraz's skin tingled. It seemed only she heard this knock, as low as it was, and there, it came again. One, two, three.

She rose, ever so slowly, and wrapped Vrej's blanket around her shoulders and held it in place with clenched fists. She stared at the inside of the door. Then, with trembling hands, she opened the door a crack and peered out.

One man stood there. He looked at Yeraz and automatically averted his head, almost in shame. The furred vest and cap, even in this heat, made Yeraz think, and then she believed she knew who this man was.

"*Merhaba.*" She believed she had greeted him properly in Kurdish, Leaving the door open, still a crack, she rushed back into the room. She fumbled for her veil, and wiping at her eyes and face, adjusted it. It would not do. She flung it aside and covered her hair completely beneath a scarf. She then pulled the blanket more securely around her body and turned back toward the door. She looked foolish, she knew, and untidy, but all that mattered was that she discover why this Kurd had traveled through a moonless night to her door.

She stepped out into the night.

The man was confused to see her again. He asked for Vartan.

This, then, was Turgay's son. Almost two years ago he had stood over Anno and asked with pained eyes, "Have you everything you need for her care?" He could not have chosen a darker night.

Yeraz clenched her teeth to still her jaw. "My husband is dead." It was the first time she had spoken the words out loud and she had to piece them together in Kurdish.

Arsad was perplexed.

Yeraz explained that he had just died. He had not taken ill. He was trying to help protect another village. She did not finish with "It was one of your race who killed him."

He bowed his head very briefly, and then, as if he remembered why he had come, began to speak urgently.

"My tribe, I know, will continue to remain neutral while these killings of Christians continue. Our bey has traveled and seen much of the slaughter and"—he hesitated—"the violations of the women and the children that are taking place at the commands of the Turkish officials. He has said to all of us that even if Mohammed Himself were to condone this and call this just, he cannot."

Yeraz nodded imperceptibly.

"But you are Christians and we cannot help you."

Yeraz stared into his eyes and steeled herself for his next words, the reason behind his dangerous trek.

"Why do you continue your work in the fields from dawn to dusk? Your sheep graze, you gather your fruit for the next winter…" He shook his head furiously. "You must not think of next winter. You must think of *now*. *Tomorrow*. I warn you, Salor will not be spared. No village will."

Yeraz could not tear her eyes from his.

"It is more difficult to attack Salor, because of its isolation, yes, your people are right. But it is not impossible. I cannot tell you when, because I do not know, but we watch you…" He shook his head baffled. "You must *prepare*." His hands reached out to her, to the air between them, his fingers poised as if he alone could shake them into action.

"I do not know how safe the mountains are. I do not know where the attack will come from, because we do not participate in the talks and the planning." He shook his head helplessly. "I can only warn you it seems. May Xuda have mercy." His head bowed and Yeraz stared into the gnarled fur of his cap.

Abruptly, Arsad turned and left. She stared after him and then into the hardened twist of the grapevine that Vartan's mother had planted long ago against the garden wall as a warm welcome to all.

At dawn, Yeraz gripped the handle of the church doors with both hands and pulled them open. She crossed herself and made her way past the still-prone bodies to a back room. There, she knocked on the door, not nearly as cautiously as Arsad had.

She heard Father Sarkis call from inside.

"It is I, Yeraz Vartanian, Father. Forgive the early hour, but we must speak at once."

By mid-morning all the village knew of Yeraz's visitor, although his name was never revealed. No one cared to know. Messengers were sent to the neighboring villages and hamlets at once, telling them of the warning Salor had received. Living their days, using their seclusion and elevation as a reason to believe they would be spared, was no more. Pray God, their men and sons would return soon, but for now, the sentries would be doubled. Girls could see for a distance as well as boys. Escape routes into even higher mountain ranges were again reviewed.

The villagers of Danz gathered together and decided to return to their own homes. They had thought to seek safety, but Salor seemed no safer than where they had come from. They would return to their husbands and fathers. How foolish they had been, they murmured.

When warning came from the sentries, it was planned, all but the men would race from the village. Bread and cheese, root vegetables and dried yogurt were already wrapped and stored in the coolest corners of their dwellings. They would be gathered and without a glance back, the men ordered, the women and children would escape.

The men could not go to Talvorig for more swords, more cartridges. Talvorig itself was under attack.

Some spoke of not waiting, of hiding in the woods, in the caves, this minute. They would not wait for the attacks to come. Then they remembered the wolves and the bears and hesitated to leave without the comfort of numbers.

Leaving never occurred to Anno. Daron was coming back. She could feel it. She just did not know which day.

Still they carried on with their work. Standing idle would drive them mad, and they slept better at night when tired.

Anno wished she had weaned Sossè. Then she could have taken her turn standing sentry with the others. Takoush had already joined them. She said she would be the first to see Kevork's return that way. Still, her cycle had not come.

"Takoush, what will you do?" Anno hissed at her.

"It is simple, Anno. When Kevork returns, we will be married."

Anno glared at her. "Our brothers, so well trained, did not return, Takoush."

Something passed over Takoush's face at the truth of Anno's words, but then she lifted her chin. "If he does not return, then I shall drown myself."

Now Anno was dreaming. Takoush was screaming at her for taking her baby. Anno, uncomprehending, stared at her own stomach, swollen and aching. In her dream, she could not speak, could not tell Takoush that of course she had not, would not ever do that to her. The child inside her pressed down and twisted and Anno felt a terrible discomfort. Takoush's face pressed closer, screaming still.

Anno jerked awake. Her heart pounded and her neck was bent painfully.

She heard noises coming from the front room. Steps. Heavy booted steps. Nairi and Sossè slept deeply and did not hear. She swung her legs to the side of the mattress and stood. Daron was home! She had searched for him so foolishly during the day. Of course they would make their way through the night. She should cover herself. She heard more commotion than one man could make. He and Kevork had most probably returned together!

In the dark her tears began to fill her eyes with joy as she picked up something to cover her shoulders with. She lifted a head scarf in her fumblings. It was small, but she did not care. She wanted only to see him, to hold him!

She raced into the front room and stopped short. Daron's grandfather was lying still on the floor. Near him, Nevart lay limp against the wall.

It was like her dream again. Anno tried to scream, to speak, but could not. There were three, four, she did not know. Naomi struggled furiously with one and then Anno remembered Sossè behind her and the entire room blurred. Holy God, Sossè would be next, and with that realization she did scream. She screamed for help but saw that

Naomi lay with her mouth gaping open and there was just one Kurd now and he was before her.

She moved quickly. She led him away from her little room where Sossè lay. Her back sidled against the wall, toward the kitchen area. The utensils clanged together and crashed to the floor. What did not fall she threw at his face.

He stared at her through her thin nightdress.

Where were the other Kurds? Where had they gone? she thought frantically. Again she screamed, unable to control herself any longer. He moved closer. She picked up a ladle, she thought, and hit him repeatedly on the head, on his ears. He closed his fist and struck her against her jaw. Anno fell to the floor. There, she saw boots, many boots, and they were making their way to her bedroom, where Sossè lay. And Nairi. She crawled after the boots. She crawled to her bed and reached under her pillow. The boots did not stop, did not turn toward her. She did not know why. She could no longer hear. But with her tiny knife now in her hand she reared up and stabbed at the boot. Someone caught her hand. She squeezed her fingers around the knife's handle, not relinquishing its hold. Long nailed, determined fingers pried at hers. She stabbed at his hands, at the air, believing with her entire soul that she would save her daughter from death with just one blade.

He snapped her wrist and Anno's knife fell into his hand. He fumbled at first with its smooth, tiny handle but then leaned forward and with one wide sweep sliced Anno's throat.

CHAPTER 49

*U*ncle Hagop's voice bellowed, to Yeraz, to himself, and to the walls that stood between them and the pillage that had come to Salor.

Yeraz felt him fly around the room. He held their remaining pistol and rushed toward the door. Then he whirled and ran back toward the grain room.

Blood pounded in Yeraz's head as she gathered her prepared bundles. She could not see or grasp what was before her. She saw only visions of her daughters. And Kurds.

Uncle Hagop, clutching a pistol and a hoe, ran again for the door. He turned to Yeraz at the last moment. "Leave it, my daughter! Run from here," he choked, and was gone.

Yeraz bent to retrieve the bundles she had dropped and straightened to find herself looking into the bloodshot eyes of a man. She stood before him, motionless. The Kurd came toward her, a stocky man with dark curls, and quite young, she saw. Her stillness confused him, and her soft voice as well, as she spoke.

"You do this devil's work for those Turks. You may kill the very last one of us, but do not think you will benefit from it. You are a race of scavengers, and this land of ours...it will not yield for *you*. *You do not belong to it*. Remember me. Remember my curse."

DARON APPROACHED THE village. He and Vrej came alone. Mihran was somewhere behind and would likely hobble in a few hours after them. The rest would not come. Kevork would not come. They had died days ago.

They hurried, almost running at times. Rounding the last knoll, they raised their arms in greeting to the sentries. There were none.

Daron felt his breath strangle and his eyes sting as they ran past the benign fields and then the orchards to catch the first glimpse of the village dwellings. Like rag dolls, they fell to their knees. There was no movement, no sound. They knew.

Vrej rose first and staggered up the lane, past bodies strung together and shot, past women stripped and mutilated. He fell and stood again and stumbled the remaining distance home. He did not need to push open the door. It hung awkwardly, slanted and broken. Yeraz was by the kitchen, where he always found her, her glad, warm eyes covered with blood.

Vrej held her hands to his cheek and rocked with grief.

DARON HARDLY KNEW that he was half crawling past the vegetable garden, trampled and torn. He found himself at the foot of the mud staircase. His boots pounded on each step as he ached and strained to hear some sound from within. Reaching the top step, he slowly turned and looked inside. He gripped the hair on his head when he saw the bodies and a gurgling sound came from his throat. He stepped among them and struggled to recognize their faces through the blood.

Choking from grief and from the sights and smells, he stood on the edge of the toneer and spun around, wild-eyed. He was not mistaken. Anno's body was not here. He looked again. Anno, Sossè, Nairi! They were not here. He knew where he must look next.

Kitchen utensils lay scattered on the floor. Daron stepped over them and turned the corner into his and Anno's room.

Here he found them, hardly disturbed at all. Tiny Sossè's belly was stabbed but her face was untouched and her lids lay closed and smooth. Nairi's throat had been sliced. And Anno's.

Anno's beloved face was caked with blood. It ran from her ear and her mouth and her teeth were bared and feral. She had tried to protect what he could not. He fell to his knees and his hands came away from his head with tufts of his own hair as he gathered her to him. He threw back his head and, scarlet-throated, screamed her name.

LUCINE, TAKOUSH, AND the others watched each other between the flaps of the Kurds' tents whenever they could. They would not remain together. They would be sold off.

Takoush watched the filthy flaps fold and billow, fold and billow. "Kevork's son will live," it seemed to say.

EPILOGUE

California, USA 1976

"*You* look good."

"Shut up." Her back was to him, but he sat on the corner of their parents' bed and she could see him fully in the mirror's reflection. "Like, we should get into it. Today." She tried to sound serious but her mouth turned up anyway and they both laughed.

In their secret brother-sister language, "good" had always meant "gross." It had taken their mother a while to understand why a sweet, thoughtful compliment from one to the other often ended up with slaps or shoes flying.

He was leaning forward, lanky, pointed elbows digging into lanky, pointed knees. His black leather shoes, absurdly polished, pressed into the green shag carpet.

"No." His dark head shook and she looked again. "You look good."

His black eyes met her blue-gray ones and they smiled.

Armen looked past the pillow of white veil the hairdresser had anchored to his sister's head, past the layers of powders and shadows and the large pearl and gold cross suspended from her neck, to try to share a word of parting with her. He had been born one year and one month after his sister; only the spinning of time would make them admit how close and interdependent their existences had been.

Their cousin's voice came to them from another room. "Susie! Can we pull the shoulders down just a little more? They're gonna fall anyway when we walk into church. Look!"

Heels pulled along the carpet and she burst in, hands clasped together as if to hold a bouquet. As her shoulders came forward, the puffs of material slid unevenly.

Susie turned to her mother, Sona. Sona turned to her mother's sister, the oldest female present.

"That would leave bare shoulders. In *church*."

They did not need to say more and the older women's lips pursed and their minds raced to find a solution.

Susie's best friend was the only one of the bridesmaids who was not Armenian and so had no inkling of what a calamity this bare-shouldered-ness could be and did not care. While the others girls argued and tugged at their dresses, she hummed and checked the mirrors to see if her blond hair still flipped as evenly as it had five minutes ago. Meanwhile, all the bridesmaids' shoulders were lifted and shifted backwards and forwards in hopes of finding a pose that would hold the slippery muslin.

Armen had been the one who had changed his sister's name. He had had to do it. His own name was bad enough, but his sister's would never have worked.

They lived in two worlds in one small California suburb, and hand in hand, sometimes literally, they had navigated both. Now there was only one person who ever called her anything but Susie, and that was Grandpa Daron. He only called her Sossè.

Susie looked at all the bared shoulders and remembered how long it had taken her mother to allow her to wear a halter top when she was dating Johnny. They had compromised. She had taken along a sweater.

Susie had given in quickly that day, before her mother had said "the words."

"Don't forget who you are. We are Armenian." Their list of rules was different than most, and longer.

The fact that Johnny was also Armenian—because what else would he be if she were allowed to date him?—didn't matter. You could never be reminded enough.

At first Susie and Armen thought that the older folks were just not getting it, but then as they grew, they realized rage forced those words out. "They killed us. They drove us out. But we do not forget."

Outdoors, at school, at the library or the stores, they dressed and talked like everyone else. As kids, they played in the streets with the other neighborhood children, Ditch It and Red Rover, sometimes into the night on those long, sticky summer days. They loved the after-school playground activities and they begged their mother to make sandwiches for them with peanut butter and cream-filled cupcakes for dessert.

But it was so hard meeting someone for the first time. Adults weren't any easier than the kids, but the kids mattered more. They gave their names, and sometimes their strange, unpronounceable last names. And then waited for the inevitable.

"But what kind of name is *that?*"

As if the answer was going to clear things up. As if the other kids would understand what they were told and all could get on with sizing each other up according to things that mattered, like softball skills, bell-bottoms, and transistor radios.

"*Armeeeneean?* What's that?" would inevitably follow. And another kid or two would gather and snicker. It was never easy. It had never been easy. Not even once, Armen remembered.

Indoors, Susie and her mother cooked and cleaned and washed and ironed for the men. Precious vinyl records produced by Armenian singers living now in Lebanon or Syria or somewhere twirled round and round on the record player in the corner of their living room. They drowned out the Watergate hearings and all that Walter Cronkite or Archie Bunker ever had to say on their black-and-white TV perched on its four wooden legs.

Once a month, up until Grandma Bayzar died, it was baking day. Anyone who could escape did, because Grandma Bayzar needed the whole kitchen and the dining room beyond to bake and lay out trays of bread, cheese and meat pies, date cookies, and salted, braided cookies. On holidays there was even more. Chorek. And bakhlava. Trays and trays of sticky, flaky bakhlava filled with pine nuts, pistachios, and walnuts.

Grandpa Daron had been a baker in Syria for many years after leaving his village. After he married Grandma Bayzar, he had begun to teach her all he had learned. The baking was still done for him, really. He sat in the corner of the dining room, a cigarette between his fingers, and watched Grandma Bayzar knead and roll the dough as her fingers expertly shaped and filled tray after tray. The heat of the oven blew the sides of her hair free of its bun and her nose grew pinker as the day progressed. Grandpa Daron never spoke while she worked and never, ever helped. Their mother was there in case Grandma Bayzar needed anything, but the baking took place with basically no conversation at all, until the very end, when an especially well-shaped cookie or pastry was placed on a tiny glass plate and presented to him to taste. But just one. Grandpa Daron never spoke much and he ate even less. It was when their father would come in after a long day's work, when Armen and Susie thought the coast was clear and ventured back indoors, that true appreciation was shown for Grandma Bayzar's skills.

He and Susie were groomed and dressed and stuffed into the car between his parents and grandmother nearly every Sunday as they headed off to church. Grandpa Daron usually saw them off with a nod, then turned his back as he made his slow way to the backyard to sit in a shaded corner.

Church wasn't too bad once they got there. He and Susie went to Sunday school with kids who *all* had hard-to-pronounce names. Some even worse than their own. And many of their grandmothers, too, had tattoos on the inside of their forearms, where they had been branded as property by the Arab tribes who kidnapped them during the long death marches away from their lands.

Grandpa Daron had been working for another man in a small bakery for a few years when he saw Bayzar in an orphanage in Syria. The first thing he had noticed about her was that large tattoo on the inside of her thin arm. The owner of the bakery, misreading Daron's stares in Bayzar's direction, began urging him to marry, to have a wife and bring some warmth into his life. For years, Daron did not even consider it.

"It is over," the baker would insist. "Whatever happened to us happened. They took our lands and we cannot change that. God has spared you, now live your life."

Had he said it was over? Daron could only stare back at the man. "It was this morning," he would begin to say. It was one hour ago.

He relived the last time he had held Anno to him again and again. The memory of her did not fade. It became even more clear and real each day.

Alone, he had dragged himself south, hiding from the caravans of walking corpses. A corpse himself, he had drawn in one shallow burning breath after another, heading for a place he could barely conceive of.

He sloughed through the desert, watching from a distance as his people were driven like broken animals. An old man had dropped to the ground next to two other children and a woman. He too began reaching for the bread the Turkish gendarme dangled at them an arm's length away. The other three had no strength to lift their arms. It was no matter. The gendarme ground the bread deep into the sand with the heel of his boot.

At last in Syria, he had huddled, ragged and emaciated, with others like him, surprised to find himself still drawing one shallow breath after another. He was no longer threatened by death by a Turk or Kurd, but by starvation.

The people behind him were eating a cat. At least that was what he believed it to be. They did not speak. They did not share.

He leaned against a stone wall at the mouth of an alley, his skin the same color as the dirt he sat on. He was at the end of a row of shops. The sun beat down on his head and he considered dragging himself to the fountain behind him for more water. At the turn of the road was the opening to the Aleppo Bazaar, a covered, cave-like maze of stalls of fabric and plates, spices and candles, fruits and vegetables and baked goods. He had stumbled in earlier today and the smells of food had made him retch until, unable to breathe, he had collapsed on his face on the ground. He had been dragged here, to the mouth of the alley, or he had crawled, he could not remember, but the water had revived him enough to sit up and take in his surroundings.

Not far away, three men argued. They had gotten their load to the door of their shop, but their cart was too large to roll it inside. The shop was filled wall to wall with carpets and ottomans and pillows. Their load would have to be lifted off the cart and pulled in. From what Daron could tell, it was more heavily rolled carpets, pale fringes hanging at both ends. Another man sat inside the shop on a low stool in front of a low, three-legged table, watching them argue as he chewed something and drank his tea.

Daron was on his feet making his way toward the Arabs. A few quick hand motions made it clear that he would get those carpets inside, on his back, in exchange for the bread that sat piled on the low tea table.

The Arabs agreed, mostly out of curiosity, and one hour later, Daron sat with his belly full for the first time in many weeks. His mind began to work.

He had never told any of them the story of what had happened to him.

Only Grandma Bayzar told them some things. She told them that Grandpa Daron had had another family, another wife before her, but they had all died. Susie and Armen always asked about them, how many there were, their names, how they died, but Grandma didn't answer them because she didn't really know.

"We should get moving, Mom." Armen rose. The limousines had been waiting outside for a half hour. "You want me to get the guys together and head out for the church already?"

"Yes," Sona answered him, "but first"—she held Susie's wedding dress, still on its satin hanger—"let me check on my father. Did he finally put his tuxedo on?" Her English was heavily accented, but she chose her words carefully, and the *Reader's Digest,* old and new issues all over the house, had improved her vocabulary immensely.

"Yep, he did." Armen followed her out of the bedroom, leaving Susie and her dress in the hands of the bridesmaids until her return.

In the living room, Armen's father stood surrounded by young men in matching tuxedoes. Medium height and stocky, he held a wide glass of whiskey on ice in his large mechanic's hands. Without even checking, Armen knew that all would have been served drinks of their choice, many times over, by him. He liked Johnny, and he liked nothing more than a house full of friends and family, so today he was one person their mother did not need to even think about.

She found Daron sitting in his usual tufted leather chair by the wide window that looked into their backyard. One large apricot tree stood in the middle, its branches bent with fruit.

Sona stopped short at the sight of her father. He was sitting almost languidly with his arms draped carelessly over the arms of the chair. His back was straight as always and his glasses were gone from his face as he watched the activity in the room. The midnight black of the tuxedo and the white of his collar were becoming against his olive skin. His eyes, dark and knowing, watched her. A small gray velvet pouch lay on his knee.

Sona did not comment on his looks. He would not like her to draw attention to that.

"So you are ready, Hayrig. We shall be leaving soon. Did you want anything?" Spoken in their own language, the words flowed without thought or hesitation.

He took in her long silvery gown and upswept hair. "Is Sossè ready?" he asked.

"She is putting on her dress, and then yes, she will be ready."

Sona waited. She could feel he had not finished.

"I have something to say to her."

Sona nodded. If there was anyone he ever did speak to with true traces of enjoyment, it was Susie. But the pouch puzzled her.

"Would you like to go in to see her?"

"Yes. Call me when she is ready."

Daron had grown uncomfortable. Sona hurried away to prepare his granddaughter.

Daron watched the men, boys really, smooth their hair and examine themselves in the mirror time and again. They had greeted him first upon arrival, but that was a while ago. They drank and ate and joked among themselves, in English.

He faced their direction, he dressed in whatever they asked, but he thought of a wedding, so different, long ago.

A day did not pass when he did not think of her, her honey-brown eyes and her coarse hair, and of Sossè, with her wisps of black hair and shimmering blue-gray eyes. He thought of all of them, but he could not speak of them. They lived, a layer of lead wrapped around his heart.

Armen came back to him. He looked at the pouch his grandfather held and decided to hang around and see what this was all about. "*Harse badrasd e, Dada,*" he said. His Armenian was broken, the words twisted, but that was all they spoke with their grandfather. "The bride is ready."

Daron usually held a string of worry beads in his hands. He pushed them round and round on their string between his thumb and forefinger all day long. The beads were unusual, golden brown, and all his older friends commented on their color. They shifted in his pocket now as he stood up.

The bedroom was cleared when Daron entered. Only Susie stood there, waiting for him, with Armen close at his side.

Good, Daron thought, and fumbled with the cinch on the pouch.

Neither Susie nor Armen moved as they watched Daron remove a single bangle from its depths. He held it with the tips of his fingers and looked closely at it, as if to be sure, before lifting his eyes to his granddaughter.

Susie stared at the bracelet, at its aged finish, at the delicately stretching tendrils and flowers etched onto its surface, and knew she was at last seeing into her grandfather's past and her own.

Unmoving, she waited for him to speak. Armen checked the door to the bedroom and knew that if anyone tried to pass through that door now, he would break their legs.

Daron lifted his hand, worn and thick-veined. Still Susie dared not move. Slate-blue eyes locked with tear-filled black ones.

"This is for you." His voice was gentle and uncommonly hesitant.

Susie's hand trembled as she took the bracelet between her own fingers, daintily, as if it might be snatched back at any moment. Tears flooded her eyes. "Dada, whose was this?" Her question was beseeching, her eyes pleading.

Armen stepped closer.

"This..." Daron began. His voice rasped and his shoulders fell before he started again. "This belonged to my wife, in Sassoun."

Susie held the bracelet now in both hands and looked into the past.

"Before your grandmother..." Daron's voice sounded a bit more strongly. "I had a wife and a daughter. You carry my daughter's name,

Sossè." This last he said more warmly. He looked to her, almost waiting for approval.

Susie nodded furiously. "Yes! I know." She quickly dried her eyes, afraid that her grandfather would decide he had said enough. "Grandma told us. Mom too. I am so glad. I have always been glad."

Daron nodded slowly. "And you resemble her, too."

"I? I do?"

Daron nodded again and leaned heavily into Armen. If he let the tears flow at last, could he stop them? This was not the day, not the time. He had made a mistake, he knew.

Susie pulled a chair close to him. Holding the bracelet, she extended her arm.

Seated and shaken, Daron looked up into her face framed by dark, wavy hair and was startled to see joy there.

He looked at his grandson and saw that now he held the bracelet with, surprisingly, the same reverence he had himself for so, so many years.

The times he had thought to sell it, for food. And the times he had, instead, held it, as if he held her, and somehow carried on, as if filling himself instead with her presence.

"Put in on, Dada," Armen urged.

And Daron clasped it high on Sossè's forearm using the further opening, just as Anno always had.

"This is the best wedding gift," she whispered. "The best gift."

"Will you tell us more, Dada?" Armen bent to him.

"Tell us everything?" Sossè asked.

Suddenly Daron breathed. His chest expanded in a way he could hardly remember. His grandchildren beamed at him, and his mouth curved, surprisingly, upward.

"Do you not wish to be married first?" he asked. "Later, I will tell you everything."

They want to know, he realized. *They deserve to know.* And his mind raced. He would tell them of Maratuk, of the fields and the fruits they ate from the orchards, and of the Sassoun River. And of course, of Anno. Anno and Sossè, Kevork and Nairi and Mgro, and of how the poppies bloomed.

AUTHOR'S NOTE

I am the granddaughter of four genocide survivors. As a child of nine or ten, my day began with whisperings from my grandmother as she knelt on her cushion near my bed, faced east, and raised her arms to God in prayer. Those who had kidnapped her during the Armenian Genocide march had forced her to kneel and worship Allah. She had learned to mimic their motions precisely and continued to do so even after she was freed, but in her heart she had always prayed only to her God. I could never understand how she sustained her will in the face of all that she had lived through and suffered.

All four of my grandparents were born and raised in Armenian cities of Anatolia, in the eastern part of the Ottoman Empire, today's Turkey. When they were children, official government policy targeted all Armenians in the empire, and the overwhelming majority were killed or, at best, deported across deserts, only to die along the way. This intentional campaign to eliminate all Armenian citizens became known as the Armenian Genocide. The term *genocide* was coined after the Second World War, using the tragedy that befell Armenians during the First World War as an example of a government's crime committed against a religious minority—the intent to wipe out an entire people. From 1915 through 1922, a million and a half Armenians lost their lives.

My mother's mother was kidnapped by various tribes along the deportation route until my grandfather, a traveling merchant whose wife and adult children had been killed during his absence, found this young Armenian girl who was almost a child, bought her, and married her. Years later, they found themselves in Aleppo, Syria's second largest city, home to tens of thousands of Armenian refugees. My father's family, who were from the area of Sassoun and had been through a similar ordeal, also arrived in Aleppo. My parents met and married there and our family emigrated to the United States when my sister, brother, and I were very young children.

My maternal grandmother lived with us, and her torn memories of loss and love haunted me in childhood. I was left trying to comprehend the enormous pain and larger-than-life terror she had endured and her ability to raise a family while plagued by those memories. I wondered how she had transformed herself from the genocide survivor she was to the grandmother who offered unconditional love, hope, and faith.

I was a teenager when I realized that the image I held of my grandmother in her early years was of a helpless, desperate young woman. It dawned on me that I no longer wanted to hold that isolated picture in my heart. I wanted to know her as she was before the carnage, before the violence, when she was still whole and healthy and happy.

Years later, when my daughter was a freshman in college, she told me of more than one friend who had never heard of the Armenian Genocide. That was the fuel I needed, both to delve into my grandparents' stories and to share the pain of the loss and the love that was an irrevocable part of their lives—and mine. And so my five years of research and writing began. My goal was to complete *As the Poppies Bloomed* in time for the 2015 centennial commemorating the Armenian Genocide.

When I had completed three-quarters of the manuscript, I was suddenly overcome with self-doubt. What if my depiction of the villagers and their bond to each other and to their land was incorrect, insufficient, less than faithful? Feeling that I could possibly be doing an injustice to the people who had lived and loved and prospered in those valleys and on those hillsides, I traveled straight to the very folds of the mountains of Armenian Sassoun (today in eastern Turkey), where this novel takes place.

I wept when I saw hills and fields just as I had imagined them. Even the hues and tones of the deep, red soil were as I had known they would be. It was the very earth my grandfather had walked on.

This is a work of fiction, but some events in the novel are based on true-life stories I have inherited. Raffi, the fedayee (freedom fighter), just as my husband's maternal grandfather decades before him, escaped scrutiny and imprisonment as he passed soldiers bent in prayer. Daron, like my husband's paternal grandfather, earned his bread by lifting a heavy rug onto his back in the bazaar in Syria while survivors around him fought off hunger by eating a cat.

Finally, Mgro, the merchant in the story, was crafted around stories of my maternal grandfather, who gave my grandmother a silver bracelet when their daughter was born. It was a lovely bangle with tendrils all around it joined by twin roses—the same one Daron gives Anno in this novel. I have that bracelet with me now. It was given to me when my grandmother passed away. I keep it, and all the memories that came with it, in a silver pouch.

Maral Haroutinian Boyadjian

ACKNOWLEDGMENTS

Many thanks to those who picked up my newly completed, very raw manuscript with enthusiasm and for all their markings in the margins: Vahe Berberian, James Sabina, and Markar Melkonian. Thanks to Helena Gregorian for her many talents and for her passion for the characters themselves and to Michael Nahabet for his ready and skillful assistance.

I thank Nigel Yorwerth and Patricia Spadaro of Yorwerth Associates for their warm guidance and expertise in all aspects of publishing this book as well as their editorial and design team, including Anne Barthel, who transformed my words into a living, breathing adventure. A special thanks to Salpi H. Ghazarian for a priceless amount of everything, but mostly for handing me my first book to read in our little room all those years ago.

There are two brothers, Garabed and Diran Bag, who made my journey to Sassoun possible. I will be forever grateful to them for their kindness and generosity.

Lastly, all my gratitude and love go to my daughter, Kareen; my son, Kevo; my niece Nahreen; and most especially my husband, Shahe, for their belief and pride in me.

All the characters in this book are fictional, but they are as real to me as the members of my own family. I had to tell their story because they could not.

GLOSSARY

Terms from Arabic, Armenian, Kurdish,
Turkish used in the region

Asdvadz: God

baba: Daddy

bakhlava: Pastry made of flaky dough, filled with nuts
and honey

barakata: Blessing

chorek: Sweet, doughy bread, like a brioche, baked,
patterned and decorated for Easter

dada: Grandfather

dade: Grandmother

dan pesa: A usually penniless son-in-law who has
married the daughter of a family and comes to live
with her family

daross: Good wishes bestowed upon participants and
guests at weddings, baptisms and happy occasions

divan: A long backless, armless sofa, set against a wall

fedayee: Freedom fighter

fez: Brimless, cone-shaped, flat-topped hat, usually with
a single tassel attached

gata: A golden, disc-like pastry filled with butter, flour
and sugar

gendarme: Police

giaour: Infidel; used to slur non-Muslims, particularly
  Armenians, Greeks, Assyrians
han: An inn or hostel; a caravanseray
hars: Daughter-in-law, or bride
hayrig: Father
khnami: A family member through marriage,
  male or female
kiz: Girl
merhaba: Hello
mixtar/mukhtar: Village leader
oghee: A clear distilled spirit made from fruits or berries
pasha: Honorary title for highly ranked officers, placed
  after the person's name
pesa: Son-in-law, or groom
Sassountzi: A resident of Sassoun
shalvar: Wide-legged, wide-seated trousers worn
  throughout the Ottoman Empire and farther east
tahn: A beverage of yogurt and water, beaten until
  smooth, with salt and dill or mint
toneer: An oven dug into the ground or floor
vilayets: Administrative divisions in the Ottoman
  Empire, provinces
Xuda: God

Photo by Mher Vahakn

MARAL BOYADJIAN wove together the memories of her four grandparents, all survivors of the Armenian Genocide, with her love for historical fiction to create the beautiful love story in *As the Poppies Bloomed*. She lives in Granada Hills, California, with her husband and two children. To learn more about Maral and her work, visit www.maralboyadjian.com.